The Final Day At Westfield Arcade
By Andy Hunt

January 6, 1997

Scattered snowflakes drift in the morning air like ash as a four-beater, late-80s model Buick LeSabre pulls into the parking lot outside of Westfield Mall in Indianapolis, Indiana. Leaving fresh tire tracks in the light snow dust sprinkled on the asphalt, the car cuts through the expansive lot, on a direct path towards the mall's entrance. This early in the morning, a full thirty minutes before the mall opens, the LeSabre is the only sign of life outside the mall--there are no other cars anywhere to be seen, no pedestrians wandering about, no shoppers waiting outside the entrance for the mall to open.

The car pulls nose-in into one of the empty vertical parking spaces that align the edge of the mall and idles in the spot for a few seconds, brake lights illuminated, tailpipe spewing plumes of foggy exhaust. The brake lights go dead and the exhaust cloud slowly dissolves as the car is turned off. A man emerges from the car, slamming the driver's side door shut behind him. Bundled up in a heavy parka with a fur-lined hood pulled over his head, he trudges up to the mall's entrance and enters through a revolving door.

Directly inside the mall's entrance, Westfield Mall's night security guard sits on a metal folding chair. Scrolling through the contacts on his silver Nokia flip phone with one hand, he gives a disinterested look up when he hears the revolving door rotating on its hinges. His face widens into a grin upon seeing the man in the parka.

"Look at what the cat dragged in," he says, flipping his phone shut and walking over. He's a younger guy-- blonde-tipped hair spiked with gel, earrings in both ears, looking like someone straight out of N'Sync or Backstreet Boys or one of the other hundreds of boy bands dominating

4

the current music charts. "Mike Mayberry. The man of the hour."

The security guard reaches Mike and extends an open palm to him. Mike looks at the palm, then looks back up to the security guard's face. He tentatively slaps the open palm. The greeting looks about as awkward as one would expect a high five between a thirty-seven year old man and someone half his age to look.

"There we go," the young guard says, still smiling. "So today's the big day, huh?"

"Yeah," Mike says, unzipping his parka, shaking free of his hood. "Today's the big day, all right."

"Damn. You feeling nervous?"

"Nah."

"Excited?"

"Not really."

"Sad?"

Mike looks at him.

"Sad?" He thinks about it for a moment. "Yeah. Of course I'm sad."

The guard nods once, a quick bob of the head. He opens his mouth to say something but is interrupted by the ringing of his cell phone. He looks at the number displayed on the phone, then looks back at Mike.

"Shit, I gotta take this," he says. "But good luck today. I hope it goes well."

The security guard answers the phone and begins speaking into it as he returns to his metal folding chair. Mike turns away from the guard and walks down the mall's main corridor, which is as dead as the exterior at this early hour. A light melody plays from the speakers hidden throughout the mall as Mike walks past the metal security gates that cover the entrances of the darkened storefronts that line both sides of mall's main walkway. At the end of the walkway, he reaches Westfield Mall's food court. The food court is a sea of empty tables with chairs resting legs-up on top of them.

At the far end of the food court, nestled away in the corner, is a lone storefront. Westfield Arcade, reads the neon sign above the entrance. When Mike reaches the metal security gate that covers the entrance to Westfield Arcade, he fishes around in the pockets of his parka and finds his set of keys. He fits one of the keys into the gate, unlocks it, and slides the gate upwards.

The overhead lights inside Westfield Arcade are off, but he can still make out the silhouettes of the eighty-four video game cabinets that comprise the arcade's current selection. Each one of the arcade games is powered off, and everything inside the arcade is eerily silent and still.

Mike walks towards the back of the arcade. Like slumbering giants, freestanding arcade cabinets with darkened monitors are all around him. Some of the games he passes are of the modern design, with bucket seats resembling a car interior and steering wheels mounted to the cabinets. Others have plastic machine guns and pistols mounted onto the control panel. One game he passes, Hang-On by Sega, has a replica plastic motorbike for a player to sit on while playing. Towards the rear of the arcade--where old video games go to die--are the leftover relics from the golden age of video games in the early 1980s. These games are of the simpler variety, most with nothing more than a joystick and a few buttons on the control panel below the monitor.

In back of the arcade, sandwiched between the Missile Command and Asteroids cabinets, there is a door. When Mike reaches it, he opens it a crack. He snakes his arm inside and feels around the wall until his fingers find the main power switch for Westfield Arcade. He flips the switch on.

And just like that, the arcade comes to life.

Every one of the games in the arcade powers on at the exact same moment. The arcade is illuminated with light from the 24-color display monitors of the older games and the 3000-color LED monitors of the newer games. The arcade is flooded with sound--monotone blips and bleeps and archaic sound effects emitting from the older machines in back, Dolby-enhanced explosions and synthesized voices drowning them out from the surround sound speakers of the newer machines in front.

Mike Mayberry has been opening Westfield Arcade in the mornings for the past seventeen years of his life, and this one moment of the day, the moment when every game in the arcade powers on simultaneously, never fails to give him goose bumps.

Mike closes the door in the rear of the arcade and walks back towards the front. Each game he passes stirs up emotions and rekindles memories from the nearly two decades he has worked at Westfield Arcade. He passes the Pac Man machine, and remembers the craze that swept the nation when it was released in the early 1980s--every teenager at the time had at least a couple Pac Man t-shirts, every grade schooler took their lunch to school in Pac-Man lunchboxes, every little kid slept on beds outfitted with Pac Man bedsheets. Mike passes the Defender machine, and remembers the time his friend Willie played the game for almost two hours straight on a single quarter, a crowd of thirty people huddled around the machine, everyone jostling for position and cheering like crazy whenever he zapped an alien spaceship. He passes the Street Fighter 2 machine, and he remembers when the game was in its heyday in the early 90s and groups of kids would show up with pockets full of quarters and have elaborate tournaments in the game against one another.

He walks over to the front counter of Westfield Arcade. Various candy bars and other sugary delights are displayed within the glass countertop, and a gunmetal gray cash register rests on top of the counter. Behind the counter is a Coke fountain machine and a popcorn machine. Mike takes off his parka and hangs it on the back of a chair next to the cash register.

He looks out at the arcade, at all of the games he oversees, a king observing his kingdom. The undying passion he feels for the arcade is rivaled by nothing else in his life. The *memories*--he could rattle off thousands of them from the nearly two decades he's spent at Westfield Arcade. If he were to list the ten greatest moments of his life, each one would've happened in the arcade; if he were to list his ten greatest friends in life, he met each of them at the arcade. The arcade is everything to him, hands-down his favorite place in the world. To him, Westfield Arcade is nothing short of magical.

Resting in front of Mike on the countertop is a tan-colored manila envelope. He grabs this envelope and opens it up, thumbs past an airline ticket for a flight leaving tonight and the receipt for the purchase of the ticket, and finds what he's looking for: a single 8x11 sheet of paper with a message typed on the front of it. He rummages around inside a drawer until he finds a roll of scotch tape, and tears four equally-sized pieces of tape from the dispenser. He affixes the four pieces of tape to each corner of the sheet of paper, then tapes the sheet of paper to Westfield Arcade's front window so the side of the paper with the typing on it faces outward to the food court.

Mike walks around the counter and briefly steps outside the arcade. He looks at the sign in the window to make sure it's visible to those walking by the arcade. It is. The typeface is easy to read.

FINAL DAY OF BUSINESS, the sign reads in large bold letters. Under that, in a smaller typeface: THANKS FOR SEVENTEEN GREAT YEARS.

# # #

No-one shows up for the first hour that Westfield Arcade is open.

Not that this comes as any big surprise to Mike. The days of Westfield Arcade being *the* local hangout for kids are long gone. Back then, during the golden age of arcade videogames in the early 1980s, groups of adolescents and young adults excitedly ambled around the arcade with five, ten, sometimes fifteen or more dollars worth of quarters weighing their jeans' pockets down, feeding those quarters into machines and competing against their friends in their favorite games. But these days, few teenagers have any desire to trek halfway across town to pay .50, .75, sometimes 1.00 to play an arcade game for a few minutes when they have a collection of quality games to play from the comfort of their homes on their Playstations and Nintendo 64's and souped-up personal computers, games they can play against friends halfway across town (or halfway across the country) via high-speed internet connections if they so choose.

The crowds at Westfield Arcade haven't just shrunk since the arcade's heyday; the crowds have almost disappeared entirely. During the glory days, it wasn't uncommon to see a line ten people deep waiting to play that month's hot game; now, Westfield Arcade is lucky to get ten people in total to visit the arcade over the course of a day.

And as the first hour of the day stretches into the second, it appears as if today will be the same monotonous slog that Mike has become accustomed to over the past few years--hours crawling by, not a customer in sight, every arcade cabinet powered on with no-one to play them.

He drums his fingers on the glass countertop as he stands behind it. Outdated Chamber of Commerce stickers adorn the glass case, peeling at the edges. There is one from 1987. Another from--

"I'm here for the Space Invaders machine."

Mike looks up and sees an African American male, early thirties, a few years younger than Mike himself. Skinny guy. He wears a pair of glasses and a red Indiana Hoosiers cap.

"Space Invaders," Mike repeats. "We talked on the phone, right?"

"Yep," the man says.

"The game's in the back," Mike says. "Let's go check it out."

Mike and the first customer of Westfield Arcade's final day of business walk down one of the walkways towards the rear of the arcade. Game cabinets are all around them, and the man's head is on a swivel as he checks out the demo screens of all the games.

"What's going to happen to all of these games once this places closes?" the man asks Mike.

"I'm selling them all. People will be showing up all day to cart off the games they purchased. This place will be almost empty by the end of the day."

They reach the Space Invaders cabinet in the back, sandwiched between a Donkey Kong cabinet and a Galaga cabinet.

"Looking good," the guy says, examining the cabinet.

"Can't beat Space Invaders," Mike says. "One of the most popular games of all-time."

"Cash transaction okay for you?"

"Sure."

The man retrieves his wallet and pulls out five crisp one-hundred-dollar bills. He hands them to Mike and Mike puts them in his pocket.

Mike walks over to the corner of the arcade and grabs a metal dolly resting against the wall. He wheels the dolly back to the man. They unplug the Space Invaders cabinet and the screen goes black. Mike tilts the Space

10

Invaders cabinet backward and the man slides the ledge of the dolly underneath the cabinet.

"I'll run this out to my truck and bring your dolly back in," the man says to Mike.

Mike watches as the man tilts the dolly and the cabinet backwards until the weight of the Space Invaders cabinet is balanced over the wheels. The man rolls the Space Invaders cabinet out of Westfield Arcade, and Mike continues watching as the man rolls the arcade cabinet through the food court and disappears down the mall's main walkway and the machine is gone forever.

Space Invaders, Mike thinks to himself, shaking his head slightly, alone in the arcade. The game that started it all.

And he remembers.

1. SPACE INVADERS

My college academic advisor was a small, compact man named Robert Johnson who worked out of a small, compact office on the third floor of Northwestern's Robert A. Johnson Center for Professional Development. He liked to joke with students that the school had named the building after him because of his prowess as an academic advisor, but in reality the building was named after a different Robert Johnson, one who had made a sizable donation to Northwestern many decades ago.

Though it was a mere coincidence that he bore the same namesake as the building he worked in, I always liked to imagine that the building had been named after him because of his eyebrows.

Directly above his eyes were two dark-haired beasts that were nothing short of magnificent. His eyebrows were thick monstrosities made up of full and voluminous hair, looking as if they'd never been trimmed or groomed in his life.

As I sat in his office and watched him look over the transcripts from my junior year of college, I looked at those eyebrows. Studied them. They twitched, furrowed, and seemed to slither all over the lower half of his forehead as he read over the sheet of paper in his hands.

Finally, he looked away from the sheet of paper and up at me. He smiled, causing his left eyebrow to suddenly arch.

"Looking over your transcripts, I would declare the first three years of your college career to be nothing short of a rousing success," he finally said. "Congratulations, Mr. Mayberry."

"Thank you," I said.

His left eyebrow lowered as he looked back down at the transcripts.

"3.87 GPA," he read. "Multiple honors classes, all completed with the highest of marks. Tell me, how has this semester gone?"

"It's gone well," I said. "I took my last final this morning."

He smiled, causing the right eyebrow to curve, forming an arc.

"Excellent, Mike. Excellent. And you enjoy Accounting as a major?"

"I do."

He nodded a few times.

"On the straight and narrow--I like it," he said.

He got up from his desk. He wore a corduroy blazer with patches sewn on the elbows and a pair of tight Wrangler jeans, the height of business casual fashion in that year of 1980. He walked over to a row of filing cabinets that lined the wall behind his desk. Each drawer in the cabinets was labeled in ascending order of year, dating all the way back to 1969. After placing my file in a cabinet with a M-Z, SPRING 1980 label on it, he sat back down at his desk and looked across it at me.

"There's just one problem," he said. "You haven't signed up for any coursework for next year. We'll need to get right on that. The Advanced Accounting courses fill up quickly. And there are a few required economics classes that you haven't--"

"I'm actually not coming back to school next year," I said.

He looked at me. The right eyebrow moved upwards so suddenly that I thought it was going to crawl off his face.

"Pardon?"

"I'm not coming back to school next year."

He considered this for a moment.

"Have you had an unpleasant experience during your junior year at Northwestern?"

"Not at all. I've enjoyed it."

"Are you transferring to a different school? If an opportunity at another school has presented itself, we'll do everything in our power to retain you as a student. A more appealing scholarship package, involvement with our Alumni Outreach program--"

"I'm not transferring to another school."

"So...what are you plans?"

"I'm taking a break."

"A break." He paused. "In other words, you're quitting college altogether."

"Yes."

"All of that hard work that you've put into school the past three years means nothing without a degree," he said.

"I realize that," I said, "and, eventually, I'd like to return to school. In fact, I plan to. But right now, I have to take a break from school. Something has come up."

"Is this something you'd care to discuss?"

"I'd prefer not to," I said.

He looked at me for a few seconds, then got up from his desk.

"Then, I wish you the best," he said.

He extended his hand across the desk, and I shook it.

"Just know that the time has a tendency to disappear very quickly," Robert Johnson said to me. "A brief break from college can turn into a permanent break from college very easily. You have a bright, bright future. If you're going to put that future on hold, it better be for a very good reason."

I looked him in the eye.

"It is," I said.

# # #

After meeting with my academic advisor, I packed up my meager possessions and made the three-hour trip east from Chicago to my hometown of Indianapolis. I moved everything into the one-bedroom apartment I'd arranged to rent on the edge of town, and then set out for Westfield Mall. I knew I needed a job, and the mall was the obvious first place to look.

The mall had opened up in my hometown of Indianapolis a year prior, and as I walked through the mall's double-door entrance, I could see that the excitement surrounding the opening had yet to wear off. The place was absolutely packed. Directly inside the entrance was a small fountain surrounded by fake plants, and standing around the fountain was a group of at least twenty teenage girls and guys talking with one another. The girls had big hair and most wore skin-tight jeans by Gloria Vanderbilt and Sasson and Chic, the jeans riding high on their hips. A few others opted for the baggy sweatshirt over leggings look. Many of the guys wore Members Only jackets over polo shirts; others wore ringer t's and jeans with Nike Cascade sneakers.

Beyond the group next to the entrance, the well-lit walkway of the mall was bustling with activity. Standing around a bench in the middle of the walkway was a group decked out in punk attire--studded black leather jackets and combat boots and jeans splattered with bleach. A few wore Ramones t-shirts, and most sported a Mohawk or a similar spiky hairstyle. Other groups of teenagers and young adults walked around, ducking in and out of stores while carrying shopping bags from JC Penney and Montgomery Ward and countless other stores.

15

I started walking down the walkway of the mall, through the sea of people, and spent the afternoon ducking into every store I was interested in working at, filling out applications and introducing myself to assistant managers. Eventually, I ended up in the food court and spotted a lone storefront nestled away in the corner. The neon sign above the entrance read 'Westfield Arcade' in bright pink cursive writing. From my vantage point, I could see that it was a video game arcade. The place looked packed, with a crowd of people huddled around a few games towards the front of the arcade. But what grabbed my attention was the sign in the window: HELP WANTED, it read in orange letters.

I made my way over to Westfield Arcade. When I reached it and walked inside, it was like entering into a completely different world. The well-lit, inviting atmosphere of the mall was replaced by the arcade's dim, dungeon-like lighting and dark maroon carpeting. The calm, soothing music being played throughout the mall gave way to explosions and bleeps and thousands of other arcade game sound effects coming from every single direction. Warbled conversation surrounded me. There were cheers. There were jeers. Every few seconds, I heard people yell out, either in frustration or celebration.

The arcade was massive, around half the size of a regulation basketball court, and there looked to be around fifty arcade cabinets throughout the arcade, with room for more. These cabinets were arranged in two vertical rows that bordered each wall and extended to the rear of the arcade, where more games were placed. Between these two rows were ten games that were arranged back-to-back in the shape of a rectangle, forming an island in the middle of the arcade.

People were everywhere--hunched over arcade cabinets, rapidly mashing FIRE buttons with their index fingers, ramming joysticks left and right with forceful movements. Some of the more popular games--Space

Invaders, Missile Command, Asteroids--had groups of four or five people around them, some waiting in line to play the game, others just standing there and watching.

The first cabinet inside the entrance was a game named Berzerk, which was occupied by a white-collar worker—shirt unbuttoned, tie and jacket resting on his briefcase on the floor. The businessman stood alone at the cabinet, and there was not a hint of anxiety in his tight movements and rapid button presses, his cold-faced expression remaining stoic as he blasted away at enemies onscreen.

To the left of the businessman was a Defender cabinet. A high-school-aged Hispanic kid wearing a red Radio Shack vest huddled over the machine, moving the joystick around and rapidly pressing a series of three buttons on the right-hand side of the control panel. Behind him was a scrawny kid who observed the game, holding a large Coca Cola cup. The kid watching the game had thick-framed glasses and messy hair, and wore a small blue ringer t-shirt with red trim around the edges that hugged tight against his pencil neck and skinny arms.

"You just wasted a Smart Bomb there," the scrawny kid watching commented on the game being played. "No need to use a Smart Bomb on two baiters. You can conserve those and use Hyperspace to escape the baiters."

The kid in the Radio Shack vest ignored the advice being given to him, continuing to stare straight ahead and play the game. A few seconds passed.

"Oh, that was a mistake, too," the scrawny kid with glasses said as he continued to watch the game being played. "Should've done a reverse-and-kill there. You could have maintained most of your forward velocity while--"

The kid at the arcade cabinet turned around, his face contorted in fury.

"Rufus, would you *shut up*?!?" he yelled. "I have my own strategy for playing Defender!"

He then turned around, resuming his game.

"Keep it down over there!" It was a thunderous voice that was loud enough to be heard over the sound effects of the arcade machines. I looked in the general direction of the voice and saw a burly bear of a man who looked to be considerably older than everyone else in the arcade. He wore a gray button-up shirt that was tucked into a pair of khakis, the buttons on the shirt straining against his protruding belly. He had on a pair of glasses, and a full beard covered the lower half of his face.

He stood in a small alcove in the far left corner of the arcade, behind a glass counter top that had boxes of candy bars displayed inside. On top of the glass counter top was a gray cash register, and resting on a ledge behind the counter was a popcorn machine and a soda dispenser with an illuminated Coca Cola sign above it.

I circled around the arcade and headed towards the counter. After cutting through a few crowds, I reached him. He was huddled over the glass display case while working on a crossword puzzle. He briefly looked up over his glasses at me, then returned his attention to the crossword.

"Change machine's over there," he grumbled, pointing to the left of me.

"Pardon?" I said.

He sighed.

"We don't let you blast away at space critters for free. You need quarters to play the games. The machine over there gives you four quarters for a dollar bill. Last time I checked, that was the going exchange rate."

I looked over and saw that even the change machine had a line five-deep at it, with people waiting in line to feed their dollar bills into the machine for quarters in return.

"I'm actually looking for a job," I said. "I saw the sign out front."

"Can you work nights?" he instantly asked.

I told him I could.

"Can you work weekends?"

I told him I could.

"You're hired," he said.

I looked at him.

"That's it?"

"That's it. I need to fill the position soon. The job's yours if you want it."

It was an easy decision. The place seemed like it'd be fun to work in. I told him that I'd take it.

"Good. My name's Ed, by the way."

"*Shut up*, Rufus!" came a yell from across the arcade at that exact moment.

Ed and I both looked over to see that the same scrawny kid who'd been giving advice at the Defender cabinet--Rufus, apparently, was his name--had moved on to the Lunar Lander cabinet and was dispensing advice on how to effectively play that game to a different kid.

"Rufus, I told you to keep it down," Ed yelled at him.

"I'm not the one yelling," Rufus said to Ed. "I'm just giving him advice on how to play."

Ed shook his head, then turned towards me.

"I oughta ban that little shit Rufus from the arcade."

For the next hour, Ed explained everything I needed to know about working at Westfield Arcade, practically shouting at times to be heard over the sounds of explosions and synthesized music and yelling ringing out all around the arcade. He explained how to work the popcorn machine and how to replace the CO2 canisters and other parts for the Coke machine when it ran out. He opened up one of the arcade games, showing me the inner workings of it and explaining the common malfunctions with the units.

"Candy is a quarter per," Ed said, pointing at the rows of candy bars and gummy delights displayed behind the glass countertop. "Same with the Coke machine. Popcorn is fifty cents. Any other questions?"

"What's that?" I said, pointing to a large chalkboard that hung from the wall behind the glass counter top, right next to the Coke machine.

"That's where we list the high scores for the arcade. People get very worked up over high scores. When someone's getting close to beating one of the high scores, you'll know. A crowd will form around the machine. If someone beats one of the scores, get their initials and their score from them, then erase the old score and write in the new one."

I looked at the high score chalkboard. On it was written:

Asteroids WLC 997,800
Missile Command WLC 711,450
Battlezone WLC 679,810
Galaxian WLC 221,750

And on it went, with the initials WLC and a score listed after every single one of the roughly sixty games on the high score leaderboard.

"WLC," I said, looking at the list. "Who's that?"

"That's Willie. Willie Cardinal. In here quite a bit. You'll meet him eventually."

For the first time since he'd started talking with me, Ed smiled.

"He's a character, that's for sure."

The smile remained on his face for a moment before Ed turned back towards me.

"You'll start tomorrow night, and we'll get a schedule worked out after that," he said. "And another thing I forgot to mention: You can play arcade games for free in the off-hours. Small perk of working here. And if it's dead during business hours, go ahead and play a game or two. I have no problem with that."

"Thanks, but I don't really play arcade games."

"You don't?" He seemed surprised. "Why not?"

"No real interest in them."

"Well, the offer's the table in case you start—and it wouldn't surprise me if you did start," he said, looking out at the madhouse scene of teenagers huddled around the games on the arcade floor. "This place has a tendency to rub off on you."

\# \# \#

Before work that next day, I showed up to Cedar Grove Senior Care Center. It was an unassuming, one-story brick building with a small, well-kept lawn out front. To the left of the senior center home was a parking lot filled with five cars and twice that many empty spots. I pulled my 1976 Chevy Nova into the parking lot, killed the engine, and walked up a sidewalk that led to the entrance. After walking through a pair of double doors, I entered into the senior center.

The smell of the place was what hit you first. I'd been to the senior center two months ago, and I still remembered the overwhelming stench of disinfectant of the place. It was an industrial, artificial minty smell, like someone had doused every square inch of the facility in mouthwash.

The double doors opened up into a room that was referred to as the recreation room, though the word 'recreation' was being used liberally. It was a smaller room with shag carpeting, no artwork or decorations hanging from the walls, and low, dark lighting. The recreation room had just enough space for two flower-patterned recliners and a wooden card table. A group of three older folks sat at the card table, putting together a puzzle. To the left of them, sitting in one of the recliners, was an even older lady who appeared to be engaged in a staring contest with a wall.

I walked through the rec room and down the main hallway of the senior center until I reached a door with John Mayberry scrawled in marker on a sign hanging from the wall. The door was open, and I stepped inside the room.

I stood there in the doorway for a moment, looking at the room. The walls and floor were painted a matching beige color. A Chicago Cubs pennant hung from the wall, directly above the headboard of the bed. The lights in the room were off and the only illumination came from slivers of sunlight creeping through the closed blinds and the dim glow from a small color television that sat on top of a dresser. The television volume was turned up, and there were no other audible sounds in the room.

My grandpa lay on the bed in the middle of the room. He had thinning gray hair that spilled onto his forehead and thick Buddy Holly-style glasses perched on his nose. He was propped up in bed with a mountain of pillows behind his head, and he stared straight ahead at the television.

"Grandpa," I said.

He looked over at me. His face broke out into a sweet, beautiful grin.

"Michael," he said.

I walked over to him in bed, leaned down, and gave him an affectionate hug. I held him in my arms for a few seconds. He'd always been wiry and skinny and had lost even more weight in the two months he'd been in the senior center, so much so that I could feel the bumpy ridges of his spinal cord through his thin white t-shirt as I hugged him.

I gently laid him back onto the bed of pillows that supported his neck and back, and I sat down in a chair next

22

to his bed. I reached over to the television and turned down the volume.

"You're home from college," he said. "How did the semester go?"

"It went well."

"You kept your grades up?"

"Of course."

"You didn't miss too many classes?"

"No, not at all."

"Good, good," he said. "Now for the important question: How many hearts did you break this semester?"

"None."

"Ah, you're lying," he said, his smile returning. "I bet you left a whole trail of broken hearts around the campus."

I laughed at his comment.

"So how are they treating you here?" I asked.

"Can't complain. I've got pretty women waiting on me hand and foot. I shoulda come here back when I was in my twenties."

"How's the food?" I asked.

He started talking about his love for the mashed potatoes they served at the senior center, and as he talked, I glanced around his room again. I'd first seen this room two months ago, when he'd moved in, and my first impression was that it was a very depressing room. It still looked just as depressing.

Other than the Cubs banner above his bed, the decorations were sparse. My grandpa had a few baseballs and other paraphernalia displayed on a small shelf next to his bed. Directly above this shelf, he had taped various cut-outs and articles from the local newspaper to the wall. The newspaper articles, I noticed, were all about me. One article was a list of honor roll students from my junior year of high school, and my name had been circled in Sharpie marker. Another small, two-sentence blurb had been clipped from a different newspaper: it announced that I'd made the dean's list at Northwestern for the Fall semester of 1979. A few of my yearly school pictures were taped to the wall as well. All in all, there were at least twenty articles and pictures taped to the wall.

My grandpa finished talking about the mashed potatoes, and we watched the television for a few moments.

"So how many hearts did you break this semester?" my grandpa asked me eventually.

I tried not to show any reaction to the question.

"None, Grandpa," I said, the same answer I'd given when he asked the question a few minutes ago.

Just then, there was a knock on his open door. I looked over and saw a middle-aged, overweight lady with a smile on her face and pudgy, rosy-red cheeks. She had a notebook in her hand.

"How are you today, John?" she asked as she walked into the room.

"Good," he said.

The lady looked at me and extended her hand.

"Kim Franklin," she said, as I shook her hand. "I'm one of the therapists here."

"I'm Mike. John's grandson."

"It's so very nice to meet you," she said. She gestured towards the newspaper article cut-outs taped to the wall. "John's very proud of you."

She walked over to my grandpa's bed. She looked down at him, smiled, then looked over at me.

"Is it all right if I ask John a few quick questions?" she asked.

"Sure."

"Great," she said, opening her notebook and taking the cap off of a pen. "So how are you feeling today, John?"

"Good," he said.

"Can you tell me the name of your favorite baseball team?" she asked.

"The Cubs!" he practically shouted.

"Good. Did they win their game yesterday?"

"No."

"What was the score?"

My grandpa thought about it for a second.

"Five to two."

"Good," Kim said, writing something in her notebook.

"Can you tell me what state we live in?"

"Indiana."

She pulled a flashcard from a pocket in her notebook. It was a white flashcard with a black circle in the middle. She held up the flashcard for my grandpa to see.

"Can you tell me what shape this is?"

He stared at the flashcard for a few moments. He looked up at Kim, then over to me, then back at the flashcard.

"A square."

She wrote something else in notebook.

"Can you count backwards by sevens, starting at 100?"

He looked at me again.

"What does that mean?" he asked me.

"Sorry, John," the therapist immediately said. "You'll have to answer by yourself. Can you count backwards by sevens, starting at 100?"

"I don't understand the question," my grandpa said.

"That's okay," she said. "Let's go on to the next question. What country are we in?"

"America," he immediately said.

The therapist asked my grandpa a few more questions, which he was able to answer correctly. She told my grandpa she'd be back to visit with him next week, and then left the room.

My grandpa and I watched the evening news on the television after Kim left. The main story was about the upcoming 1980 Summer Olympics in Moscow and a potential boycott of those games by the United States and other countries. My grandpa and I watched the news for awhile and continued to talk.

Halfway through the news broadcast, there was a knock at his door and a different nurse stuck her head into the room.

"It'll be dinner time in five minutes, Mr. Mayberry," the nurse said. "Your guest will have to go then."

She disappeared as quickly as she'd appeared. I looked over at my grandpa. He nodded his head at me.

"I'll have to introduce you to that one," he said. "Belinda is her name. She's way too much of a woman for me, but I bet you could handle her. And if you did, I'd want you to give me every last detail about it."

I smiled at my grandpa once again, then stood up out of my chair.

"I'll be back tomorrow," I said.

And, once again, he smiled. I missed that smile.

# # #

That next night, during my initial shift working at the arcade, I met the man who was soon to become the greatest friend I'd ever had in my life: Willie Cardinal.

I didn't know a thing about him or what he looked like, but when he arrived at Westfield Arcade early in the evening, I knew it was him. He sauntered in through the entrance alone, clad in a pair of Toughskin jeans and a Barracuda jacket with the sleeves rolled up past his forearms, the epitome of 1980s cool. The jacket was unzipped, showing a skin-tight baby-blue Space Invaders t-shirt underneath. His blonde hair was long and curly, his skin with a natural-looking tan. The Sony Walkman was the latest craze in electronics, and he had a rectangular Walkman clipped to his belt, a pair of headphones around his neck.

Once again, the arcade was absolutely packed and bustling with activity on that night, but when Willie arrived, everything stopped. Those who weren't engrossed with playing games stopped talking in mid-conversation and turned their attention towards him. Others abandoned their games mid-game and watched his entrance. A couple of people waved at him, and he gave a cocky nod of his head in acknowledgement.

I stood behind the front counter, and watched Willie walk over to the change machine. Five people were already in line waiting for the machine, and they quickly got out of the way and let Willie bypass them. He fed a one-dollar bill into the machine. As he waited for his quarters to be dispensed, he casually glanced at the high score chalkboard behind me, as if to confirm that his WLC initials were still listed for the high score in every game.

Four quarters clambered down into the coin return slot of the change machine, and he scooped them up. He walked over to the counter and looked at me behind it.

"You the new guy?" he asked me.

"Yeah."

"I'll take a Coke, new guy," he said, sliding a quarter across the glass countertop. "No ice."

I filled a cup with Coke, put a plastic lid on the soda cup, and handed it back to him with a straw. He took a long sip of soda, and gave a nod of his head to a college-aged, Hispanic guy in a red Radio Shack vest standing at the Berzerk cabinet. I recognized him as the guy who'd been playing Defender when I'd showed up to the arcade for the first time last night. The guy came over and exchanged fives with Willie.

"Gonzo, how's it hanging?" Willie said.

"Can't complain," Gonzo said. "I was beginning to wonder if you'd show up tonight."

"'Course I showed up--if it's Thursday night and my name's still Willie, I'll be at the arcade," Willie said. "Anything good happened yet?"

"Not really. Some kid had over 310,000 points with three lives left in Star Castle, but he got his ass kicked by level 17. Lost all three lives within a minute."

"No surprise there," Willie said. "Level 17 in Star Castle is a nasty bitch."

"Oh, and I got a new personal best in Centipede," Gonzo said.

"What'd you get?"

"96,000."

"Shit, I could get 96,000 in Centipede while wearing a blindfold," Willie said. "That ain't even close to half of my high score."

Gonzo extended his middle finger towards Willie, and Willie laughed. They both looked out at the crowds of people in the arcade.

"Oh, and Rufus..." Gonzo began.

Willie looked at him.

"What's that little weasel up to now?" Willie said.

"You know that cousin he's always talking about?"

"The one he claims got 40,000 in Space Invaders?"

"Yeah, that one. Rufus brought him in tonight."

I'd recognized Rufus from the previous night, too. He'd been at the arcade all evening, and he and a friend had been posted up at the Space Invaders cabinet for the entire night, never once leaving. His friend looked almost identical to him--diminutive, thick glasses, pimply skin.

I looked over towards the cabinet, and saw them both still there--Rufus watching, his friend playing. As if he heard his name being mentioned, Rufus looked over to the counter and his beady eyes lit up behind his glasses when he saw Willie. He tapped the shoulder of his pimple-faced friend playing Space Invaders in front of him, and they both walked over to Willie.

"Willie, what a pleasant surprise," Rufus said once he'd arrived. "I was hoping you'd be here. This is my cousin, Teddy."

"So you're the infamous cousin?" Willie said, eyeing the kid over. "I've heard a lot about you. Rufus won't shut up about his cousin Teddy, the best Space Invaders player he's ever seen. All he ever talks about is this cousin of his who scored 40,000 in Space Invaders."

"41,840, to be precise."

"I call bullshit," Willie said instantly.

A few people had come over to where the confrontation was taking place. They stood on the periphery and listened to what was being said.

"You calling my cousin a liar?" Rufus said.

"If he's claiming that he got 41,000 in Space Invaders, then, yeah, I'm calling him a liar," Willie said. "My high score is 38,000, and I've never seen anyone come within 10,000 points of beating that."

"Trust me, I scored 41,000," the cousin said. "41,840, to be precise."

"I saw him do it," Rufus said. "He's not lying."

"If he's done it once, maybe he can do it again," Willie said. Willie looked around at the small crowd that had accumulated. "Let's have ourselves a challenge," he said.

Upon the mention of a challenge, there was an excited undercurrent of commotion that swept over the crowd. Eager, anticipatory looks flashed over everyone's faces. A few people called out to their friends throughout the arcade, motioning them over. Clearly, this was a big deal.

Led by Willie and Rufus's cousin, a crowd of twenty walked over and formed a semicircle with the Space Invaders cabinet in the middle. I walked out from behind the front counter and joined the crowd, remaining towards the back to keep an eye on the front counter.

Rufus's cousin Teddy stepped up to the machine first. He inserted a quarter into the coin slot and hunched over the cabinet, legs shoulder-width apart. He gripped the joystick in his left hand and placed the index finger of his right hand on the fire button. A few sound effects rang out from the speakers and the game began.

I'd never played Space Invaders before, but after a few minutes of watching, the simple objective of the game became clear. You controlled a spaceship at the bottom of the screen and tried to kill off a series of fifty-five aliens by firing your ship's gun at them. As you eliminated aliens, the remaining aliens started to move faster and faster towards the bottom of the screen. If any one of the aliens reached the bottom of the screen, it was game over.

The one aspect of the game that stood out was the background music. It was a simple monotone 'Thump, thump, thump,' sound that came from the game's speaker each time the aliens moved. The noise sounded like the beating of a heart, and the closer the aliens came to the bottom of the screen, the faster the 'thump, thump, thump,' sound effects came. After awhile, the thumping sound became so frantic and nonstop that it sounded like a jackhammer.

Though I didn't know much about the game, it was easy to see that Teddy was an expert player. I watched the game screen as he moved his ship around the bottom of the screen and deftly dodged enemy fire while eliminating the aliens one by one. He played with a savage, unrelenting concentration. A sweat stain formed on the back of his shirt between his waiflike shoulder blades, and as the game progressed the stain slowly expanded until a majority of the upper half of his shirt was damp with sweat.

He continued playing for twenty minutes on a single quarter, then half an hour, as the waves of aliens moved increasingly faster and faster down the screen. The jackhammer-like 'thump, thump, thump' background effects of the game only heightened the intensity of the game. Those in the crowd exchanged impressed looks with one another on the rare occasions that they tore their eyes away from the game. Finally, after almost forty solid minutes of playing, a lone alien reached the bottom of the screen. The words GAME OVER appeared onscreen.

Teddy stepped away from the cabinet and turned to face the crowd. He looked like he'd just run a marathon. A thin sheen of sweat covered his forehead, and his cheeks were flushed red. His breathing was deep and labored.

"42,660," he said, repeating the score displayed at the top of the game's screen. "My personal best score."

Teddy stuck out his dainty chest in pride, and Rufus pumped his fist in celebration.

"That's a new arcade record, too," Rufus said excitedly. "He just killed Willie's high score."

An awed silence overtook the crowd surrounding the game. People looked around at each other as if they couldn't believe what they'd just seen. Willie, their guy, had been beaten.

"My initials are TGL," Teddy announced. "For the high score leaderboard."

"Don't put his name up yet," Willie immediately said, looking directly at me.

Willie hit play on his Walkman and put the headphones over his ears. He walked up to the Space Invaders cabinet and produced a quarter from his pocket, flipping it around a few times with his index and middle fingers. He inserted the quarter, then cracked his knuckles on both hands. He hit the one player button, and the game began.

He played the game with equal parts concentration and casualness. He nonchalantly stood at the cabinet, slightly slouched over, and the look on his face didn't change in the slightest as he stared directly into the screen. The veins in his forearm bulged as he maneuvered the joystick and rapidly tapped the fire button.

First, he took out each of the aliens in the far-left row with five quick, precise taps of the fire button. Next, he immediately moved to the right side and took out the aliens on the far right side. From there, he took cover behind the bunkers at the bottom of the screen as he eliminated each alien row-by-row. He continued with this strategy and passed through the first five waves of aliens.

"Looking good so far," someone beside me commented.

"Willie's zoned in," the person next to him said.

He continued on, passing the next two stages by using the same technique. Word had spread around the arcade about the scene at the Space Invaders machine, and even more people had joined the crowd watching the game. There were now people all around me, everyone jostling for position to get a clearer look at the screen, crammed in like sardines.

He got to 20,000 before he lost his first life. Then Willie reached 25,000, 30,000. Someone started up a "Wil-lie, Wil-lie, Wil-lie," chant, and soon everyone in the crowd was chanting Willie's name.

He kept playing. 35,000. Even more people joined the crowd around the Space Invaders machine, and the chants of his name grew louder: "Wil-lie, Wil-lie, Wil-lie." Then, Willie was at 40,000. 41,000. Finally, there was a collective "OHHHH" from those who could see the game, and the word filtered back to everyone in the crowd: Willie had beaten Teddy's score.

Willie died for the final time and turned around to face the crowd behind him. He took off his headphones and wiped the sweat from his forehead with the palm of his hand. His face was a deep shade of red, and his chest expanded and contracted with deep breaths. He, too, looked like he'd just run a marathon.

"44,310," he announced to the crowd. He'd beaten Teddy's score by nearly two thousand points.

He ran his hand through his long blonde hair and his face broke into a large grin. The entire crowd exploded in a cheer, and everyone started mobbing Willie. Someone handed him his Coke, and he took a long sip through the straw.

Eventually, the crowd dispersed, and I retreated back to the front counter. I served up a few bags of popcorn, refilled a number of Coke cups. I looked up and saw Willie making his way over with Gonzo trailing behind him.

"Add it," he said once he'd arrived at the front counter. "44,310. WLC."

I walked to the board and erased Willie's old Space Invaders high score. I grabbed a piece of chalk and added the new one, then walked back to the counter.

"So what's your name, new guy?" Willie asked.

"Mike," I said.

"Well, Mike, let me introduce you to the crew. This here's Robbie Gonzalez, but everyone calls him Gonzo. Comes in here every night after his shift at Radio Shack."

Gonzo stepped forward and I shook his hand.

"The guy playing the Lunar Lander game over there is Bearclaw," Willie said, pointing out a larger guy engrossed in a Lunar Lander game. "Don't even know what his first name is, but he's got the biggest damn hands you've ever seen. Arcade game joysticks look like toothpicks when he's holding them."

Willie motioned towards the back of the arcade.

"There's Rufus, that dorky piece of shit who just made a fool of himself."

Willie pointed out a few other regulars who were situated throughout the arcade.

"But Gonzo and I, we run this arcade," Willie said.

"Damn right," Gonzo said.

"You up for a few games?" Willie asked Gonzo. "I'm thinking an ass-beating in Galaxian is just what the doctor ordered."

"Not tonight," Gonzo said. "I got plans for the night."

"The latest <u>Sports Illustrated</u> swimsuit issue and a bottle of Jergins hand lotion don't count as plans in my book," Willie said, smiling.

"Nah, man, I have other plans," Gonzo said. "I have a date."

"A date?" Willie said. "What's his name?"

"Very funny. It's a date with a girl."

Willie started laughing.

"I'm glad you find my sex life so funny," Gonzo said.

"It's only a sex life if there's actually sex in it."

Gonzo opened his mouth to say something, a quick-witted comeback in response, but he shut his mouth and simply shook his head.

"It was nice meeting you," Gonzo said to me.

"And you," he said to Willie, "you can go fuck yourself with a spoon."

Willie cackled at the comment as Gonzo walked out of the arcade. Willie remained at the front counter for a few moments, sipping his soda.

"Looks like I'm playing Galaxian solo tonight," Willie said.

Before heading over to the game, Willie turned back towards me.

"Nice meeting you," he said to me. "I'm sure we'll be seeing a lot of each other."

2. DONKEY KONG

On an unremarkable Wednesday night that turned out to be very remarkable indeed, a group of us stood around the Donkey Kong cabinet, watching Willie expertly play the game. Though I still never played any games myself, I enjoyed watching others play, particularly Willie. It was mesmerizing to watch a true master like Willie play the games, how he would precisely maneuver his character around the screen to snag a power-up or avoid death at the hands of an enemy by mere millimeters.

"You left a few points on the board there," Rufus said as Willie cleared a stage.

"You giving me advice on how to play Donkey Kong--that's a joke," Willie said, remaining staring directly ahead at the game screen as he continued to play. "My high score in Donkey Kong is twice what yours is."

There were a few laughs and comments from the peanut gallery gathered around the game.

"I'm not giving you advice," Rufus said. "I'm just pointing out a fact. You could've had a few more points on that last game board. You didn't even grab the hammer."

Rufus was still in junior high, and was the youngest member of the Westfield Arcade regulars, as well as being the smallest. It had become clear from the start that he was the piñata of the arcade, the butt of most jokes. Not that I really felt sorry for him--he brought it on himself, as he was constantly giving advice on how to play games and seemed to go out of his way to annoy others. In a way, I imagine that he liked the ridicule he received, because it was better than the alternative, which was simply being ignored by the older crew.

A debate arose between Willie and Rufus about the best strategy in Donkey Kong, but I was scarcely paying any attention. I was focused on something entirely different.

One of the things I quickly noticed about Westfield Arcade was that the crowds who visited the arcade were so varied. You had some people who were still in junior high, some who were in high school, and some who were older than that. Some had full-time jobs, and others treated the arcade as their full-time job. Some were there for the social aspect of the arcade and viewed Westfield Arcade as a hang-out; others were anti-social and rarely talked with anyone--they came to Westfield Arcade to pump quarter after quarter into arcade games and do nothing else. But there was one constant in this varied collection: almost everyone who came to the arcade was a guy.

Women just didn't frequent the arcade. Westfield Arcade was more like a men's club, and the only requirements for membership were being a male and loving arcade games. If you fit those criteria, you were in. Unless a girl was tagging along to watch her boyfriend play games, women simply didn't come to the arcade.

Which is why I was so surprised on that day to look up and see a girl in the arcade. She was by herself, and she tentatively stood on the outskirts of the arcade, right inside the entrance, close to a small group huddled around the Galaxian cabinet. She had wide, expressive eyes and milky white skin. This was the era of the blondes, when every teenage girl lightened their hair to resemble Cheryl Tiegs and Suzanne Somers and Blondie, but she had rich, jet black hair that was cut short and fashioned into a tousled bob. She wore a pair of dark blue Chic jeans that rode high on her hips and a small black t-shirt depicting the open mouth, tongue-out logo of The Rolling Stones. The U.S. Tour, 1978, the shirt read underneath the logo.

As Willie continued playing Donkey Kong in the background, I looked at this mystery girl. She stood just inside Westfield Arcade's entrance, and her eyes scanned the arcade and all of its inhabitants. As she looked around the arcade, her eyes locked with mine for the briefest of moments before she looked away. She spotted the change machine in the corner of the arcade, and walked over to it.

"Who's the fox?"

I turned around. Willie had abandoned his Donkey Kong game and he and the crew watching him play were right behind me, focused on the girl.

"I dunno," I said.

"She's a cutie, whoever she is," Willie said.

We watched as she reached the change machine in the corner of the arcade. She stopped directly in front of it and started going through her purse. Her back was now to us, but I could see her pull a dollar bill from her purse and insert it into the dollar slot on the change machine. The machine sucked the dollar bill in, then spit it back out a second later.

"You guys see the babe?" Gonzo asked, appearing at our side. The word of an attractive girl in the arcade had apparently spread like wildfire--a quick look around showed that at least half of the guys in Westfield Arcade had abandoned their arcade games and had their eyes fixated in the direction of the change machine.

"I saw her, all right," Willie said.

I watched her as she inserted her dollar bill into the change machine again. Once more, the machine promptly spit it back out. She took the dollar bill from the slot and attempted to smooth it out using the edge of the machine.

"The machine won't take her dollar," Rufus said.

"No shit, Einstein," Willie said.

We watched as she inserted her dollar bill into the change machine a third time. Once more, the machine rejected her dollar.

"Go over there and help her, Mike," Willie said. "That's your job, ain't it?"

"And while you're over there, put a few moves on her," Gonzo said. "Maybe get her number."

"Hell yeah," Willie said. "What's your best pick-up line, Mikey-boy?"

"My best pick-up line? I don't know."

"You have a go-to line, right? The one that women fall for every time? Go over and fix the machine for her, then feed her your best pick-up line. Try to get her number."

I looked at the change machine. The mysterious girl still stood at the machine, her back to us, trying to feed her dollar bill into the machine.

I started walking over to the change machine, trying to portray a calm, cool confidence that I in no way actually felt. I walked down the row of arcade cabinets, on a direct path to the change machine, and I could feel the eyes of every single person in the arcade on me. I passed a group around the Berzerk cabinet, each one of the four guys at the cabinet turned towards the girl at the change machine as if none of them had ever seen a woman before.

I reached the change machine and stood there for a few moments, the girl's back still towards me. I cleared my throat, and she turned around and looked at me. I froze. Up close, she was even more beautiful. There was a hint of eyeliner around her eyes. I could see light freckles on the bridge of her nose. She had on red lipstick that contrasted perfectly against her light skin.

"Having some difficulty?" I said.

"Yeah, a little," she said. "I need some change for the tolls on my drive home, but the machine doesn't want my dollar."

She inserted her bill into the machine again. The machine spit it back out. She turned towards me and shrugged.

"It must only like blondes," she said.

I smiled at her joke, then grabbed the keyring from the pocket of my jeans. I thumbed through a few of the keys until I found the one for the change machine. I tried to act smooth and debonair as I inserted the key into a keyhole at the top of the machine and swung the door service door open. Unfortunately, there's a ceiling that limits how suave one can look when opening a change machine while working at a video game arcade. That ceiling is very low.

"Here's the problem," I said, pointing at a small black piece on the inside of the machine. A dollar bill was crumpled against this piece. "The change machine uses this magnetic head to read the ink on the dollar bill, and then it sends a signal to the coin mechanism to dispense the proper number of coins from the storage compartment."

"I see," she said.

"But this dollar bill got jammed into the machine, and it's obscuring the magnetic head. So the head can't read your dollar bill."

"Fascinating stuff."

"So the message doesn't get sent to the coin mechanism and the dollar bill just gets spit back out and--"

I looked at her. She had a numb, thoroughly unimpressed look on her face.

"I'm just boring you to death, aren't I?" I said.

Her face lit up with a smile and she laughed. She had a cute laugh.

"Sorry, but the inner workings of a change machine isn't exactly a topic of interest for me," she said, still smiling.

"I apologize," I said. "I'm just rambling like a complete fool."

I shut the door of the change machine and reinserted her dollar. A moment later, four quarters clambered down into the coin slot. I reached down and scooped them up. When I gave them to her, my hand briefly brushed up against hers.

"You're my knight in shining armor," she said.

She took the quarters and put them in the pocket of her jeans, then looked back up at me.

"See you around, cutie," she said as she started walking away.

The feeling in my stomach was not unlike the feeling one experiences when a roller coaster passes the top of the hill and begins its rapid descent back downward. My legs nearly gave out from under me, and I had to concentrate to remain standing upright.

Cutie. She had just called me cutie. I tried to think of some sort of smooth, snappy response, but at the moment simply breathing was enough of a challenge; actually coming up with a suave retort that didn't sound like the world's most pathetic attempt at flirting with a girl was impossible.

I watched as the girl (never did get her name) walked away from me before I could respond to her. She passed the Missile Command and Defender cabinets at the front of the arcade, the crowds at both quickly turning back around and focusing on the games in front of them to avoid making eye contact with her. She reached the entrance to Westfield Arcade, but before disappearing into the crowd of shoppers outside the arcade, she turned around and looked back in the direction of the change machine. Our eyes locked for what seemed like an eternity but was probably only a second or two. The faintest smile crossed her lips, then she turned back around and walked outside of Westfield Arcade.

I remained standing by myself at the change machine. My hand still tingled where I'd touched her. Her casual smile had melted my heart. Literally. The warm sensation in my chest felt as if my heart was slowly liquefying under intense heat.

Through Westfield Arcade's window, I looked out into the crowd of people outside the arcade. I scanned the various faces, trying to spot her. Amidst the sea of shoppers, I couldn't find her anywhere. She was gone for good.

But as it turned out, she wasn't gone for good at all. Not by a long shot.

# # #

I watched as a large red truck with 'Freight America Distribution' painted on the side of its trailer backed into the loading dock beneath Westfield Mall. The truck slowly inched backwards until its rear bumper was up against the cement ledge of the loading dock. The brake lights illuminated and engine shut off. An overweight guy in a stained red t-shirt stuck his head out of the driver's side window and motioned to me. I walked over to him.

"You the guy from the arcade?" he asked me.

"Yeah."

"Need you to sign something."

He reached out the open window and handed me a pen and a sheet of paper on a clipboard. I briefly scanned the invoice, then scrawled my name on a dotted line at the bottom of the sheet.

"What game is this one?" I asked, handing the pen and clipboard back to him. "We've got a few on order."

"Dunno," he said. "I just deliver the things, kid."

He exited from the truck's cabin, then walked to the rear of the truck and extended a ramp that formed a bridge from the rear of the truck to the loading dock. He slid the trailer's rear door upwards and jumped up into the cargo area. I looked into the cargo area and saw that it was filled with two rows of arcade cabinets, each game draped in a brown padded protective cover to prevent dings and scratches during transport. Each arcade game had a pink invoice taped to the protective cover. The delivery driver scanned the invoices of a few cabinets until he found the one he was looking for.

He retrieved a dolly from the front of the cargo area and wheeled it over to the arcade cabinet. He slid the dolly underneath the cabinet and secured it in place by looping a few safety straps around it. He wheeled the arcade cabinet down the incline of the ramp into the loading dock area.

"Where do you want it?" he asked.

"Follow me."

I walked across the loading dock, the delivery driver wheeling the arcade cabinet behind me, and reached the service elevator in the corner. The service elevator provided access from the subterranean loading dock to a second storage area on the first floor of the mall, from which a pair of double doors opened into the food court. I pushed the up arrow when we reached the service elevator, and we waited for the elevator to arrive.

I'd spent nearly every single day over the previous few months working at the arcade, the part-time job quickly turning into a full-time one. My schedule was practically set in stone: I visited my grandpa in the morning for an hour or two every day, grabbed a quick lunch at the mall's food court, then worked the evening shift at Westfield Arcade until close. The more time I spent at Westfield Arcade, the more I fell in love with the place. It wasn't the arcade games I loved--I'd still managed to resist the lure of arcade games and had yet to play a single game since I'd started. For me, it was the social aspect of the arcade. The fast-paced banter among the regulars at the arcade. The jokes that flew endlessly. The constant debates and arguments that we had amongst each other--debates about whether Farah Fawcett or Jaclyn Smith was hotter, debates about whether it was actually possible to solve a Rubik's Cube, debates about that year's hottest tv question, Who Shot J.R.?. Regardless of the topic, everyone had an opinion they didn't hesitate to voice, and I soon developed something close to a friendship with all of the regulars at the arcade--Rufus, Gonzo, Bearclaw, countless others.

And of course, there was Willie.

He was an entertainer in the truest sense of the word. The guy was a force of nature, a runaway freight train who stormed around the arcade and made himself the center of attention every time he showed up at Westfield Arcade. If Willie didn't have a crowd around him as he set a high score in an arcade game, he had a crowd around him as he told a joke or relayed a story or voiced his opinion in a debate with someone. He was the most obnoxious person I'd ever met, and I mean that in the best way possible. He never shut his mouth, but he was so entertaining that you never *wanted* him to shut his mouth.

As I started working more hours at the arcade, Ed had given me more responsibility. He worked at a fertilizer sales company in addition to owning Westfield Arcade, and was more than happy to pass off some of the day-to-day work to me. I had taken to balancing the books for him, a responsibility I performed with ease thanks to a few accounting courses I'd taken at Northwestern. I'd started to work with various distributors of arcade games to secure the best price for games we ordered. When it came to the delivery of the new games, I did it all--determining where in the arcade we'd place the game, securing space in the local newspaper to advertise the newer games, then dealing with freight companies to coordinate the delivery of the games.

The elevator arrived and the delivery driver and I took it up to the first floor. We stepped off, and the driver wheeled the cabinet behind me as we walked through a pair of double doors out into the food court. It was a Friday afternoon and the place was starting to fill up with the weekend cinema and shopping crowds. I led the delivery driver over to Westfield Arcade, and as we approached, I noticed there was a group standing at the front of the arcade, waiting for the delivery.

The delivery driver wheeled the cabinet into Westfield Arcade and the crowd at the front of the arcade watched him with anticipatory, anxious eyes. I'd already opened up a space next to Missile Command at the front of the arcade for this new game, and the delivery driver positioned the cabinet in the open space, then expertly slid the dolly out from underneath it. He pulled the brown protective cover off of the arcade cabinet and wadded it up in his hands.

"Anything else?" he asked me.

"Nope. Thanks."

The anticipation and buzz that surrounded the arrival of a new game was unrivaled by anything else in the arcade, and even more people walked over to the new game, forming a crowd around it. They examined the game and talked amongst themselves while looking at the cabinet.

"Pac Man," Willie said, reading the name of the game on the marquee. "What the hell kinda name is that?"

"Is this supposed to be a good one?" Bearclaw asked me, pouring a handful of M-n-M's out into his meaty paw.

"No clue," I said.

"Looks like a dog if you ask me," Willie said. "I mean, look at the controls."

I looked at the game's control panel. There was a one-player button, a two-player button, and a joystick. That was it. No 'fire' button. No 'jump' button. No accelerate or decelerate or thrust or hyperspace buttons. Just a joystick that you could move in four directions and nothing else.

"Only one way to find out if the game's any good," I said.

I reached around the back of the cabinet and plugged the power cord into an outlet on the ground. The screen flickered to life and the theme music started playing through the speakers. Everyone watched the demo screen, as a computer-controlled yellow circle moved around the screen and ate pellets while four ghosts chased him.

"Looks like a maze game or something," Bearclaw said.

"Lemme give it a shot," Willie said. "See if it's as shitty as it looks."

Willie stepped up to the game, a bored, indifferent look on his face. He fished a quarter from the pocket of his jeans and put it in the game's quarter slot. The coin clinked metallically after he deposited it into the machine, and he hit the one-player button. A blue-lined maze with various small pellets (and four large pellets in each corner) appeared on screen. After a brief wait, the game began.

For the rest of the night, there was a line ten-deep to play it.

3. PAC MAN

It is impossible to overstate just how huge Pac Man became after it was released. The game grossed over 3.5 billion dollars in quarters during its first few years of release, making it the most successful video game of all-time by a wide margin. The lines to play the game were so long that Ed bought a second Pac Man cabinet, then a third. We lined them up side-by-side-by-side in the corner of the arcade and unofficially dubbed it Pac Man Corner. The crowd around Pac Man Corner would often get so big that it would spill out of Westfield Arcade and into the food court.

But that doesn't even tell half the story. The game's popularity transcended the arcade. Pac Man appeared on the cover of <u>Time</u> magazine. Stories that talked of the game's popularity led the evening news. Pac Man was licensed to appear on all sorts of memorabilia, and everywhere you looked, you saw kids carrying Pac man lunchboxes to school, people wearing various Pac Man t-shirts, teenagers eating Pac Man power pellets candy stored in Pac Man candy tins that they washed down with Pac Man Power-Up fruit drink. Two separate strategy guides for Pac Man made <u>The New York Times</u> bestseller list. A song about Pac Man was recorded by an unknown

Ohio rock band, and, like everything associated with the yellow pie-shaped guy, it turned into a huge success, making the Billboard Top 10 Singles chart despite the fact that it was a brutally terrible song. Pac Man Fever was the name of the song, but describing the popularity of Pac Man that swept over the nation during the early 1980s as a fever was an understatement. It was a craze, a national obsession. Pac Man was absolutely everywhere.

# # #

On a Thursday night a few months after the game's release, a group of around fifteen people stood in Pac Man corner. Willie played on one of the cabinets, and most of the crowd watched his game as they waited for their turn in line. I walked over to the crowd.

"Place is closing, guys," I said when I reached them.

This was immediately met with protests. A few people groaned and shook their head in frustration. I couldn't blame them--most had probably been waiting in line for at least twenty minutes to play the game.

"The game will still be here tomorrow," I said.

Everyone started leaving Westfield Arcade. I walked to the back of the arcade and started emptying the quarters from the various machines into a large bucket, recording how much money each machine had generated in a small notepad. I made my way around the arcade, unlocking the service door for each cabinet and emptying each out into the bucket. When I reached the front of the arcade, I walked to the change machine. I noticed that Willie still stood at the Pac Man cabinet. He was the only other person in the arcade.

"Hey, Willie, the place is closed," I said to him.

"Not yet, it isn't," Willie said, not looking away from the screen. The rapid *wokka-wokka-wokka* noise that

Pac Man made whenever he ate a pellet sang from the game's speakers. "I've got a killer game going here. Almost four hundred thousand points and I haven't died yet."

"Doesn't matter--I still gotta kick you out," I said.

"Chill, man. Cops aren't going to show up if I stay here a little after nine. Just lemme finish this game and I'll be gone."

"Fine," I said. I knew it was pointless to argue with him.

I opened up the change machine and replenished its stock of quarters, pulling handfuls of quarters from the bucket and dumping them in the storage compartment of the change machine. Once I emptied the bucket, I walked over to the front counter and logged the amount generated by each machine in a ledger. After performing some general cleanup duties, I walked over to Willie at the Pac Man cabinet. He was still playing the game by himself.

"Almost done?" I asked.

"Yeah," he said over his shoulder. "Sort of."

I looked in the upper left-hand corner of the screen and saw that his current score was 71,230.

"I thought you said your score was almost 400,000," I said.

"It was," he said. "That was last game."

"You started another game?"

"Maybe..." Willie said. In the reflection of the Pac Man screen, I could see a smile creep over his face.

"This is the last one," I said. "We're out of here after this."

I retrieved a chair from behind the front counter and pulled it over to the Pac Man cabinet. I sat down in the chair and watched Willie play Pac Man over his shoulder. As Willie played, the rapid *wokka-wokka-wokka* sound continued to ring through the speakers every time Pac Man swallowed a pellet.

"Doesn't that sound drive you crazy?" I asked him.

"Nah, man," he said. "I love it. When I die, I want that sound to be played on a continuous loop at my funeral."

He continued playing the game, focused on the screen as he maneuvered the little yellow sphere around the blue-lined maze and ate pellets.

"So what's your story?" he eventually asked me, still staring straight ahead at the screen.

Even though I'd spent countless hours hanging out with the regulars at Westfield Arcade, the conversation amongst us rarely strayed beyond the arcade's current crop of games or a debate about a television show or movie. Or women--we talked about women constantly. We lived in the moment, had fun talking about mindless shit with one another, and we left it at that. I didn't know where any of the guys lived or what any of them did when they weren't at the arcade, and I didn't really care, either. We had a blast every night at the arcade, and that was enough for us.

"My story?" I said. "Not much to tell."

"Sure there is. Everyone's got a story."

I didn't say anything in response.

"Are you in college at all?" Willie asked.

"I attended Northwestern for awhile. Decided not to go back for my final year."

"Too cool for school—I can dig that," Willie said, his eyes still focused on the Pac Man screen. He rammed his joystick to the left to escape a ghost in hot pursuit.

"Not really too cool. Just had to take a break from college for awhile."

"'Take a break from college'—sounds like code for 'My grades sucked and Northwestern kicked my ass to the curb,'" he said, laughing.

"I had a 3.9 GPA."

"Sure you did. And I won the Nobel Peace Prize."

"I'm serious."

"Guys with a 3.9 GPA don't just drop out of school. You're either full of shit, or you actually do have a story. Which one is it?"

I didn't say anything at first. I just watched him play Pac Man. But for some reason, I felt like talking with Willie. It was nice to be here one on one with him, away from the large groups that typically populated Westfield Arcade. And, I decided, it might be a refreshing change to discuss something more substantive than women and movies.

So I pulled my chair in closer to the Pac Man cabinet and began telling Willie my story.

"My parents both died when I was twelve years old," I said, raising my voice slightly to be heard over the sound effects coming from the Pac Man game. "My dad had a convention for his job in Florida, my mom joined him, and their plane crashed in the middle of Tennessee before they arrived. It was a small, private jet that my dad's company paid for. All thirteen people on board died in the crash."

Willie stopped playing the game of Pac Man, abandoning it in mid-game, and he turned around and looked at me.

"Jesus, man. I'm sorry."

"It happened. It was almost a decade ago, and it seems even longer. I've come to grips with it now, but at the time, it was more than I could handle. Twelve years old and I was suddenly on my own. I had no-one—no siblings, no relatives in the area, nothing. I didn't know what was going to happen to me. I thought I was going to have to move away to a foster home or get adopted by a random family I'd never met, something like that.

"I was just a mess. And the one person who was there for me was my grandpa. He flew in from Oregon when it happened, and he was the shoulder I cried on in the days after the crash. He'd lost his wife a few years earlier, and he helped put things in perspective, helped me to cope. He stayed by my side through it all, and when the funeral was over, he told me that he was going to move to Indianapolis to raise me.

"Thing is, I barely even knew him at the time. He'd lived in Oregon his entire life, and we only saw each other once every year or two. But he uprooted his entire life in Oregon, moved away from his friends and everyone he knew, to move here so I wouldn't have to start over somewhere else. He sacrificed everything for me. And for the next few years, he raised me. Drove me around before I was old enough to drive, then helped me buy a car when the time came. Ate dinner with me every night, then helped me with homework afterwards if I needed it. Yelled at me if I came home too late on a Saturday night. He completely devoted his life to my life, through junior high and high school and then he saw me off to college."

I paused to compose myself. Willie remained staring at me, listening to the story.

"A couple months ago, when I was away at college, I got a call one day. The police had found my grandpa wandering in the middle of a street a mile from where we lived. It was ten degrees outside, and he was wearing a t-shirt with no coat. Long story short, after some tests, it was determined that he has early-onset Alzheimer's. He couldn't be trusted to live on his own--he might forget to turn off a stove burner and cause a fire, something horrible like that--so he had to be moved to a senior care facility. And this senior care facility he moved into...it's just the most depressing place I've ever been to in my entire life. He's got this small, dark room. No-one ever comes to visit. He has a small television that he watches constantly. I just pictured him, alone in his room day-after-day, no-one ever coming to visit, nothing to look forward to all day. And it broke my heart to think of how lonely he must be.

"So I decided not to go back to school, and I moved back home to be there for him. He sacrificed everything to be there for me when I needed him, so the least I can do is be there for him. I visit him every single day, and it's always the highlight of my day to see his face light up when I arrive to his room."

I let out a deep breath. Willie stood there, looking at me, his game of Pac Man long-forgotten.

"I don't even know what to say to something like that," Willie said.

"Nothing to say. That's life."

"So you just work here and visit him, every single day?"

"Pretty much," I said. "I thought about transferring to a college here in Indy, but it'd be too much of a time commitment. Plus, I'd graduate in a year, and starting out a career and caring for my grandpa would be too much. Maybe I'll be able to handle that in the future. But not now."

"How's your grandpa doing so far?" Willie asked. "Has the Alzheimer's gotten bad?"

"Not at all. He's doing good. I mean, he forgets things from time to time. But his condition hasn't gotten super-serious."

Willie gave a slight nod.

"So your grandpa--he's cool?"

"The coolest," I said. "The best."

"I want to meet him."

"My grandpa?"

"Yeah. I want to meet him."

"Why?"

"Would you believe I have a grandma fetish? I figure he can introduce me to some of his lady friends, maybe score me a hot date for Saturday night."

He smiled at me.

"Nah, I just want to meet him. He sounds cool. I like meeting cool people."

"Sure, if you wanna," I said. "I've got the night off tomorrow and I'm heading to watch the Cubs game with him."

"I'm in," Willie said. "I love baseball."

I gave him directions to the senior care center, which was only a short ways from Westfield Mall.

"So do you care if I get another game in tonight?" Willie asked, eyeing over the Pac Man cabinet.

"Sure, let's stay. Ed will never know. I'll grab some sodas"

Willie reached down to put a quarter into the slot.

"Oh, and make it a two-player game," I said as I walked towards the front counter.

"You're playing?" he asked.

"Sure, why not?" I said. "I'll play a quick game."

"Oh, this oughta be good," Willie said, laughing. "Looks like Pac Man's about to claim another victim."

# # #

I pulled my car into the parking lot of the senior care center and killed the headlights before shutting off the engine and exiting the car. I yawned, taking in a breath of the brisk evening air. Willie and I had stayed at Westfield Arcade until just after three in the morning the night before, playing game after game of Pac Man. It was the latest I'd been awake since college, and the late night had wreaked havoc on my sleep cycle. I'd felt tired and groggy all day.

I looked around the parking lot. Ten open spaces, three parked cars, and not a single sign of Willie. I leaned on the hood of my car and waited for him. As I waited, I thought about Pac Man. The simple, quick game of Pac Man last night had quickly turned into a couple of games, which then turned into Willie and I playing Pac Man on

53

separate side-by-side cabinets, talking to each other the entire night over the combined wokka-wokka-wokka sounds of Pac Man chomping away on pellets in our separate games. When I finally drug myself away from the game to check the time, I was shocked to see that we'd been playing for almost four consecutive hours. The time had absolutely disappeared.

I'd fallen in love with the game. Even here, in the darkened parking lot of the senior center, I was thinking about Pac Man in the back of my mind. The layout of the various mazes in the game. The best strategy for conserving power pellets. The most efficient route to take to access the bonus fruit that appeared in the middle of the screen. I still had my high score from last night memorized—49,150—and couldn't wait to get started on besting it.

The thoughts of Pac Man were quickly interrupted by a Trans-Am that pulled into the parking lot, tires squealing on the asphalt. It was a car straight out of Smoky and the Bandit--jet black paint job, t-top windows, screamin' chicken painted on the hood. Despite the relatively chilly evening weather, the windows of the Trans-Am were down, and "When You See a Chance" by Steve Winwood blared from the speakers of the car.

I could see Willie behind the wheel. He pulled into the parking spot next to me, and I waved at him. He extended his middle finger towards me in response. Through the windshield of his car, I saw him smile.

"Sorry I'm late," he said, exiting from his car.

"Don't worry about it," I said.

We walked inside the senior care center and passed by the recreation room. A few older folks sat around a card table, working on the exact puzzle that they seemed to have been working on putting together for months. Another sat in a recliner, watching them put together the puzzle with a dazed expression on her face.

After signing in, we walked down the hallway to my grandpa's room.

"Man, this place smells worse than the arcade," Willie said.

At the end of the hallway, we reached my grandpa's room. The door was open and Willie and I took a few steps inside. My grandpa was in a recliner, right to the side of his bed. A few feet in front of him, the television was on, and he stared into the screen.

"Grandpa," I said. He looked over and broke into a smile when he saw me.

"Come in, come in," he said. Using the armrests for support, he slowly got up out of his recliner. He walked over to his bed and laid in it. The mound of pillows behind his head propped him up.

He looked up at me, then over at Willie.

"It's good to see you again," he said to Willie, even though they'd never met before.

For a second, there was a flash of confusion on Willie's face.

"Good to see you again, too," Willie said.

The game was on the television, already in the top of the third. The voices of Jack Brickhouse and Milo Hamilton came through loud and clear on the television's speakers.

"What's the score?" Willie asked.

"Already 1-0 Phillies," my grandpa said.

Willie sat down in the recliner and I sat next to him.

"Are you a Cubs fan?" my grandpa asked Willie.

Willie unzipped his Baracuda jacket, revealing a baby blue shirt with CUBS written in red lettering.

"You know it," Willie said. "Too bad that season's shot already."

"They can't pitch," my grandpa said.

"Can't hit, either."

"Other than that, they're a great team," my grandpa said. Willie laughed at him.

"They need a new manager," Willie continued. "That's the real problem. Fire Amalfitano, go out and get a guy who know what he'd doing, maybe then they—"

He stopped in mid-sentence.

"What the hell do we have here?" he said.

His eyes focused on the newspaper cutouts on my grandpa's wall, and he walked over to them to get a better look. He leaned in close to one of the pictures.

"Look at the ladykiller over here," Willie said. "Mike, dude, you were a hound back in high school."

I walked over and looked at the picture he was referring to. It was a school picture from my sophomore year of high school. I wore a multi-colored plaid sport jacket over a mustard-colored argyle sweater, the finest of 1970s fashion. The photograph of me looking into the camera had been superimposed upon a different shadowed picture of a side-shot of my face looking into the distance.

"Wow, that is just great," Willie said, delighted. "That's fantastic. Do you still have this sweater?"

"No," I said.

"What about the jacket?"

"Don't have that, either."

"That's a shame," Willie said.

On the television, Dave Kingman struck out with a runner on third base to end the inning. My grandpa slowly shook his head.

"Blew the heater right by him," he said.

Willie continued to look over the assortment of newspaper cutouts and article on my grandpa's wall, then shifted his attention to the shelf with various collectibles and knick knacks.

"What's this?" Willie asked. He picked up a baseball from my grandpa's shelf.

"It's a baseball," I said.

"No kidding," Willie said. "Looks old as hell, though."

"It is," my grandpa said. He looked at me and winked. I knew exactly what was coming next.

"1932 World Series," my grandpa continued. "Game 3. That's where I caught that ball."

Willie looked at him, impressed.

"You were at the game?"

"Sure was. I was twenty years old"

"Wait a second. Game 3, 1932 World Series. That was—"

"Babe Ruth's called shot. That ball you're holding in your hands, that's the ball he hit."

Willie looked at the ball in his hands, his eyes widening to saucers.

"This is the ball from Babe Ruth's called shot?" he asked, awed.

"It is," my grandpa said. "I was out in the bleachers for the entire game. The sixth inning rolls around and the Babe steps to the plate. And he points directly at me in the outfield stands. He steps back in the batter's box, the next pitch comes, and he kills it to centerfield. And the ball's coming right at me."

I looked at Willie. He was amazed by the story, his jaw practically unhinged from his mouth.

"My entire section stands up," my grandpa continued. "The ball keeps sailing through the air, coming straight at us. Then it starts coming back towards the ground, looking like it's traveling at a million miles an hour. It's still headed straight for my section but looks like it's going to land over my head. So I jump as high as I can and—"

My grandpa paused for a second, then started laughing.

"What's so funny?" Willie asked. "Finish the story."

"He's pulling your chain," I told Willie.

At that, my grandpa lost it, laughing even harder.

"Oh, that is just mean," Willie said.

"Sorry," my grandpa said, coming back. "Sorry. But I had to. You should have seen the look on your face."

It was a prank that my grandpa had pulled on countless friends of mine growing up, convincing them that his baseball had some significance and history behind it. Sometimes, he'd concoct a story about the ball being from Roger Maris's record-breaking 61st home run in 1961. Other times, he'd claim that the ball was from Hank Aaron's very first homerun in his rookie season. Bobby Thompson's "Shot Heard 'Round the World," Bill Mazeroski's game-winner in game 7 of the 1960 World Series, Ernie Banks' 500th career homerun--at one point or another, my grandpa had tricked a visitor to our house into believing his old, worn baseball was from each one of these famous moments in baseball history.

It made me happy to see that he was still good as ever at it. And that he still got a kick out of the old joke.

"So what is the baseball from?" Willie said.

"I don't even know where I got that old ball," my grandpa said. "I think I found it in my yard one day. I put it in a case for the heck of it, and people started asking questions about it, thinking there was a story behind it. So I gave them a story. But the truth is that it's just a regular old ball."

Willie looked at the ball again, then tossed it in the air a few times and set it back in the display case.

The three of us continued watching the game, just three guys sitting around and talking shop. Willie and my grandpa hit it off and chatted away the entire game, connected by the common bond of their love for the Cubs and their mutual disgust with the sorry season they were having. They complained about the manager, complained about he pitching staff, complained about the offseason trades the ballclub had made.

"My glasses," my grandpa suddenly said in the middle of one of their conversations. "Where are my glasses?"

"You have them on," I said.

He looked down at his left wrist, then his other wrist.

"No, my glasses. Where are they?"

He looked at his wrist again, and I realized he was talking about his watch. I found it on his bedside table, in plain sight in a small dish with some change, where he always put it when he took it off. I grabbed it and handed it to my grandpa. He looked at the time displayed, then set it back on the bedside table.

From time to time when I visited, my grandpa would have lapses like these. He'd ask about his shirt when referring to a pair of pants, or refer to the dining room as the rec room. Once, he'd asked me when we were going back to Hawaii, despite the fact that he nor I had ever been to Hawaii. It was never anything major, but these brief lapses served as a stark reminder that his disease was indeed real, that not all was well inside of his head and his mind was slowly deteriorating away.

Around the eighth inning, a nurse appeared and told Willie and I we had to go--it was past visiting hours. Willie and I bid my grandpa farewell and walked outside to the parking lot.

"Thanks for coming," I said to Willie once we were outside. "That was nice."

"Your grandpa's fifty times cooler than you are," Willie said.

"I told you he was."

"I had a great time," Willie said. "I can't wait to visit him again."

And in that moment, I knew that there was much more to Willie Cardinal than the side he showed at the arcade. There was a genuinely nice person in there somewhere. Beyond the guy who was boisterous and foul-mouthed and hurled insults when he was at the arcade, there was a caring person. A nice person who'd just spent the entire evening sitting around and talking with my grandpa.

Right then, I knew that Willie Cardinal and I would be great friends.

"See you tomorrow?" Willie said as he entered his Trans-Am.

"I'll see you tomorrow," I said. "I'll play you in Pac Man."

Willie laughed.

"I told you that game would get you."

4. ROBOTRON: 2084

After Pac Man, Donkey Kong, and Galaxian had set the industry on fire, sequels to each came out in the next year--Ms. Pac Man, Donkey Kong Jr., and Galaga. Each sequel was hugely popular. Revolutionary games were released on what seemed like a weekly basis. Q*Bert was a blast. Tempest was unlike anything we'd ever played. Pole Position was the first truly realistic racing game. Even the relics of the arcade from years prior--Asteroids, Space Invaders, Battlezone--still drew crowds.

It didn't seem possible after the otherworldly success of Pac Man, but arcade games became even more popular than ever before. When the year ended, the video game arcade industry as a whole took in $8 billion in quarters in 1982, surpassing the combined totals of the film ($4 billion) and the music ($3 billion) industries. It also exceeded the revenues of all major sports combined, earning three times the combined ticket and television revenues of Major League Baseball, NBA basketball, and NFL football. The sheer popularity of arcade games was unparalleled.

The crowds that showed up to Westfield Arcade were bigger than ever and the lines to play the newer releases were longer than ever. Friday and Saturday nights, in particular, were truly amazing sights--Westfield Arcade was usually as packed as a popular nightclub on those nights, with huddled crowds of teenagers and young adults moving from game to game.

The enormous crowds at the arcade made money hand over first for Ed, and with some of the extra money, he pulled out his pocketbook and bought a television for the arcade. We cleared out a section of games next to the entrance of the arcade, and moved in a hulking, wood-grained, 50-inch monstrosity of a television that was absolutely state-of-the-art for the time.

Even better, Ed also sprung for cable television, an extreme luxury back then. Having cable television meant that we had a mind-boggling twenty-seven channels to choose from--but more importantly for us Westfield Arcade regulars, having cable television at the arcade meant that one of those channels was MTV.

We got our MTV right as the network started to blow up. All day, every day, MTV played on the television and the music accompanying the video blasted from the speakers. Westfield Arcade was one of the only places for miles that actually had MTV, and even bigger crowds began showing up to check out MTV. People couldn't get enough of it, and arcade games started to be played with one eye looking out the corner at the television. If a popular video was showing or a new video was debuting, the crowd at the arcade would gravitate over towards the television, watch the video together, then return back to our beloved arcade games once it ended, the music video providing endless fodder for conversation and debate.

# # #

My heart thundered in my chest. Sweat beaded on my forehead. I concentrated. In my left hand, I firmly held a joystick and rammed it to the left to avoid a wave of five enemies by mere millimeters, then quickly rammed the joystick back to the right. My right hand gripped a second joystick, and I took out a row of five HULK robots by forcing the joystick upwards.

I was playing Robotron: 2084, the latest, greatest, most nonstop game the arcade had to offer. The premise of the game was simple enough: You controlled a human being as he ran around the screen and shot robots. But what separated Robotron: 2084 from every other game that had been released up to that point was just how relentless the waves of robots that chased your character were. In the later stages of the game, the screen was literally covered with what seemed like thousands of robots chasing you around the screen. It was the most nonstop game we had at Westfield Arcade.

I continued playing the game, solely focused on the screen in front of me. Since my first game of Pac Man on that late night with Willie, I'd turned into a one-hundred percent arcade game addict. Whenever I worked at the arcade, I played games in the down time. Most every night, after Westfield Arcade closed, I stayed at the arcade and played games, Willie usually right by my side. Working at the arcade had turned into so much more than a fun, time-killing way to make a few dollars. The arcade was my home, my life. If I was awake, I was either visiting my grandpa or I was at Westfield Arcade, even on days I wasn't scheduled to work.

Each joystick gripped firmly in my hands, I took a wave of enemies out, directing my character into the upper left corner of the screen. When I got practically surrounded, I quickly moved down the left side of the screen. Another thing that set Robotron: 2084 apart from every game that had been released before was the controls of the game. Instead of a single joystick to control your player and a variety of buttons to fire, jump, or perform other actions, there were two joysticks and no buttons. The joystick on the left controlled your player's movements around the screen, and the joystick on the right controlled which direction your player's gun fired in. The dual joystick controls took awhile to get used to, but once you

63

had them down, the game was impossible to step away from.

The television across the room was cranked to MTV. I heard "Who Can It Be Now?" by Men at Work come to an end, then the opening guitar riff for "Eye of the Tiger" by Survivor kicked in through the speakers. It was perfect background music to play to, upbeat and electrifying.

Always on the move, I made my character zig and zag across the screen while working the right-hand joystick in a circular motion to direct the gunfire and take out the robots that closed in on me from every angle. A dull throbbing sensation had started to radiate throughout my right hand. My eyes quickly darted to the running scoreboard in the corner. 1,887,650 points.

Behind me, I was well aware that a crowd had started to form. I could see the huddled mass in the reflection of the arcade screen. I could hear them, moving around, sipping their sodas, conversing with one another.

"He's got a chance to beat Willie's high score," Rufus's awed voice said to the crowd behind me.

"Trust me, he'll choke," I heard Willie say, raising his voice so he was sure that I could hear him over the guitar of "Eye of the Tiger." Willie, in particular, loved Robotron: 2084. He'd quickly racked up a two-million-point game in the game's first month of release, and no-one had come close to his score. Until now.

"Almost 1.8 million, still three extra lives remaining," Rufus said. "This is incredible."

I rammed the joystick on the right to the left and the joystick on the left to the right, firing at enemies on the right side of the screen as my character retreated towards the left. Took out a row of five GRUNTs, the rapid fire sound effects of gunfire singing out through the game's speakers.

It was the game of a lifetime, and when I died for the final time, I stepped away from the cabinet and let out a deep, relieved breath. The frantic intensity of the game had left me exhausted--a thin sheen of sweat covered my forehead, and my heart hammered in my chest. I looked at the scoreboard in the corner of the monitor: 2,451,400 points. I'd beat Willie's score by nearly 300,000 points.

I turned around and faced the crowd that had gathered, which numbered almost twenty people. Some mobbed me. Others offered more subdued congratulations. I noticed Willie on the periphery. Instead of looking at me, he eyed down the Robotron: 2084 cabinet, as if it had betrayed him by allowing someone to top one of his high scores.

I walked over to the chalkboard behind the counter. Most of the crowd watching my game had dispersed to other games in the arcade, but a few people, Willie included, followed me. I jumped behind the counter and grabbed an eraser, erasing WLC and the high score listed next to Robotron: 2084. In its place, I put my initials— MRM—and the new high score.

"Damn, my hands are wrecked," I said after updating the high sore chalkboard. I looked down at them. The left one was slightly trembling from repeatedly ramming against the joystick, and the throbbing sensation had intensified. There was a nasty, red abrasion on the outside of my right index finger where the skin had been rubbed raw by the joystick, and I knew that there'd be a blister forming over the sore before long.

"Battle scars," Willie said. "They happen to everyone. Man up and quit complaining like a Sally."

"Someone sounds a little bitter about their high score getting destroyed."

"Ain't no big deal," Willie said, though we both knew it was indeed a very big deal. "Beat my score in Pac

Man or Space Invaders, then we can talk. Or Asteroids. Ha! I'd love to see you even crack 200,000 on Asteroids."

Willie retreated back to the Robotron: 2084 cabinet and I stayed behind the counter, serving up a few sodas. I turned around and looked at the high score chalkboard. There it was. Right there amid the sea of WLC's. Robotron: 2084. MRM. 2,402,350.

The night ended, and Willie and I stayed in the arcade after it closed, which had turned into practically a nightly occurrence for us. It was usually just the two of us, Willie and I playing arcade games and listening to MTV After Dark blaring from the television speakers. We'd usually stick around until midnight, but occasionally, we'd stay late into the night, until three or four. This was particularly true if Westfield Arcade had just received a newer game that we both enjoyed playing. On the memorable night after the arcade had first received Dig Dug, we'd stayed until five in the morning without even realizing it, alternating games and sucking down Cokes, before stumbling out of the arcade, bleary-eyed, the morning sunlight stinging our eyes. The time had a tendency to just disappear when we were playing arcade games.

I walked over to Willie, playing alone at the Robotron: 2084 cabinet. I watched over his shoulder for awhile. Waves of GRUNTs and Hulk assassins flooded the screen, and he moved his player around the screen, firing his gun in every direction, doing anything he could to avoid the onslaught of enemies. He rammed his joystick to the left to avoid an electrode and collided with a projectile shot from the cannon of an Enforcer tank, killing off his player.

"You died there," I said.

"No shit."

"The point of the game is to avoid dying," I said.

"I'm aware of that."

"Just making sure."

He continued playing. I started emptying quarters out of a few machines near the Robotron cabinet. A few minutes later, I heard Willie kick the base of the cabinet and yell out in frustration. I chuckled at him, and he looked over at me.

"You know, when I finally beat this score of yours, it is going to be the absolute greatest," he said. "Just putting my name on the high score chalkboard won't be enough. I'm gonna take an ad out in the newspaper to announce my new high score. Nah, forget that. I'm going to go to the bakery, get a personalized cake made with my new high score written in frosting, and give it to you."

"At least I'll get a cake out of the deal. I love cake."

"And then I'll take the cake and eat it all myself right in front of you."

I emptied out the remaining cabinets and logged the information in the ledger up front. After performing a few general closing chores, I walked over to Willie, still at the Robotron cabinet. Next to it was Pole Position. I slid a quarter into the slot, gripped the steering wheel mounted to the control panel, and started up a game.

We played side by side at our respective cabinets, the only sounds between us the rapid fire sound effects coming from his Robotron game and the constant hum of the engine in the Pole Position game.

"I almost forgot," Willie eventually said. "I got a story for you."

"Do tell."

"Remember that girl who came in here that one time?" Willie said.

It was a vague description but was the only description I needed. I still remembered her. The girl who'd called me cutie. It had been over a year ago, but I could count on one hand the number of girls who'd come into the arcade since then. None had been as memorable as her.

"The one who used the change machine?" I said.

"Yeah, her. I ran into her today."

One of the things about arcade games that I fell in love with was the escape they provided. When you were truly locked into a game, nothing else mattered. Everything else--every problem, every worry, every single thing around you--simply ceased to exist for that that moment that you were playing the game. It was just you and the game.

Point is, it took something major to distract me from an arcade game when I was playing. But Willie's statement had accomplished just that. I stepped away from the Pole Position cabinet in mid-game and turned towards Willie. The sound effect of my car's engine slowly petering out came through the speakers.

"Go on," I said. "Where'd you see her?"

"I was at the Sam Goody music store on the other side of the mall, looking for a new tape to buy. And I'm in there, just browsing around, when she comes up to me and asks me if I need any help."

Willie went silent for a moment, focusing on playing his game of Robotron.

"And?" I eventually said.

"And, nothing. That's the story. I saw her. She works there. Nothing major, but it was just kinda weird seeing her again. Wish I could say that she drug me to the back room and I made sweet love to her, but, sadly, nothing of that sort happened."

"How'd she look?" I asked, as if we were talking about some long-lost friend I hadn't seen in awhile and not someone I'd had a five-minute interaction with over a year ago.

"She looked great."

Willie continued playing his Robotron game, but my focus was effectively shot for the night. I walked by the Sam Goody every single day on my work to work at the arcade. I'd even stopped in before to buy a couple of tapes. To think, all this time, she was only a few stores away.

"I can't believe she actually works at the mall," I said to Willie.

# # #

The very next day I went to the Sam Goody store on my break.

It was a smaller store that was jam-packed with all sorts of music-related paraphernalia and accessories. Directly inside the entrance was the Top 20 section, with singles of that week's top 20 songs on display next to one another in a row, numbered one through twenty. The cassette tape version of the song was displayed at eye level, with copies of the lp version displayed on a rack directly underneath the tapes. Even more tapes and albums were on display behind the top 20 section, in rows of storage containers that extended to the rear of the store. On the right side of the store was a section displaying a number of Walkmans and ghetto blasters and other music playing devices. Hanging from a few pegs fastened into the walls were t-shirts that depicted various popular artists.

On the left side of the store was the front counter, and she stood behind the front counter. She looked exactly as I remembered on that day she'd come to the arcade. The short, jet-black hair. Those wide expressive eyes. The flawless, pearly white skin. She wore a t-shirt that showed an artist's rendition of David Bowie in front of a shadowy silhouette--the album art for his Scary Monsters album-- and a nametag was pinned to the shoulder of the shirt. Maddy, it read.

I was the only customer in the store. Maddy spotted me the moment I entered. She immediately stepped out from behind the front counter and started walking over.

A baseball-sized knot formed in my stomach, and for a moment, I considered quickly exiting the store and sprinting through the mall back to the arcade. I hadn't come here to actually talk with her; that was far too daunting. I'd merely come to verify that Willie hadn't been mistaken, that she did indeed work here.

Well, it was definitely her. And before I knew it, she was directly in front of me.

"Can I help you with anything?" she asked.

"Just browsing," I choked out. "Looking. For music. I like music."

The words came out in choppy, fragmented bunches, sounding like they came from the mouth of someone who was learning English as a second language.

"Cool," she said. "Lemme know if you need any help. The new John Cougar album came in today. Haven't had a chance to put it out yet but I've got some in back if you're interested. Highly, highly recommended."

She looked at me and, for the briefest of moments, there seemed to be a glimmer of recognition, a don't-I-know-you-from-somewhere look. She then turned around and started walking back up towards the front counter.

A voice in my head told me to simply leave. Right now. Before she even reached the front counter and turned around, I'd be gone. I came here to verify that she did indeed work here, and I'd accomplished exactly that. No need to stick around anymore. Just head back to the arcade, contemplate my next move, and go from there.

Instead, I walked over to the TOP 20 section and browsed the selection for awhile. Out of the corner of my eye, I looked over at Maddy behind the front counter. The latest issue of <u>Rolling Stone</u> was open on the counter in front of her, and she flipped through it. I stared at her for a moment as she studied the issue.

I walked over to the other half of the store and looked at the t-shirt selection, then checked out a few boom boxes. I examined the side of the boxes and compared the various models. Again, I snuck a quick look out of the corner of my eyes at Maddy.

She was staring directly at me.

Hunched over the front counter, she stood there and studied my face with her penetrating eyes, the <u>Rolling Stone</u> in front of her momentarily forgotten. She once again had a look on her face like she recognized me from somewhere but couldn't place where.

My heart hiccupped in my chest and I quickly broke eye contact and turned away from her. As I did so, my hand clipped the edge of a large display-model boombox on a waist-level shelf. I watched in slow motion as the boombox slid to the edge of the shelf, teetered for a brief moment, and fell to the ground. The thing was a beast, a true ghetto blaster, and the impact sounded like an earthquake as it collided with the ground. The cover for the tape deck splintered off. The digital interface above the tape deck shattered. The plastic casing that housed the speakers snapped and a few large chunks split off from the boombox.

I quickly reached down and picked the demolished boom box off the ground and set it back on the shelf. Various wiring and inner circuitry were exposed. Maddy arrived at my side and looked at the boom box on the shelf.

"God, I am an idiot," I said. "I'm so sorry."

"Don't worry about it," she said.

"I am such a klutz."

"It happens all the time," Maddy said. "Well, actually it doesn't happen all of time. This is the first time I've ever seen a customer completely smash a boom box like that."

"I feel absolutely terrible," I said.

"Chill out. You're fine. I've gotta take this to the back, though."

She grabbed the boom box and carried it towards the rear of the store. She reached a door that was marked EMPLOYEES ONLY and she walked through it.

Time to leave, I told myself. Time to leave before I make an even bigger fool out of myself. I'd come back tomorrow, apologize once again and bring some money with me to pay for the boom box. Maybe Maddy and I would even have a good laugh at my clumsiness. But right now, in the heat of the moment, I didn't feel like laughing at all. I felt like disappearing, vanishing into thin air.

I walked over to the front counter and wrote my name and the phone number to Westfield Arcade on a piece of paper. I left the piece of paper on top of her Rolling Stone magazine and got the hell out of the record store. I speed-walked through the mall, feeling utterly humiliated. When I arrived at the arcade, I immediately went to the front counter and stood behind it, as if it would provide cover.

The rest of the early afternoon was relatively dead at the arcade. At four o'clock, as happened almost every day, the rush of teenagers coming to the arcade from school showed up. In the span of ten minutes, the place went from moderately busy to absolutely packed, and it stayed that way for the rest of the night. Rufus was there with a few friends. Willie showed up for a little while. Gonzo stopped by after his shift at Radio Shack ended.

Willie couldn't stay late that night, so I was alone in the arcade after the place closed. I walked around the empty arcade, collecting money from each cabinet. When I finished, I walked to the front of the arcade and stood behind the counter, logging that day's totals into the ledger.

I was halfway through with this task when a voice outside the arcade interrupted me.

"Excuse me."

I looked over and saw Maddy standing outside of the security gate. She wore the same David Bowie t-shirt as she'd worn earlier, with a black leather bomber jacket worn over it.

"Hi," I said, shocked. I walked over to the security gate and stood behind it.

"I was going to come back tomorrow to pay for the boom box," I said. "I promise, I was. That's why I left my name and number."

"That's cool," she said. "But that's not why I'm here. When you were in the store earlier, I thought I recognized you, I just couldn't place where from. And then, all of a sudden, it hit me: I've seen you at this arcade before."

"Right," I said. "I fixed the change machine for you one time, didn't I?"

"You did," she said. "Saved my life. Without you, I'd probably still be standing at the change machine, feeding my dollar bill into the machine and getting it spit back out for the nine millionth time."

I laughed.

"So I assume you're here to give me a bill for the boom box," I said. "Again, I'm so sorry for just running off like that. I felt like such a fool."

"I actually got a laugh out of it. You should've seen the look on your face after the boombox had shattered on the ground. You were all like..."

She contorted her face into a horrified look, then started laughing.

"It was pretty funny," she said.

"I didn't really make that exact face, did I?"

"Oh sure, you did," she said. "It was exactly like that."

She remained looking at me through the security gate.

73

"Anyway, I wanted to stop by and let you know that we get fully refunded from our distributors on stuff that's broken. We just tell them it was damaged in transit. So you don't have to worry about paying for the boom box."

"That's good," I said.

She opened her mouth to respond, then her eyes focused on something inside the arcade and she remained staring at it for a moment.

"Oh my God, you have MTV here?" she said.

"Yeah."

"How awesome," she said, still staring at the television. Onscreen, the video for "Bette Davis Eyes" by Kim Carnes was playing.

"Come in and watch!" I said. Too forward. You fool. "I mean, if you want to. I have some stuff to finish up. The tv's going to be on the whole time, anyway."

"You don't mind?" she said.

"No, not at all," I said.

I slid the security gate upwards and she stepped into the arcade. I brought her a metal folding chair from behind the front counter, and she sat down in it. I finished my closing duties for the night, sneaking the occasional glance at her out of the corner of my eye. She had opened up some sort of packet of papers on her lap. Between watching the television, she'd take an occasional glance at the packet of papers and read them for awhile.

Finally, I finished logging all of the necessary information in the ledger. I placed it in its drawer and looked over at Maddy.

"You want a Coke or anything?" I yelled over to her.

"Sure," she said.

I retrieved Cokes for both of us and brought them over to the television. I grabbed my own chair and pulled it next to her, and it was just the two of us, sitting in front of the television. I felt different around her than I did earlier, more at ease. As if being in the familiar setting of the arcade was giving me a rush of confidence.

Onscreen, the video for "Shake it Up" by The Cars was playing.

"Great song," I said.

"For sure," she said.

She folded the packet of papers in her lap and placed it back in her purse. We watched the video in silence for a bit.

"So what are you reading?" I asked, gesturing to the packet of papers.

"Oh, nothing. A script. For a play I'm in."

"You're an actress?"

"Yeah. I mean, not a famous one or anything. But yeah. I act in a lot of plays. I love it."

We watched the "Shake it Up" video for awhile. Onscreen, the artist info for the video flashed onscreen and the video started to come to an end.

"'Beat It' by Michael Jackson," I said.

I turned to her.

"I like trying to predict what the next video will be. We play this game at the arcade all day. It's actually pretty thrilling when the prediction is right, as stupid as that sounds."

"Cool," she said. "I'll go with "We've Got the Beat" by The Go-Go's"

"Shake it Up" came to an end. After a brief pause, the opening stanza of 'Beat It' by Michael Jackson started to play through the television speakers.

Maddy looked over at me and smiled.

"How did you know?" she asked.

"Lucky guess," I said.

"A lucky guess? Really? Of all the thousands, of videos that MTV has, you just happened to guess the right one?

"Sort of. Lately, MTV has been playing this video at some point every single hour. Never fails. They last played it around nine o'clock, right before I closed the arcade, so I was just playing that odds."

"Cheater," she said.

I smiled. Things were going well so far.

We started talking some more and soon found the rhythm of conversation. Maddy talked about her childhood spent growing up in Indianapolis, the job at Sam Goody that she'd held for almost two years now, and told me about her acting career, going so far to describe a few of the plays she'd been in over the past year.

"That's sort of the dream," she said. "Acting is. It's my ticket out of this town."

"You don't like this town?"

"I don't mind it. But I've also lived here my entire life so far. There's also a big world out there. I want to see it."

Maddy also mentioned dropping out of college a week into her freshman year to devote more time to acting, and I, too, told her a shortened version of the story about dropping out of school to care for my grandpa.

"So you just dropped out of college to be there for him?" she said.

"Yeah. Pretty much."

"That's incredible. That's so nice."

For the next hour, we continued talking, about anything and everything. The entire conversation, the videos airing on MTV provided the background music for us. Every time a video would come to an end, we'd guess what the next video would be.

At a little before midnight, she finally got up from her chair.

"I better be going," she said. "Seeing Olivia Newton John's 'Physical' video twice in one night is enough. If I see it a third time, I'm going to start doing aerobics right here in the arcade. And you really don't want to see that, trust me."

I got up from my chair and opened up the metal security gate at the front of the arcade. She stepped outside.

"You should come around more often," I said before she left. "I'm here almost every night, watching MTV after the arcade closes."

She looked back in at the television, then looked at me.

"I just might do that," she said.

# # #

I could list any number of things about Maddy that I came to adore over the months that followed, when she would show up to the arcade three or four nights a week to watch MTV after she'd closed down the Sam Goody store. There was her endearing personality and her quick, sharp wit. There was her sheer energy, a vitality that instantly won over everyone who met her. There was her vibrant smile, a smile that always blew me away no matter how many times I saw it.

She was a dreamer. I came to adore that most about her. She had had a firm, unwavering belief that acting was *it* for her, and she attacked this dream with an all-encompassing devotion. She'd always spend her late nights in the arcade perched on a chair in front of the television, with MTV blaring in the background as she read over the script for whatever local play she currently had a part in. When she wasn't reading over scripts, she was reading over books that dealt with acting, books with titles like "Method Acting Basics" and "Acting for the Stage," writing notes in the margins of the books and dog-earing important pages.

She loved talking about her acting dreams, and I love listening to her talk about them. Whenever I asked her about her current play, I was awed by the passion she'd speak with as she talked of her character's backstory and how that character fit into the play as a whole. The parts she played were usually small roles at various local venues around town, bit parts with no more than a few lines, but she'd prepare for the part as if it were the lead in a Broadway production. Occasionally, she'd have me read a part with her as she practiced a few scenes, and I always loved it--I felt as if I was, in a small way, helping her achieve her dream.

Usually, it was Maddy, Willie, and I in the arcade late at night. Throughout these late nights, Willie and I would play arcade games. Sometimes against one another, sometimes at separate cabinets. When we needed a break, we'd go over and watch MTV with Maddy. When she needed a break, she'd come over and watch us play.

And every night we'd talk, about a whole range of topics. Maddy's personality seamlessly fit right in with us, and she never hesitated to voice her opinion in a debate about a video on MTV or the latest episode of a television show. And movies--we talked about movies endlessly, and every single Sunday night, Maddy, Willie, and I had a standing date to go to that weekend's latest release at the movie theaters. We were blown away when we saw Return of the Jedi during the summer. Maddy cried when we saw Terms of Endearment a few months later. All three of us felt like crying after wasting two hours of our lives watching Psycho II.

The more we hung out, the more I got to know Maddy. And the more I got to know her, the more apparent it became that she was, quite simply, everything I ever wanted in a woman.

# # #

"There is no hope for you as a human being if you think this is a good song," Willie said.

It was another late night at the arcade, and it was Willie, Maddy, and I lounging around after the arcade had closed, sitting on metal folding chairs in front of the arcade's television. Onscreen, the video for "I Know There's Something Going On" by Frida was showing.

I looked at Willie.

"You don't like this song?" I said.

"Hell no, I don't like this song," he said.

The refrain of the song kicked in. Onscreen, Frida pulled a photograph out of a tub of developing solution and looked at it. It was a picture of her boyfriend out on the town with a different girl.

"You're crazy, man," I said. "This is a fantastic song."

"Sure it is, if you like shitty music," Willie said.

"Maddy," I said. "Settle the debate. Is this a good or bad song?"

A script was open in Maddy's lap. She'd been reading it all night. She briefly looked up from the script and glanced at the television before looking back down at the script.

"It's ok," she said.

"Ok?" I repeated. "That doesn't settle anything."

"Yeah," Willie said. "Come on, Mads. Is this a good song? Yes or no."

Maddy pulled a quarter from her pants pocket, flipped it in the air, and snagged it from mid-air, placing it on top of her other hand. She looked at it for a brief moment.

"Yes," Maddy said, putting the quarter back in her pocket. "It's a good song."

"Told you," I said to Willie.

Shortly thereafter, the video started to come to an end.

"'Tainted Love,' Soft Cell," I guessed.

"'Maniac,' Michael Sembello," Maddy guessed, without looking up from the script.

"'Sweet Dreams,' Eurhythmics," Willie added.

A black screen flashed for a second between videos. Then, the television showed a close-up of a pair of legs walking down an unnamed alleyway, which quickly cut away to a lone person staring into the camera and lighting a cigarette. The opening stanza of "Escalator of Life" by Robert Hazard faded out, and the synthesized beats of the song's refrain kicked in through the speakers.

"Now, *this* is a great song," Willie said.

"Agreed," I said.

We listened to the song for awhile. Before long, Maddy closed the script she was looking at and looked over at us.

"So I've got some big news," she said.

"Do tell," Willie said.

"Well, it's not really big news. It's more of...exciting news. Actually, not exciting. It's just...cool, I guess. It's cool news."

"You gonna describe it a million different ways or actually tell us?" Willie said. "Spit out."

"Well, this play that my theatre group is putting on right now," she began. "Dog Eat Dog. *This* one."

She held up the script in her lap.

"The lead actress suddenly dropped out of the play a few days ago. And the director offered the part to me. So instead of having five spoken lines in the production, I'm going to be the lead."

She had attempted to suppress a smile while talking but finally broke out into a huge grin.

"First time I've ever been the lead in a play," she said.

"Maddy, that's great," I said.

"Thanks."

"So are you gonna turn into this worldwide famous stage actress now?" Willie said.

"No," Maddy said. "I wish. I mean, it's only a local production. The theater holds like two-hundred people."

"That's really cool," I said. "I'll be one of the two-hundred."

"You'll come?" she said.

"Of course," I said.

"Plays aren't exactly my thing, but I'll be there, too," Willie said. "Maybe the ticket stub will be worth millions someday. 'Maddy Fredrickson's first lead role before she became Broadway's biggest star.'"

Maddy laughed.

"A play this small doesn't really qualify as a big break, even if I am the lead," she said. She smiled again. "But I'm still super excited. And I appreciate you guys coming."

"When is it?" I asked.

"Next Wednesday. If you know of anyone else who'd want to come, you should bring them."

"Let's bring Johnny-boy with us," Willie said to me. Willie had continued to visit my grandpa with me, joining me when he could tear himself away from the arcade, and through their mutual love of baseball, he and my grandpa had practically become best friends.

"Yeah," Maddy said. "Bring your grandpa. I want to meet him."

"Sure," I said. "I'll see if I can drag him away from the Cubs game that night."

# # #

We only saw Maddy a handful of times at the arcade in the following days, and when that next Wednesday arrived, I picked up my grandpa from the senior care center then met Willie at the theatre that was showing Maddy's play. It was named The Grandview Performance Hall/Banquet Center, although there was little that could be classified as grand about the place.

It was in an industrial part of the city, right next to an abandoned strip mall with 2x4's hammered over the doors and a few of the windows shattered. Instead of a red carpet path from curbside to the theater's entrance, the narrow sidewalk that led from the parking lot to the theatre was littered with weeds that poked up through cracks in the pavement. The theater was a few blocks from a large landfill, and the faint odor of garbage hung in the air.

"You sure this is the place?" Willie said as we walked across the parking lot to the old, weathered building that resembled a decrepit warehouse more than a theater.

"This is the address she gave us," I said.

"Feels like it's a set-up," Willie said. "Like she just lured us out here to rob us at gunpoint."

"I highly doubt that."

"If Maddy jumps out with a gun, we're using you as a human shield, John," Willie said to my grandpa. "You're the oldest one here. Mike and I still have a lot of our lives left to live."

I looked over at my grandpa.

"What are we doing here?" he said to me.

"We're going to a play, remember? Our friend Maddy is in a play we came to watch."

"Is she the pretty one you were talking about?" my grandpa asked Willie.

"Yeah," Willie said. "She is."

The entrance to The Grandview Performance Hall/Banquet Center was not a majestic entryway under a marquee with flashing lights, but instead a lone glass door with a single loose-leaf sheet of paper taped to it. DOG EAT DOG, Tonight, 7:00, had been scrawled in Magic Marker on the sheet of paper.

The three of us walked through the door and entered into the theatre. Approximately two hundred metal folding chairs had been arranged in a semi-circle, facing a small stage at the front. Less than one-fourth of the chairs had someone sitting in them. There was no curtain covering the stage but the lighting had been dimmed. I could make out the silhouettes of a few stagehands moving around on the stage.

A lone old lady sat at a table inside of the theatre's entrance. There was a small metal box on the table. We walked over to her and paid our admission fee. She placed our money in the metal box without saying anything.

We walked past the table and sat down in a group of chairs towards the back of the theatre, me in the middle, Willie and my grandpa on either side.

"What's this play supposed to be about?" my grandpa asked.

"Hell if I know," said Willie.

Truthfully, I didn't really know, either. Maddy had been very secretive about the play, telling us that she wanted it to be a surprise and didn't want to spoil the play by explaining too much of the plot. I'd helped her practice a few scenes during a late night at the arcade. I was playing the part of her character's father in the play and chastised her about some mysterious decision she'd made a few scenes earlier. Beyond that, I knew little about the play.

Before long, the lights around us dimmed. The room was entirely dark for a moment, then the lights up front lit up, illuminating the stage. A bed was in the middle of the stage. A dresser drawer was right beside the bed, and a full-length mirror was to the left of that.

There was a silent moment of anticipation. Then, Maddy walked out onto the stage alone in a pair of jeans and a white sweater. She silently sat down on the bed. An instant later, two other actors walked onto the stage and the play began.

I'd read interviews and magazine articles before that talked of actors who had presence, a special, indefinable trait that made them stand out from others who performed with them. An invisible aura that distinguished them from those around them. Maddy had presence.

Her performance was mesmerizing. Her talent and charisma were so far beyond the actors and actresses in the play that it she seemed on another level entirely. Everything about her performance was perfect. Her commanding voice that echoed throughout the almost empty theatre. The confident, domineering way she walked across the stage--head held high, shoulders straight, perfect posture. Her dialogue was interspersed with a few humorous lines, and she sold every single one of them with perfect inflection to her voice and pinpoint comedic timing.

The play itself was a shoddily-produced affair full of mistakes--actors botching their lines, a stagehand wandering onstage twice during the production, little things like that--but I barely even watched the play. Instead, I watched Maddy. My eyes were fixated on her for the entire play. Even when she wasn't speaking, I watched her reactions, her expressions, her subtle mannerisms that made her performance stand out.

It was amazing to me, the thought that I actually knew the person putting on this performance on the stage. At one point I tore my eyes away from Maddy to ask my grandpa what he thought of the play. When I looked over at him, I saw that he was asleep, eyes closed behind his glasses, mouth slightly ajar.

For the entire ninety-minute duration of the play, I did nothing but watch Maddy. When the play finally ended, the cast and crew held hands on the stage and took a bow to scattered applause from the sparse crowd. The applause rustled my grandpa from his sleep.

"Where am I?" he said, his voice slightly panicked.

"Grandpa, you're with me," I said, placing my hand on his shoulder. "We're at the play."

There was a look of complete confusion on his face as he glanced around the theatre hall.

"What—why are we here?"

"We're watching the play that my friend is in," I said. "You came here with me. And Willie. You fell asleep."

"I need my watch."

"It's right here," I said, showing him his watch on his wrist, even though I had no idea if by "watch" he actually meant "watch."

He looked at it for moment, then looked back at me.

"Okay," he simply said.

"Let's go introduce you to Maddy," Willie said to my grandpa.

I helped my grandpa get up out of his chair and the three of us walked towards the front stage. A few assorted family and friends were meeting with other cast members, and when Maddy spotted us she hurried over. When she reached us, she put both arms around me and gave me a big, emotional hug.

"Thanks so much for coming," she said to me.

"You were awesome," I said.

We remained hugging for a few seconds and she broke away. She turned towards Willie.

"You, too, Willie--thanks for coming," she said. No hug for him, I noticed.

She turned to my grandpa.

"You must be John," she said.

My grandpa nodded his head.

"I've heard so much about you," Maddy said. "It's great to meet you."

"I was supposed to watch the Cubs tonight but I came here," my grandpa said.

Maddy laughed.

"I appreciate it."

"So you're the pretty lady that these two boys were talking about," my grandpa said.

Maddy's face lit up with a smile.

"You are just too sweet," she said.

She turned back towards Willie and I.

"So what'd you guys think?"

"It was great," I said.

"Amazing," Willie added.

"Thanks for the obligatory ass-kissing, but be honest this time: What did you think?" she asked.

"I loved it," I said. "Seriously. You were awesome."

"Thanks."

She looked out at the small crowds of people around us, then back up at the theatre stage.

"It was such an amazing feeling," she said. "I know it's a small theatre that doubles as a banquet hall. I know there weren't even fifty people in the crowd. But just being onstage as the lead of the play, being involved in every single scene and not just an assorted scene here or there, it was just awesome."

We talked for a little while longer. Maddy was as excited as I'd ever seen her. She animatedly talked about the play, a smile on her face the entire time. At one point, when talking about a scene towards the end of the play that she'd been struggling with during rehearsal but nailed in the performance, she was so overcome with emotion that I thought she was going to start crying.

The cast and crew started to gather on the stage for a post-production meeting, and one of them yelled out to

Maddy. Before joining them, Maddy looked one final time at Willie, my grandpa, and I.

"Thanks so much for coming," she said, close to being overcome with emotion again. "It really means a lot."

5. SPY HUNTER

The year that followed passed by in a blur. We were young and having fun and the time period felt like one big celebration. No clue what we were celebrating. Our youth, maybe. We didn't need an excuse to have fun.

It was an incredible time for pop culture. Michael Jackson's popularity soared out of this world--MTV didn't go half an hour without airing a MJ video. When he unveiled the Moonwalk at an awards event, it was earth-shattering; when his hair caught on fire while filming a Pepsi commercial, it was all anyone talked about for a week straight. Prince, Madonna, and U2--only three of the most influential music artists of all-time--each blew up, and their videos were played on MTV constantly.

Cheers and The Cosby Show had quite possibly their best respective seasons, and were shown back to back to back on Thursday nights--one of the few times we universally agreed to flip the arcade's television away from MTV. Miami Vice premiered, and it, too, achieved the coveted switch-the-television-from-MTV-when-it's-on status. It was a television show unlike anything any of us had ever seen.

Ghostbusters was a sensation at the box office; Beverly Hills Cop was even bigger. Indiana Jones and the Temple of Doom came out. Sixteen Candles ushered in the Brat Pack era.

The arcade was full of great shit, too. Arcade games started to truly evolve past the simplistic graphics and monotone sound effects of past games. Spy Hunter was a top-down action game in which you controlled a car that shot missiles and had a machine gun mounted to the hood, and the graphics in the game were light years beyond Pole Position and other driving games from the past. A fantastic Star Wars game with color vector graphics was released a few months after Return of the Jedi appeared in theaters, and at the peak of the game's popularity, we needed two of the hulking Star Wars arcade machines to meet demand. Dragon's Lair was the first full-motion video arcade game ever released (as well as being the first game to cost fifty cents to play instead of the standard quarter), and the graphics of the game were on par with most Saturday morning cartoons.

Willie and I loved them all, competed in them all-- we'd spend hours playing games and watching MTV After Dark after the arcade had closed, usually with Maddy or a few other Westfield Arcade regulars with us. More than ever, in that year-long stretch, the arcade was my home. My apartment was nothing more than a storage unit for my clothes and a place to sleep at night. Ed barely even came into the arcade any more, instead entrusting me with almost all of the day-to-day responsibilities of running the place. He'd phone in every few days to make sure everything was running smoothly, but outside of that, I rarely talked with him at all.

The arcade regulars and I lived for the night and existed on a steady diet of MTV and arcade games and over-buttered popcorn. I loved every second of it; we all did. It was one big party that none of us thought would ever end.

And then, it ended.

# # #

"What are your plans for New Year's Eve?" Maddy asked me during another late after-hours night at the arcade for her, Willie, and I. The year was winding down, only a few days from ending.

The two of us sat in front of the television watching MTV After Dark, and Willie was behind us in the arcade, playing on the Robotron: 2084 cabinet. He'd still yet to beat my high score, and Robotron: 2084 was the only game that didn't have his initials next to it on the high score chalkboard. Despite the influx of new games being released weekly, he still continued to plug quarters into the Robotron: 2084 cabinet night after night in his quest to best my high score.

"My plans for New Year's?" I said. "Probably nothing."

"Nothing?" Maddy said. "Lame."

"We should have a party here at the arcade," Willie yelled over to us.

I didn't even respond to his statement. Instead, I looked over at Maddy. She held a script in her hands and was reading over it.

"How's the preparation coming?" I asked.

"Good," she said. "I think."

"When's the audition?"

"Not for another month," she said. She set the script on her lap and turned towards me. "This is the part. 'A Flea in Her Ear' at the Indiana Repertory Theatre. I'm reading for the lead. I mean, I've never wanted anything so much in my life."

In the past year, Maddy had followed up her lead role in Dog Eat Dog with a number of roles at various theatres around town. I'd gone to every single one of them. She'd been in a few plays at the Indiana Repertory Theatre, and it was a nice, very professional theatre in the heart of downtown Indianapolis--a far cry from the Grandview Theatre Hall/Banquet Center. Her previous roles at the Indiana Repertory Theatre had always been smaller, secondary roles, but the role that she was currently preparing to audition for was the lead. For weeks, she'd been talking nonstop about the opportunity.

"This is a big-time role," she continued. "Well, at least as big-time as it gets in Indianapolis. Five years ago, Catherine Carpenter was the lead in a play at the Indiana Repertory Theatre."

"She was? Wow."

"Do you even know who Catherine Carpenter is?"

"Absolutely not."

"She's an actress on Broadway. She was just in 'Fool for Love.' Just a few years ago, she was in the same spot I'm in. And now, she's huge. Getting the lead in a play at the Indiana Repository was her big break."

She went back to looking over her script, and I continued watching MTV. Onscreen was a commercial break. As it came to a close, I turned towards Maddy.

"'Wake Me Up Before You Go-Go,' Wham," I guessed. We still loved trying to guess what the next video shown would be. It never got old.

"'I Just Called To Say I Love You,' Stevie Wonder," Maddy said, not looking up from her script.

The image of a lone person drinking at a bar appeared onscreen, then panned over to a lady with shoulder-length black hair and a dark leather jacket walking along the sidewalk outside the bar. The opening guitar riff for "I Love Rock n Roll" by Joan Jett and the Blackhearts started playing through the television speakers.

"Nice," I said.

"Love this song," Maddy said.

We watched the video for awhile. Behind us, I heard Willie yell out. Then, a loud thump--kicking the side of the cabinet in frustration. The same sequence of events happened every night--Willie would start playing a game of Robotron: 2084 at some point, and around half an hour after the game began, he'd yell out a curse and kick the side of the machine after he'd died for the final time.

After a moment, he appeared at our side and grabbed a seat.

"I oughta take a fucking sledgehammer to that game," he said, slumping down in chair. "That game is going to be the death of me."

We watched the video for a few moments.

"So Mike, I have a question for you," Maddy said, finally looking up from her script. "I was thinking of growing my hair out a bit, kind of like Joan Jett in this video. Thoughts?"

I looked at her face, then pictured her in my head with slightly longer hair.

"It would look good," I said. I meant it.

"Really?"

"Yeah. But I still like you with short hair. It brings out your cheekbones."

"What a nice thing to say," she said.

"Keep it short, and dye it pink like Cindy Lauper," Willie said.

Maddy laughed.

"Pink, I like that," she said. "Maybe I will."

Willie turned to me.

"So whaddya think of my idea?" he said.

"What idea?"

"Having a party at the arcade for New Year's."

"You were actually being serious with that idea?" I said.

"Of course, I am being serious," he said. "It's a great idea. Have a party here. Invite all of the regulars. MTV's got a countdown of the 100 best videos of the year that ends at midnight--we can put that on, everyone can play some arcade games, and we'll have us some fun."

"If we threw a party here and Ed found out, he'd kill me. He'd fire me."

"Which would he do first, kill you or fire you?" Willie asked. "Because if he's going to kill you first, firing you is just redundant."

"I'm serious. I'm lucky enough that he hasn't said anything about the three of us staying after the arcade closes."

"Chill out," Willie said. "Ed wouldn't find out about the party. I know the mall security guard, and I'll talk with him. He won't rat us out. We'll get everything cleaned up that next morning and no-one will ever know about it."

"It'd be a blast, you have to admit that," Maddy said.

"Plus, there won't even be that many people who show up," Willie said. "No more than ten people."

I looked at him. I knew Willie too well to let a lie like that slip by.

"Okay, twenty," he said. "Twenty people tops."

I kept looking at him.

"Twenty people," Willie said. "I swear."

"What if it gets out of hand?"

"If it gets out of hand, I will end the party and personally escort every last person from the arcade. You have my word."

"And you can talk with the security guard? That's not bullshit?"

"Yes, I'll talk with Roy. He will be totally cool with it. Trust me."

"Fine," I said.

Maddy and Willie both celebrated, and we talked more about the party as we watched MTV. After half an hour, Maddy left, leaving Willie and I in the arcade.

"Up for an ass-whooping in Joust?" he asked.

"Of course," I said.

Joust had been around the arcade for awhile, but it was still one of our favorite games. The premise of Joust was simple enough, if not a little bizarre. You controlled a knight who rode on an ostrich, and you battled waves of enemy ostriches. The enemy ostriches could be killed either by landing your ostrich directly on top of them, or by pushing them into the lava at the bottom of the screen.

Willie and I loved the game because both players played onscreen simultaneously during two-player games. The screen was flooded with computer-controlled enemy ostriches, and you competed with your opponent to see who could kill more ostriches. What made the battles even more heated was that you could take out the other player's ostrich with a perfectly-timed attack, the ultimate way to screw over your opponent. Willie and I, of course, typically ignored the computer-controlled players as best as we could and focused on taking each other out.

We walked over to the cabinet and inserted a few quarters. The game started and our ostriches began flying around the screen. There was only a single button on the control panel--a FLAP button that made your ostrich flap his wings and fly higher. Willie and I both rapidly pounded on the FLAP button as we directed our ostriches around the screen.

"So are you ever going to make a move on her?" Willie asked me as we played.

"What are you talking about?" I said, hitting the FLAP button three rapid times to avoid an enemy.

"Maddy. You gonna make a move on her?"

"We're just friends."

"It's more than that and you know it. She likes you, man. I want to barf at how obvious it is."

"You're crazy," I said.

Willie stepped away from the cabinet and looked at me.

"Okay, take tonight," he said. I turned towards him, the game of Joust forgotten. "She says that she's thinking of cutting her hair. And she specifically asked you if she should. She didn't even ask my opinion. It was like I wasn't even in the room. Or when she asked about New Year's Eve plans. She asked you what you were doing, and didn't ask shit about me."

I thought back to the exchanges we'd had earlier. Willie was right.

"Or the night of her play that we went to. When it was over, she came directly to you and hugged you. Went straight for you. I didn't get a hug. She barely noticed I was even there."

He was right on that, too.

"Shit like that happens all of the time," Willie said. "You're blind if you don't notice it."

Truthfully, I had noticed her being flirtatious around me on occasion, or going out of her way to get my opinion on something. But I didn't think there was much to it. I'd always chalked it up to my overactive imagination. That, or wishful thinking on my part.

"She likes you, man," Willie said. "I don't know what the hell you're waiting for, but you should make a move on her before it's too late."

# # #

New Year's Eve arrived. Local schools were out for Christmas break, so it was a busy day. Ed briefly stopped by in the middle of the day to pick up some paperwork, and I listened to him complain for awhile about Bomb Jack, the arcade's newest game that had done minimal business since we'd received it.

"Two weeks we've had that game, and it hasn't even brought in ten dollars in quarters," he said, shaking his head. "I paid fifteen hundred dollars for that cabinet, and I'll be lucky if I make one-tenth of that back."

He complained about the game some more. As the late afternoon arrived, he announced that he was leaving.

"Have a happy new year, you guys," he said to a group of us regulars standing around the front counter.

"You, too," I said.

"And stay out of trouble tonight."

Ed walked out from behind the counter and exited the arcade. Once he was out of earshot, Willie turned towards me, a devilish grin on his face.

"Tonight, there's only going to be trouble," he said. He'd placed a backpack behind the counter when he arrived, and he walked around the counter and grabbed it. He unzipped it and showed me what was inside: Four bottles of Jack Daniels.

"We're shutting it down if it gets too out of control," I said.

"Of course."

6:00 came, and the mall closed--early holiday hours. I kicked out the younger kids and anyone who I didn't recognize. Once they'd left, Rufus, Gonzo, and some other regulars were remaining, around twenty people in total. Bearclaw showed up with his new girlfriend, a cute, pudgy girl named Sarah. Maddy, who'd been working at Sam Goody, arrived just as I was closing the security gate. She looked to have on a little more eyeliner and blush than she typically wore, and she had on a white cotton t-shirt that hugged against her slender upper body. On the front of the shirt was the crossed-out ghost logo from the movie Ghostbusters. Her purse was slung over her shoulder, and in her left hand, she carried a large shopping bag.

"Happy New Year's," she said to me.

"Same to you," I said. "What's in the bag?"

"Your belated Christmas present," she said.

"For real?"

"Yeah. You can open it later."

I pulled the metal security gate down and locked it, my mind briefly racing with the thought of this present. I walked over to the group that had formed around the television. Someone had cranked MTV at near full-blast, and the countdown of the 100 best videos of 1984 was in full swing, already in the 50s. Song #57 was currently playing on the television: "Love Somebody" by Rick Springfield.

Willie threw on a pair of wayfarer sunglasses and jumped behind the counter. He grabbed his backpack and turned the counter into a makeshift bar by setting out the bottles of alcohol and having the various sodas from the Coke fountain serve as the mixers. We put on some popcorn, and Willie began slinging drinks for everyone.

MTV blaring in the background, we started pumping quarters into arcade cabinets, going from machine to machine. I posted up at the Pole Position cabinet, right next to Bearclaw playing Marble Madness, one of our newer games. His girlfriend watched over his shoulder. Willie left the counter, walked around the arcade, and eventually decided on Robotron: 2084, his nemesis.

"One of two things is going to happen tonight," Willie announced to anyone in his vicinity. He tilted his head back and emptied his drink. "I'm either going to beat Mikey's high score in Robotron: 2084, or I am going to wheel this machine up to the roof of the mall and throw it off, give the game the proper send off it deserves."

Drink resting on top of the cabinet, I continued playing Pole Position, taking intermittent sips from the drink as I controlled the game's steering wheel with one hand. I was no stranger to alcohol, though I rarely drank. But there was no question about drinking tonight. Everyone else was letting loose, and it was a special night--

the final day of what had been the single-greatest year of my life.

The night continued. Two of the alcohol bottles were empty by 10:00, and the countdown on MTV reached the 20s. Gonzo drew up an elaborate chart listing all of the main contenders for video of the year, and everyone placed money down on their pick. The early favorites were "Jump" by Van Halen and "Like a Virgin" by Madonna.

I made myself another drink and wandered around the arcade. The place had already turned into a pig's sty. Someone had dropped a bag of popcorn near the Zaxxon cabinet and failed to clean it up, and the kernels of corn had been stepped on and smashed into the carpet. What looked to be a completely full bag of M n M's had been poured onto the ground in front of the Lunar Lander machine. The stench of alcohol and carbonated, sugary soda hung in the air.

I watched Gonzo and a regular named Jason battle it out in Joust for awhile, the loser of each game being forced to take a swig from their drink. I looked over and saw Willie, still at the Robotron: 2084 cabinet, a steely, focused glare in his eyes as he blasted away and maneuvered the joystick. I walked a little further, towards the rear of the arcade, which was practically empty compared to the party that was going on up front.

And I saw Maddy, in the back of the arcade, playing a game of Galaxian all by herself. She hunched over the cabinet, her drink within reaching distance. It was one of the first times I'd actually seen her play a game.

I walked over to her.

"Set a high score yet?" I asked Maddy when I reached her.

"There you are," she said. "No, no high score yet."

She stepped away from the cabinet mid-game and looked at me.

"I don't even understand the controls for that game," she said.

"See that button that's labeled FIRE? Tap that if you want to fire your weapon. That's the only control for this game. It's probably the simplest game we have."

"Well, I think it's confusing," she said. "But I'm glad you're around. Wait right here for me."

I took a swig of my drink as I watched her walk away from me. I waited. A minute later, she reappeared. She had the large shopping bag she'd been carrying earlier in her hand, and she pulled a present wrapped in red wrapping paper from it. The present was perfectly square and very thin--it looked like a record.

She handed the present to me. We were alone in the back of the arcade.

"Sorry it's a little late," she said.

"You really shouldn't have," I said.

I started to tear a corner of the paper off, but Maddy stopped me.

"You have to guess what it is before you open it," she said.

"An album," I said. I felt the present in my hand. "Actually, it's a little thick for just one album. So it's probably a couple of them."

"Which ones?" she said.

"Van Halen. The Boss. Duran Duran. I don't know. As long as it's not Culture Club, I'll be happy with anything."

I tore into the present and discarded the wrapping paper onto the ground. I held the unwrapped present in my hands and looked at it for a very long time.

It was a framed, blown-up photograph of the entire Westfield Arcade crew. I remembered the night the photograph was taken. Maddy had stopped by the arcade after her shift at Sam Goody ended, and there was a group of us who'd just finished a Ms. Pac Man tournament.

Maddy had a camera and she told us to pose for a picture. It had been months ago, and I'd completely forgotten about it.

I didn't know what to say, so I kept looking at the picture in silence. A group of ten of us were lined up side-by-side in the picture, right in front of the Ms. Pac Man cabinet, each of us smiling into the camera. All of the regulars were there. Gonzo, smiling into the camera wearing his Radio Shack vest. Rufus, hair disheveled, the glare from the camera flash reflecting off of his glasses. Bearclaw, standing on the edge of the group, one arm holding a Coke cup extended into the air. In the middle of it all, sandwiched between everyone, were Willie and I. He had his arm around me, both of us smiling in to the camera.

It was such a rich photograph. The subtle background details jumped out at me--a lone kid intently playing a game of Space Invaders, only his back visible as he hunched over the game and blasted away at aliens; a line of three teenagers at the change machine, one of them feeding a dollar bill into the machine; an overturned soda cup in front of the Donkey Kong cabinet that had left a stain on the carpet. Barely readable in the background, at the top of the photograph, was the high score chalkboard.

"This is amazing," I finally said.

"Thanks," she said.

"I mean, this is absolutely incredible."

"It was either this photograph or the Culture Club album," she said. "I'm glad I made the right call."

"I forgot your present at home," I said. I hadn't gotten her anything, but I couldn't accept a gift like this without giving one of my own. "I'll bring it in next week."

"You're lying," Maddy said, a wry smile crossing her lips. "You didn't get me anything."

"I di—"

"Your eyes," she said. "That's what gives you away. Your eyes are too honest."

I looked over at her, and she stared back at me. She took a sip of her drink. I took a sip of mine. Towards the front of the arcade, a commotion had started to take place. I glanced over and saw practically everyone huddled around the television, riveted to MTV. Midnight was approaching. MTV's countdown had finally reached #1, and I heard the opening of "When Doves Cry" by Prince play through the television's speakers. A few people cheered. Others complained. Someone threw a handful of popcorn at the television screen.

I turned back towards Maddy. Willie's words rang in my ears. *Are you ever going to make a move on her?*

"So," I said, "they year's almost over."

"It is," she said.

I paused for a moment. I tipped my cup back for a drink, and realized it was completely empty. I heard "When Doves Cry" come to an end, and the broadcast cut to a final commercial break before the countdown to midnight began.

"Who do you plan on kissing at midnight?" I asked seductively. At least, I thought it was seductively. Instead, I'm sure it sounded more like a slurred jumble of words that vaguely resembled a question.

"I was hoping for Rufus, but he already shot me down," she said.

I laughed at her comment and she smiled. I looked at that smile, at Maddy, and she stared back with those beautiful, expressive eyes. The two of us were still alone at the back of the arcade, everyone else focused on the television up front. For the first time all night, I started to feel lightheaded. And it wasn't just because the alcohol was kicking in.

Suddenly, I needed to tell her everything. Right then, right there, I wanted to tell her that she was amazing, that she was the most talented and incredible person I'd ever met. I wanted to tell her that her smile was electric, that her laugh sounded like a melody. I wanted to tell her that just being around her was the best, that I could spend the rest of my life simply sitting around talking with her and I'd be content. It seemed to me that this exact moment in time could not progress until I told her everything. I knew the alcohol had something to do with it but I didn't care.

I looked at Maddy, then quickly diverted my eyes to the row of arcade games behind her. I tipped my Coke cup back again. Still empty.

My heart started jackhammering in my chest. Muddled thoughts swam in my head, and I took a deep breath to help my focus. I was going to do this.

"Maddy," I began, "I—"

"What the hell are you two doing back here?!?"

I looked over and saw Willie standing behind us. His words were slurred and his eyes had a glazed, distant look to them. He held a Coke cup filled to the brim with some sort of alcoholic concoction.

"You guys are gonna miss the countdown to midnight," he said. "It's almost fuckin' 1985!"

Willie took a drink from the Coke cup and part of the drink sloshed out of the cup and ran down his chin, dribbling onto his t-shirt.

"Get your asses up here!" he said, starting to walk back towards the television. A few people around the television looked back at Maddy and I and motioned for us to join them.

Maddy looked at me, shrugged, then started walking up towards the television. I grabbed the framed photograph and followed. The moment had effectively been killed. Not just killed--murdered. Whatever small window of opportunity there'd been had closed with a resounding thud.

In front of me, Maddy glanced over her shoulder and looked at me.

"Later," she said. And that one simple word held infinite possibilities. Like she knew exactly what I'd been about to say and wanted to wait until the time was more appropriate for those words. *Later. When the time is right. We'll talk then.*

I placed the picture behind the front counter and joined the crowd at the television with exactly ten seconds until midnight. From the television speakers, Martha Quinn and J.J. Jackson started the countdown. Ten, nine, eight. Everyone in the arcade counted down along with television. Seven, six, five.

I looked over at Maddy but she was focused on the television.

Three, two, one.

And the place erupted. We celebrated and cheered. Bearclaw kissed his girlfriend, then Willie ran over and gave a hug to Bearclaw that almost knocked them both to the ground. Willie's drink spilled everywhere. I looked over and saw Maddy and Gonzo hugging. I exchanged high fives with various people. Everyone had smiles plastered on their faces.

After that, the party died down. A group of people, Maddy included, decided to leave shortly after the ball had dropped. I walked with them to the front security gate, then unlocked it and slid it upwards. I exchanged goodbyes with everyone, receiving a few compliments on the party.

Maddy was the last person in the group to exit the arcade. Once she'd stepped out into the walkway in front of the arcade, she turned towards me.

"I hope you liked your present," she said.

"I loved it."

She smiled.

"We'll talk later," she said.

"Sounds good."

I couldn't wait to see her again.

The night ended, fittingly, with Willie and I in the arcade. Gonzo stayed as well, and the three of us watched MTV for awhile. Willie grabbed the only bottle of Jack Daniels that hadn't already been emptied and poured some into a Coke cup.

"You sure you don't want to switch to water?" I said.

"Hell no," he said. He walked over and emptied the bottle by pouring the remainder in Gonzo's cup. He stumbled and almost lost his balance as he walked back over to the front counter. He set the empty bottle on the counter, then turned around and pointed at Gonzo and I, then pointed at the Joust cabinet.

"How 'bout we start the new year off right with a quick game of Joust?" he said.

"You're on," I said.

The three of us walked over to the cabinet and started alternating games against one another. As it always did, a quick game turned into multiple games, until Willie, Gonzo, and I had been at the Joust cabinet for the better part of an hour, slamming the Flap button and moving the joystick back and forth and talking shit to one another.

Willie and I played one last game against one another, then we decided to call it a night. I walked Willie and Gonzo over to the entrance and unlocked the security gate.

"You need a ride home, numbnuts?" Willie said to Gonzo.

"Yeah," Gonzo said.

"You coming?" Willie said to me.

"Nah, I gotta get some of this stuff cleaned up," I said.

Willie looked back in at the wreckage around the arcade. Bits of popcorn littered the ground, along with pieces of smashed M n Ms and other candies. The dark carpeting had multiple stains from various people spilling their drinks over the course of the night. The front counter was covered with empty bottles of alcohol and discarded Coke cups.

"Have fun," he said. He and Gonzo both found this statement hilarious, and they laughed loudly as they turned around and started walking through the food court. Willie stumbled as he walked, then righted himself. I watched as Willie grabbed his car keys from his pocket, then dropped them on the ground. He bent over to pick them, then lost his balance and fell to the ground. Gonzo laughed at him, almost falling over himself. Willie got back up and threw an arm around Gonzo to help support him as he walked. I watched the two of them walk through the food court to the mall's parking lot.

I didn't realize it at the time, but the game of Joust we'd just played ended up being the final arcade game I ever played against Willie Cardinal.

January 6, 1997

Almost twenty years ago, that was, a middle-aged Mike Mayberry thinks to himself as he sits behind the front counter of Westfield Arcade, alone in the deadened arcade. Yet he still remembers the golden age of arcade video games as if it happened yesterday, that glorious stretch in the early 1980s when classic games were released on what seemed like a weekly basis and the arcade was packed wall-to-wall with people every single night. That's what he'd love to see the arcade become again. And it saddens him to know that it never will.

With nothing to do, Mike picks up the old rotary phone that has been in the arcade since he started working here. He dials a number, and waits as it rings a few times. He's put on hold for a few minutes, and while he waits, his eyes look over the arcade. A few people have shown up to pick up cabinets in the past hour and the arcade floor is littered with open gaps scattered among the remaining cabinets. But Mike's eyes focus on the gaping hole where Space Invaders used to be, in the rear of the arcade, right next to the Donkey Kong and Galaga cabinets. That cavernous, empty hole sticks out more than the others. It's difficult to look at. A video game arcade without a vintage Space Invaders cabinet in the back just seems morally wrong.

"United Airlines," a voice on the other end of the phone finally says.

"I need to check on the status of a flight leaving tonight," Mike says, looking away from the arcade. Mike grabs the manila envelope from the counter and pulls the airline ticket from inside.

"Flight number?"

Mike looks down at the ticket in his hand.

"2841."

There is a pause on the other end of the phone.

"Flight 2841," the voice repeats. "What do you need to know?"

"Are there any delays?" Mike asks.

"None as of yet."

"Still scheduled to depart from Indianapolis International at 10:15 tonight?" Mike asks.

"Yes, sir."

"Thanks," Mike says. "That's all I needed."

Mike hangs up the phone. Good, he thinks. A flight delay--or, God forbid, a cancellation--is a headache he'd prefer to avoid dealing with. He glances at the clock behind the counter. It reads 12:31--just over nine hours before the flight's scheduled departure tonight.

He decides to grab a quick bite to eat for lunch. He walks out from behind the counter and exits the arcade. Mike heads over to the front of the food court, and as he looks over each one of the eight dining options, something suddenly dawns on him: Since he's planning on grabbing dinner at the airport before his flight later, the meal he's about to eat will, in all likelihood, be the final meal he will ever eat at the Westfield Mall food court.

This revelation has a surprisingly profound impact on him. Over the past seventeen years, how many greasy slices of pizza has he had from Luigi's Pizza, which has been open since he started working at Westfield Arcade seventeen years ago? How many plates of Kung Pao Chicken from Panda Express? How many Big Macs from the McDonalds, before it relocated a few years ago? The numbers are mind-boggling. And this meal will be the final one.

107

He decides on a slice of pizza from Luigi's, his old standby. He walks up to the counter, scans the three pizzas on display (sausage, pepperoni, or cheese), and determines that the pepperoni pie is the only one that looks like it hasn't been sitting under the heat lamp for longer than a week.

He pays for his slice and grabs a seat at a table by himself, then peels each one of the six circular slices of pepperoni from the cheese and eats them one by one. He watches Westfield Arcade from across the food court as he eats his final meal, and sees a shopper walk past the arcade, then stop and walk back to look up at the WESTFIELD ARCADE sign above the arcade's entrance. The guy is younger, mid-twenties, slightly overweight. He looks at a piece of paper in his hands, looks back up at the sign, then walks inside the arcade.

Mike shoves the rest of his pizza slice into his mouth and walks across the food court, depositing his tray on top of a trash receptacle. He reaches the arcade and immediately spots the customer up by the front counter. He walks over to him.

"Can I help you?" Mike asks.

"Is this the arcade that's closing today?" he asks.

"Sure is."

"Are you Mike?"

"Sure am."

"My brother-in-law talked with you on the phone last week," he said. "He purchased a game from you."

"What was his name?"

"Travis."

"Out-Run was the game, right?"

"Yeah. Out-Run."

"Great game," Mike says. "Out-Run's a classic."

"Never played it myself," the guy says. "My brother-in-law's got a bad back, I owe him a favor, and I told him I'd pick up his game for him. I've got a check for you and everything."

"Works for me," Mike says. "Follow me."

They walk side-by-side towards the back of the arcade. Mike looks over and sees the guy's head on a swivel as he looks around at all of the arcade games that surround him.

"A lot of arcade games in this place," he says.

"Now, there are," Mike says. "Most will be gone by the end of the day."

The guy stops walking in the middle of the arcade.

"You know, there's this one game that I used to play," he says. "I wonder if you have it."

"Gonna have to be a little more specific than that."

"I can't think of the name right now. The local arcade in my hometown had it before the place closed, so this would've been like 1984 or so. You were a secret agent or a spy or something. Trying to save the world."

"A spy trying to save the world--that could be any one of hundreds of games," Mike says.

"I don't remember much about it. It was an older game. Addicting as hell, though. I played it so much that I still remember the game's theme song."

"What'd the theme music sound like?"

"It went, DA-da-dum-dumdumdum-DA-dum," the man hums.

"Elevator Action," Mike says instantly.

"That's it! Elevator Action. I loved that game."

"We have that one. Third one from back, in the row on your left."

The man scans the row of arcade games and his eyes light up when he spots the cabinet with ELEVATOR ACTION written across the marquee at the top of the cabinet. He excitedly walks over to it, and Mike follows. Onscreen is a flashing list of high scores.

"120,985 points?" he reads. "Damn. I thought I was a good player, but I don't think I ever scored even half that."

"Took me over an hour to get that score."

"That's your score?"

"Yeah."

"How in the world did you get 120,000 points?"

"I played this game nonstop when it came out. After awhile, you can memorize the enemy patterns and know where they're going to move before they actually do. After that, it's just a matter of pure and simple concentration."

Mike pulls a quarter from his pocket.

"Here, play a game," he says, handing the quarter to the man.

"Don't mind if I do."

He takes the quarter and places it into the quarter slot of the game. Elevator Action is a side-scroller in which your character starts on the thirtieth floor of a skyscraper and takes an elevator to the basement of the skyscraper, while being shot at by enemy agents he encounters on his way. With its blocky graphics, the game is rudimentary by today's standards, but the man gets into it. He sways his body with the movements of the character onscreen. Every time he hits the jump button, he grunts. His face is a mask of concentration, solely focused on the game.

His game lasts for no longer than five minutes, and when he dies for the final time, he lets out a frustrated grunt and lightly slams his palm against the cabinet. But a few seconds later, a smile returns to his face.

"That was fun," he says. "I enjoyed that."

Mike offers him another quarter.

"It's on the house if you want to keep playing," he says.

The man looks at the watch on his wrist.

"Thanks, but I'm short on time," he says. "I need to get this arcade machine loaded up and delivered. My brother-in-law will start wondering where the hell I am if I take too long."

Mike leads him to the back of the arcade and they load the Out-Run cabinet onto a dolly for him to take out to his truck. After handing Mike a check for the game, he wheels the game out the front entrance of the arcade. And just like that, another classic game is gone from Westfield Arcade.

6. Out-Run

The first day after the party, I could think about
nothing other than my encounter with Maddy in the back of
the arcade. I constantly replayed that one moment in my
mind. Both of us alone in the back of the arcade. Looking
into each other's eyes. How the moment had just seemed
perfect to simply tell her everything about how I felt about
her before Willie came and--

"—good time?"

I broke out of my reverie. I was in my grandpa's
room, sitting in the chair beside his bed. My grandpa lay in
his bed, looking at the television at the foot of his bed. He
wore a blue sweater that had CUBS knitted across the front
in red letters. The sweater had been my Christmas present
to him, and he'd worn it every single day in the week since
he'd unwrapped it.

I turned around and saw one of my grandpa's
therapists standing in the room's entranceway. Kim was
her name. She looked at me, as if expecting an answer.

"I'm sorry, what was that?" I said.

"I'm here to ask John a few questions," she said.
"Is now a good time?"

"Sure," I said. I got up from my chair and she sat
down at my grandpa's bedside.

"Okay, John, I have a few questions for you," she
said. My grandpa didn't even acknowledge her presence
and remained staring at the television. She motioned for

112

me to turn it off and I did so. After the picture had disappeared, my grandpa remained staring at the black screen of the television.

"John?" the nurse repeated.

My grandpa looked over at her.

"Oh, hello."

"Hi John. Do you remember my name?"

"Jamie."

"Jamie's the nurse who takes you to dinner. My name is different. Do you remember my name?"

"Kim."

"Good, good."

She opened her notebook and wrote something with a pen.

"Now, can you spell your name backwards for me?" she asked my grandpa.

He thought for a moment.

"It starts with a J."

"No, backwards, John. Starting with the last letter first."

"I don't understand the question," my grandpa said.

Kim wrote something in her notebook.

"Do you know what month it is?" she asked.

"January."

"Good. Very good. What about the capitol of the United States? Do you know that?"

"Washington, D.C."

"And what did you eat for breakfast this morning?"

My grandpa blankly looked at Kim. I knew that he ate Wheaties for breakfast every single morning at the senior center--just as he'd done for his entire adult life--and I wanted to give him a hint, just a little nudge to help him answer the question. I was usually present for most of Kim's questionings, and it was always difficult to simply remain silent as I saw my grandpa struggle to respond to questions that should have been so easy to answer.

"You had cereal," Kim said. "Do you remember which kind? Nurse Sandy brought it in to you."

"I don't want to do this anymore," my grandpa said.

"Just a few more questions."

"I want to watch the Cubs."

"The Cubs aren't on, John. It's January. The Cubs only play in the summer." She made a scribble in her notebook. "The cereal, John. What cereal did you eat this morning?"

"I don't know," my grandpa said.

"What about for dinner last night? Do you remember what we all ate for dinner last night?"

"I don't know," my grandpa said instantly.

Kim asked my grandpa a few more questions, and he responded 'I don't know' to every single one of them. The response came immediately after she asked the questions, and I couldn't tell if he truly didn't know the answer or had just grown tired of the questions.

She eventually got up from the chair and turned the television back on, and my grandpa resumed watching it.

"I think that's enough for today," Kim said.

She turned towards the hallway, and gestured for me to follow her outside the room.

"I'm going to steal your guest for a quick second, John," she said.

My grandpa said nothing, remaining staring at the television.

I followed Kim out in the hallway and we came to a stop directly outside of the door to my grandpa's room. The hallway was empty.

"How did the holiday season go for you?" she asked me.

"Good," I said.

"I know that John really likes the sweater you bought for him," she said. "He won't stop talking about it."

She smiled, looked at my grandpa in his room, then looked back at me.

"I wanted to talk with you briefly about something else," she said. "The other day, there was an incident."

"An incident?"

"John became very upset at dinner," she said. "He threw his tray across the room and started verbally abusing the staff."

"My grandpa?"

"I'm afraid so," she said. "It wasn't anything major. We were able to handle the situation and calm him down ourselves, so that's why we didn't call you. But I thought you'd want to be aware of what had happened."

"That doesn't sound like him at all."

"Irritability is a common side effect in Alzheimer's patients as the disease progresses," she said. "The common misconception is that the disease only affects a person's memory, but in many cases, the disease affects much more than that. Many develop mood swings, short tempers, resistance to caregivers. Just as their memory fades in and out unpredictably, these mood swings are unpredictable, too. Another one could occur tomorrow, or not for a few months. Or not at all."

"I want to ask him about it," I said.

"He won't remember. We've already brought the subject up with him, and he doesn't remember a thing.

"It's just something I want to prepare you for," she continued. "I don't want you to be caught off-guard if he becomes irritable during one of your visits in the future. If something does happen, please do let us know. We're here to help him."

"I appreciate it."

"Hopefully, it was an isolated event," she said. "You never know. It's such an unpredictable disease."

I thanked Kim again, and she left, disappearing into a room down the hall. I walked back into my grandpa's room. He was still lying in hid bed, focused on the television. I sat down in the chair next to his bed and watched with him.

I remained with him for the rest of the day. Since it was a holiday, the arcade was closed, and there was nothing to do at my apartment. NBC had a marathon of old western movies on, and we watched back-to-back John Wayne features. We talked for much of the first movie, and he seemed fine--the same old grandpa I'd come to love over the years, albeit with a few lapses in memory.

During the second movie, he fell asleep, and I looked at my grandpa, lying in his bed, a few wispy strands of gray hair spilling onto his forehead. The news from his therapist had affected me, had even scared me a little. It was one thing for my grandpa to occasionally forget bits of information and mix-up words; it was another thing entirely for his whole personality to be altered. I wondered who he would become once the disease truly started to take hold. Would I even know him or be able to recognize him? It was sobering, this thought that the man I admired so greatly, this man that I loved, could simply turn into someone with an entirely different personality.

# # #

1985 started out slow at the arcade, and continued that way for the first few days of the year. Local schools resumed classes, and the teenagers who'd spent most of their break at the arcade returned to school. Maddy was busy preparing for her big play audition with a local actors group she was a part of and hadn't had time to stop by the arcade. Willie had even been absent from Westfield Arcade for that first week of 1985, the longest stretch he'd ever gone without showing up to the arcade.

Everything changed when Gonzo stopped by the arcade a week into the New Year. He walked through the entrance wearing a pair of jeans and his red Radio Shack vest over a black sweater. He'd rolled up the sleeves of the sweater, revealing a thick, plaster cast that covered his left forearm, running from his elbow down to his wrist.

"Gonzo," I said, walking out from behind the front counter. "Jesus, are you all right?"

I reached him. Up close, I could see a small, inch-long cut on his forehead that had been closed with a few stitches.

"What happened?" I said.

He looked at me with a distant, far-off gaze in his eyes.

"You haven't heard?" he said.

"Heard what? What the hell happened?"

His expression didn't change as he continued looking at me.

"You might want to sit down," he said.

The news one receives after hearing those words is typically either really good or really bad. I prayed for the former but expected the latter as Gonzo and I walked over to the front counter. It was early in the morning, not even noon yet, and we were the only two people in the arcade. I sat down behind the counter and Gonzo stood on the other side. He leaned against the glass countertop, his one good arm supporting his weight.

"There was a car accident," he simply said.

"What? When?"

"New Year's Eve. When Willie and I left after the party."

"Are you all right?"

"I'm fine," he said, though he didn't look like it. "The broken arm didn't exactly feel nice. But the doctors tell me the cut on my forehead is nothing major."

He paused for a moment, looking out at the arcade, then back to me.

"But Willie…" he said.

117

His words trailed off. I felt a knot forming in the pit of my stomach. I wasn't sure I even wanted to hear what Gonzo was about to say.

"Willie wasn't as fortunate," Gonzo finally said, his voice barely louder than a whisper.

I didn't know what to do, what to say. I didn't even know if I was capable of speech.

"What happened to Willie?" I eeked out.

No response from Gonzo. He'd turned his head away from me again, looking out at the games in the arcade.

"Gonzo, what happened to Willie?" I repeated.

"It was…it was a really bad car accident. He lost control of the car on the interstate and crashed into one of those cement dividers in the middle of the highway. I was wearing my seatbelt. Willie wasn't."

He turned back towards me. I could see tears welling in his eyes. He took a deep breath and continued on.

"He's in the hospital now. Intensive care. He's going to live, they say. Unless something unforeseen happens, he's going to make it. But the swelling has to go down before they can tell exactly what needs to be done."

"What happens then?"

"Surgery? Rehabilitation? I don't really know. Your guess is as good as mine."

Neither of us said anything for a few moments. I was grateful that Gonzo had me sit down before telling me the news. Had I been standing up at the moment, I was certain I would have collapsed under the weight of the news.

"I need to visit him," I said.

"The section of the hospital he's in doesn't allow visitors. Even if it did, he's on so much pain medication that he's hardly ever awake. According to my nurse at the hospital, that is. She's the one who filled me in on his condition."

He looked at me.

"My nurse mentioned that Willie has a spinal injury. That's all they knew at the moment."

"A spinal injury..." I said, those words trailing off, feeling like I was going to be sick.

I thought back to that night of the party. I remembered Willie and Gonzo leaving the arcade, drunkenly laughing with one another, neither of them barely able to stand up as they walked across the food court. I recalled how Willie had dropped his keys, then practically fallen on his face when he bent over to pick them up. And I'd simply remained in the arcade the entire time, watching them and not doing a thing.

"This is all my fault," I said.

"Don't be ridiculous."

"It is. I knew he'd been drinking. I didn't even try to stop him from driving."

"I knew he'd been drinking, too," Gonzo said. "And I didn't try to stop him, either. In fact, I got in the car with him for a ride home. So don't waste your time blaming yourself."

More silence between us. I pictured what Willie must look like at the exact moment Gonzo and I stood in the arcade--lying in a hospital bed unconscious, hooked up to various machines that monitored his status, a tube feeding him intravenously--and my spirits sunk even lower.

"I gotta get to work," Gonzo said, stepping away from the counter. "It sucks being the bearer of bad news."

"Feel better, Gonzo," I said.

"I'll let you know if I hear anything on Willie," he said.

# # #

There was no convenient way of instantly communicating with Willie or getting updates on his condition in the mid-80s, and, as the days, then weeks, passed, it was excruciating to have no idea what was going on. I called St. Vincent Hospital every day in an attempt to get some sort of update, but I was always given the same response: they couldn't give information out over the phone, and visitors weren't being accepted for Willie Cardinal at the time. After a few weeks of this, I called one day and was told that Willie had been transferred to a hospital in Boston for further testing.

It was the feeling of helplessness that was the worst. All I wanted was to visit him, maybe brighten his spirits for a moment, get an update on how he was doing. But I couldn't even do that, and on more than one occasion, it struck me just how little I knew of Willie. I'd regarded him as one of my closest friends, possibly my best friend, but it was also a tenuous friendship that was held together by the common bond of Westfield Arcade. I knew practically nothing of his life outside of the arcade--I didn't have his phone number, didn't have any idea where he lived, didn't know anything about what he did when he wasn't at the arcade.

I still spent almost every late night at the arcade, usually by myself. For me, the appeal in arcade games had always been the escape they provided, how nothing else in the world mattered when you were truly zoned into a game. And now more than ever, arcade games served that purpose for me. I immersed myself in playing games, staying in Westfield Arcade by myself late into the night, MTV After Dark blaring from the television speakers, completely lost in my own little world. It became increasingly rare for me to go to sleep at night before two or three in the morning.

Throughout all of the late nights and time spent at the arcade, I held out hope that everything would work out, that Willie would simply stroll into the arcade one day with that smile on his face and start kicking ass at arcade games like nothing had happened. But as the time passed with no word from him, that looked more and more unlikely, and I started to worry that Willie, my best friend, the greatest, might simply disappear from my life.

# # #

"Well, today was officially a total piece of shit," I said.

I sat at the front counter of Westfield Arcade, late at night, hunched over the ledger that listed every game in the arcade. I'd already emptied out all of the cabinets and logged the amount each cabinet brought in on the day. Maddy sat over by the television, watching MTV. The video for "Take On Me" by A-Ha was showing. She looked over at me.

"Bad day?" she asked.

"Beyond bad," I said, looking back down at the ledger. "Twenty-two dollars and seventy-five cents. That was the haul for the day."

"Total?" she asked.

"Yeah, total."

I closed the ledger and put in back in a drawer behind the counter.

"Oh, I almost forgot," I said. "There was one Canadian quarter that some asshole jammed up the Rush'n Attack cabinet with. So I can add that to the total. What's a Canadian quarter worth?"

"No clue," Maddy said. "Like fifteen cents, maybe."

"So twenty-two dollars and ninety cents. Still an awful day. Pac Man used to bring in twenty bucks by itself on a good day. Space Invaders, Donkey Kong, Centipede—all of them did."

Maddy said nothing in response, her attention focused on the television. It was one of the first nights she'd come to the arcade since she'd started preparing for her play audition. It was great to be with her, even with Willie's absence hanging over the arcade like a black could.

I drug the chair from behind the front counter over to the television and sat down next to Maddy. We watched MTV in silence for awhile.

"Business will pick up," Maddy finally said. "People will start coming back to the arcade once summer gets here."

I admired her optimism. I also wasn't sure if I shared it. Business at Westfield Arcade had been slow for awhile now. Willie was the ringleader of the arcade, the guy everyone looked up to, and without him, less and less people were showing up to the arcade. The place simply wasn't as fun without Willie around, and even those who did show up typically spent no more than ten or fifteen minutes in the arcade before leaving to find some other distraction in the mall--a far cry from the days when people would spend hours on end bullshitting with friends and challenging opponents to duels.

Everyone missed Willie, and his absence was impossible to ignore. The high score chalkboard still stood, high and mighty, behind the arcade's front counter. Willie's initials were still behind every single game but one, and these initials served as a stark reminder of his absence.

"The place just isn't the same without Willie," I said to Maddy.

She didn't say anything in response, and we continued watching the television.

"Today wasn't the best for me, either," she eventually said.

"What's wrong?" I said.

"That part I auditioned for last week? The play at the Indiana Repertory Theatre? I heard back from the director of the play today."

"What'd you hear?"

She looked at me and simply shook her head 'no.' The gesture said everything I needed to know.

"I'm sorry," I said.

"Not the first time I've been turned down for a part," she said. "But it definitely hurts more than the ones in the past. This play, this was a dream. Being the lead in it would have been amazing."

"There are plenty of other plays," I said. "Something will work out. I know it will."

"I used to think that, too," she said. "That something will work out. I was always so positive. When I was eighteen, nineteen, I had all of the answers. I knew exactly what was going to happen. I was going to become a stage actress. I'd start out small, slowly work my way up to the big time. I could see it so clearly.

"And now, it's like nothing has worked out. I started out small, and I'm still small. I can't continue to just act in these small plays that barely anyone comes to see, but I don't know what else to do. I'm twenty-five years old, and I'm more lost at twenty-five than I was at eighteen. It's not supposed to work like that. You're supposed to figure everything out as you get older. Not the other way around."

She shook her hand, ran her hand through her short hair, sighed. I'd never seen her so worn-out, so sad.

"It's just so frustrating," she said. For a moment, she looked like she was going to cry.

"I believe in you, Maddy, I said.

"Thanks," she said. "but I'm not even sure I believe in myself anymore."

# # #

Life at Westfield Arcade continued, and it soon became apparent that the problems with the arcade were related to more than Willie's absence.

Throughout the beginning of 1985, the market was flooded with games. Many were terrible (4-D Warriors, Buggy Boy, Spelunker), some were okay (Fantasy Zone, Gradius, City Connection), and a few were actually pretty good (Commando, Gauntlet, Space Harrier). But none were memorable. None were special. Not a single one had that addictive quality that made games like Pac Man and Donkey Kong so exceptional and caused people play the game for hours on end.

But the mediocre games that were released masked another fact, possibly the most-important reason the crowds visiting the arcade were dwindling: The regulars, the people who showed up every single night and helped turn Westfield Arcade into such a special place, were all growing up. Gonzo had been promoted to assistant manager at Radio Shack and now worked almost sixty hours a week. Bearclaw's relationship with his girlfriend had gotten serious and he spent almost all of his free time with her. Rufus was now a senior in high school and was busy visiting colleges to determine what school he'd attend in the fall. Even Maddy started to come around less frequently--after being turned down for the part in the play, she'd taken on a second job bartending at a local bar, and usually went straight from her shifts at Sam Goody to the bar.

I could see with my own eyes as the arcade started to become a shell of what it used to be. I kept waiting for things to magically go back to how they'd once been, and it just wasn't happening. I'd even stopped updating the high score chalkboard. The board still stood behind the arcade's front counter, but none of the arcade's newer games had been added. Getting the high score in a game didn't have the same prestige that it used to. No-one seemed to care anymore.

It broke my heart to see the arcade, the place I loved more than anything, as it slowly rotted away.

7. Gauntlet

It was a Thursday evening when Willie Cardinal showed up to Westfield Arcade for the final time.

I stood by the Out-Run cabinet, towards the front of the arcade, when I spotted him. He was out in the food court, slowly making his way over to the arcade. An older, middle-aged lady walked at his side. When they reached the edge of the food court, she said something to Willie. He nodded his head and she sat down in one of the empty food court tables. Willie continued on towards the arcade.

He wore a white t-shirt and a pair of black sweatpants, a pair of white L.A. Gear hi-tops on his feet. As he approached, I could see that his unruly mop of blonde hair had been cut short. The tanned tone to his skin had faded into an ashen, pasty white. Even from a distance, I could see a scar on the left side of his face, right around the same place as the scar on Gonzo's face, but Willie's was a more pronounced scar that extended down from high on his forehead to the middle of his cheek.

He was in a wheelchair. His arms pumped the wheels forward as his chair slowly rolled across the food court up to the entrance of the arcade. His head was up, looking at the arcade the entire time. He spotted me watching him but didn't register any sort of acknowledgement on his face.

I watched him as he continued slowly rolling through the food court. Eventually, he reached Westfield Arcade and wheeled himself over to where I stood.

"Willie," I said. I realized I'd been holding my breath, and I let it all out in a rush.

"Hey, man," he said.

I'd thought a lot about this moment over the past few months, the moment of Willie's triumphant return to the arcade. I envisioned him strolling in, taking stock of all the new games we'd received. I imagined him walking up to one of the newer games--Gradius, maybe, or Rush'n Attack--dropping a quarter down the slot, and picking up on the game instantly, setting a high score on his very first try as a crowd of onlookers slowly gathered behind the game and watched him play.

I never imagined he'd be in a wheelchair, and I never imagined that he'd have such a beat-down, drained expression on his face.

"How's it going?" I said. I didn't even know what 'it' was referring to. His legs? His rehabilitation? His life?

"In case you didn't notice, I got a new set of wheels," he said. He spoke in a slow, monotone voice that I barely even recognized.

"I noticed," I said.

"They look pretty slick, don't they?" he said.

"They look great," I said. "They really compliment your eyes."

He didn't smile or acknowledge my remark; instead, he looked around at the arcade. There was a teenager playing a game of Defender in the back of the arcade and another playing Galaxian a few cabinets down from him. Other than that, Willie and I were the only people in the arcade.

"What the hell happened to this place?" Willie asked. "I remember Thursday nights being not so...dead."

I looked back at him.

"It's been slow for awhile now."

"I quit showing up, and everyone follows suit?"

"That's part of it," I said. "There hasn't been a truly good game come in out in awhile. That's the main problem."

Willie pushed forward on his wheels, and I walked behind him as he rolled a few feet over to the group of cabinets near the front of the arcade. He stopped when he reached the Out-Run cabinet and watched the demo screen for a few moments, as a computer-controlled Ferrari Testarossa zoomed down an unnamed stretch of California coastal highway.

"This one looks cool," Willie said.

"It is," I said. "Best game we've received in a long time."

"Kinda like Pole position," he said. "Only the car actually looks like a car."

He watched the Out-Run demo screen for a few seconds longer, then wheeled past the cabinet to the one next to it. It was a cabinet with imitation bicycle handlebars mounted to the control panel.

"Paperboy," he read off of the marquee. "What's this one about?"

"You're a paperboy," I said. "And you ride a bicycle around and deliver newspapers to houses."

He looked up at me.

"Are you serious?"

"Yeah. You get points for delivering newspapers and avoiding obstacles like dogs and manholes and stuff like that."

"Jesus, that sounds horrible."

"Sad thing is, Paperboy's one of the better games we've received over the past few months. Some of the others are just awful."

He gave a final glance at the Paperboy cabinet, then started wheeling down the far-left aisle of the arcade, looking at the cabinets on either side of him. I walked behind him.

"Alpha Mission?" he said back to me as we passed that cabinet.

"It sucks," I replied.

"Junior Pac Man?" he asked, looking at the game across the aisle from Alpha Mission.

"Not the best," I said. "It's basically the exact same game as Pac Man and Ms. Pac Man."

"Choplifter?"

"It's a waste of space."

"Dig Dug 2?"

"It's awful. Like, monumentally bad. Nothing compared to the original."

He came to a stop at one of the cabinets in the middle of the row: Gauntlet.

"So what have you been up to these past few months?" Willie asked as he watched the top-down view of a wizard and a knight battling a few goblins on the Gauntlet demo screen.

"I've mostly been working," I said. "That, and worrying about you. Praying that you were ok."

"I shoulda wrote you guys a letter, gotten word to you somehow," Willie said.

He remained staring at the Gauntlet demo screen.

"But I kinda had some other stuff to focus on," Willie continued, his voice even. "You know, like four three-hour-long spinal surgeries over the past few months. Taking enough painkillers to drop a horse. Those types of things."

His expression didn't change as he continued talking.

"And before you ask, no, the surgeries weren't successful. Four specialists, all across the country, and none of them could help me. The last one was the final straw. It's over. I will be in a wheelchair for the rest of my life."

There was a feeling in my gut like being hit with a sledgehammer. I looked at his stationary legs in the wheelchair and imagined those legs never moving on their own will ever again. This was Willie, the guy who used to prance around the arcade, going from game to game like he had an invisible jetpack attached to his back? And he'd never walk again? It didn't seem right. Didn't seem fair. Didn't seem possible.

"It sucks," he said. "It fucking sucks so badly."

He wheeled past Gauntlet and continued moving towards the back of the arcade. The two kids who'd been in earlier had left, and Willie and I were the only two people in the arcade.

"I'm sorry for not stopping you that night," I suddenly said.

He looked over his shoulder at me.

"It wasn't your fault," he said.

"I knew you'd been drinking. I should have done something."

"I wouldn't have listened. You and I both know it. I would've called you a pansy, I would've laughed and told you to go screw yourself. You had nothing to do with this. This is all on me. I'm just glad that Gonzo is all right, that no-one else was injured."

We reached the back of the arcade, home to most of the old games we used to play against one another. We passed Pac Man, Space Invaders, Defender. We passed the Joust cabinet that we'd played our final game on, then reached the Robotron: 2084 cabinet. Willie briefly stopped at it, watching the demo screen for awhile.

"Still can't believe you had a 2.4 million-point game," Willie said.

"The record still stands," I said. "You're the only one to come anywhere close to it."

I pulled a quarter from my pocket and held it out for him.

"Wanna take a crack at beating it?" I said. "It's on the house."

"No thanks," Willie said.

"Come on. My treat."

"Don't really feel like it."

Willie turned his wheelchair around and I followed him as he wheeled back down the aisle. We reached the front of the arcade, back up by the Out-Run and Paperboy cabinets. Willie stopped his wheelchair and spun it around, looking out at the arcade. Neither of us said anything for a few moments.

"You have no idea how much I missed this place," Willie said, scanning the various games in the arcade. His voice cracked a little as he spoke. "For awhile, I wasn't sure if I'd ever make it back."

"Next time you come, give me some notice. I'll get the whole crew in here."

He shook his head.

"There isn't going to be a next time. I have to move back home to live with my parents. When your legs don't work, it's pretty difficult to live on your own. At least, it is until I learn to deal with this. So I'm moving back to California."

I looked at him.

"Bet you didn't even know I was from California, did you?" Willie said.

"No, I didn't."

"Yep. Moved out to Indy after high school. Followed my high school sweetheart out here, she dumped me within the first month of being here, and I liked it so much I decided not to move back home."

He paused. Glanced at the high score chalkboard behind the front counter for a moment, then looked back out at the sea of games in the arcade.

"The memories, man," he said, his voice cracking once more. "How many hours did I spend in this place?

131

Jesus, I don't even know if I can count that high. And the thing is, I don't regret one second of any of it. If I could do it all over again, I'd spend even more time here. I had a blast every single night I showed up, just dicking around with friends and playing arcade games. It was a guaranteed fun evening every single time I came here. There aren't too many places in the world you can say that about."

He remained looking out at the arcade for a moment, then looked up at me.

"So, goodbye," he said. "Not much more to say than that. I'll miss you, man. We had us some great times here, and I'll never forget them."

I looked down at Willie, in his wheelchair. I thought of all of the late nights when it had been just him and I and our favorite arcade game.

"I'll miss you, too," I said, feeling emotional. "Good luck in California."

"And tell your grandpa that I said goodbye. I'll miss him."

He spun his wheelchair around so it was facing the entrance, but then looked back at me. For the first time since he'd arrived, his eyes had a hint of a spark to them.

"So I gotta ask," he said. "Did you ever make a move on Maddy?"

"No," I said.

"Still being a pussy, I see."

"It's not that," I said. "It just didn't seem right to worry about making a move on her when I didn't know what was going to happen to my best friend. Everyone's been pretty down without you around."

"Well, I made it. And I'll be fine. So you don't have any more excuses."

And with that, he started wheeling his wheelchair out of the arcade, arms pumping. I watched the back of his wheelchair as he wheeled over to the middle-aged lady who'd been walking by his side earlier--his mother, I presumed. She said something to Willie, and he wordlessly shook his head. She walked around behind the wheelchair and started pushing Willie away.

For one final time, Willie looked over his shoulder at Westfield Arcade. He waved at me, and then disappeared.

# # #

"Maddy, I have something I want to talk about," I said. I took a deep breath to compose myself. "I think you're amazing. You're the greatest person I know. The absolute best. By far. No-one else even comes close."

I paused for a moment, letting the full weight of those words sink in.

"I'm in love with you," I continued. "In fact, that seems like an understatement. Love isn't a strong enough word. I'm infatuated with you. I'm—"

I looked at my reflection in the bathroom mirror, then glanced back down at the crumpled sheet of loose leaf paper resting on the edge of the bathroom sink in front of me. The entire sheet was a jumbled mishmash of words written in pencil. Some of the words had been erased, others were scribbled out, other important words were underlined with dark, thick pencil lines.

I was alone in the bathroom of Giovanni's, a nice Italian restaurant that had recently opened up next to Westfield Mall. Maddy was out in the restaurant, sitting at our table.

I took off my linen sport coat, then noticed the sweat stains visible in the underarms of the button-up shirt I wore underneath and quickly put the sport coat back on to cover them. I looked back at my reflection in the bathroom mirror. Looked down at the sheet of loose-leaf paper. I shook my head, and let out a long, slow sigh.

Shortly after Willie's visit to the arcade, I'd decided that I was going to finally say something to Maddy and tell her exactly how I felt about her. I knew that I couldn't just wing a speech like that and hope to come up with something off the top of my head, and so, for weeks, I'd been working on a speech to fully express my feelings for her. I'd gone over the speech with a fine-tooth comb, performing countless rewrites and revisions to it.

As I was finishing up the speech, Maddy had made an offhand remark that she wanted to try Giovanni's, a new upscale Italian restaurant that recently opened up less than a block from Westfield Mall. I told her I wanted to try it out, too (which was a slight exaggeration, as I'd never even heard of the place), and we made plans to have dinner on a night she didn't have to bartend.

And here we were. Me, in the bathroom alone, sweating bullets, a complete nervous wreck. Maddy, sitting at our table in the dining area by herself, most likely wondering why I was still in the bathroom ten minutes after I excused myself.

I checked my teeth in the mirror. Looked back down at the sheet of paper a final time, then carefully folded it up and stuck it in the pocket of my sport coat.

Butterflies in my stomach as I walked back to our table, past tables of friends out for a nice dinner and couples on dates, past the dark-grain mahogany bar with a few people sitting at it on barstools. I arrived at our booth and slid in across from her. She reached over and grabbed a piece of bread from a small basket in the middle of the table.

"This bread is incredible," she said.

I glanced across the table at her. She looked great. Her short hair was effortlessly held in place by a small, light blue headband, and a pair of hoop earrings that were the exact same color as the headband dangled from her ears. The earrings were more sensible than gaudy. She wore a black sleeveless blouse tucked into a pair of Guess jeans--I knew they were Guess because I'd noticed the small upside-down triangle logo on her rear left jeans pocket as we were walking to the restaurant.

She looked up at me and caught me staring at her.

"Seriously, you have to try this," she said, sliding the basket across the table to me. "It tastes like a little slice of heaven."

I grabbed a piece of bread and tried it.

"Well?" Maddy said.

"It's good."

"It's better than just good. I'm thinking of canceling my entrée order and just having our waitress bring me out a gigantic loaf of bread instead."

I took a drink of wine. Then, I took another drink of wine. Then another, which finished off my glass. I could feel a droplet of sweat sliding from my armpit down my left ribcage. My heart thundered in my chest.

"So," I said. "I have something I want to talk about. Something I want to tell you."

"I have something I want to tell you, too," she said. "Thumb wrestle to see who goes first?"

"You can go," I said. I needed time to try and calm myself down, maybe order another glass of wine.

"Well," she began, then paused. She skittishly looked away from me, at the table next to us, towards the front entrance of the restaurant, out the window next to our table. She stared out the window for a moment. She seemed nervous, preoccupied.

"Is everything all right?" I said.

"Everything's fine," she said, still looking out the window.

Finally, she turned back towards me.

"I'm moving to New York," she simply said.

My heart went from hammering in my chest to not beating at all. My entire body went cold, the pools of sweat underneath my armpits turning to icicles. I had no words. Even if I was able to speak, I had no idea what I'd even say.

She stared at me, waiting for some sort of response, her statement hanging in the air between us.

"You're moving?" I said, barely recognizing my own voice.

"Yeah," she said.

"To New York?"

"Yeah."

I looked at her. She stared back. An eternity passed.

"Oh," I finally said.

Oh. It pretty much summed up my feelings. I'd been kicked in the stomach, blindsided by a roundhouse punch, run over by a freight train.

"You looked shocked," she said.

"Yeah," I said, dazed. "Yeah, I am."

There was another brief moment of silence, and then she started talking. I was only able to comprehend parts and snippets of what she was saying. A friend from Indianapolis had gotten a job. As an Assistant Director of a play in New York. The play was named 'Sensible Alternatives.' The friend told Maddy that she could get her a part in 'Sensible Alternatives.'

"And so, I figured, why not?" Maddy continued. "I mean, it's not a huge production or anything. It's not even off-Broadway. It's like off-, off-, off-Broadway. But it's New York, the theatre capitol of the world. This is my chance. They don't come around often. If I fail, I fail. That's life. But I at least have to try."

She looked at me, expecting a response. But I had nothing to say.

"It's not exactly like things are working out here for me," she continued. "Twenty-six years old, still making barely more than minimum-wage at Sam Goody. When I didn't get that part in 'A Flea in her Ear,' that was the last straw. I knew that something had to change. Acting was always going to be my ticket out of this town. I figured some talent scout or producer would just randomly discover me one day, be blown away, and give me a job in his latest production to get me out of this town. But it's the other way around. I need a ticket out of this town before I can do anything with my acting. I can't make it big and then move out of this town--I have to move out of this town first, then make it big."

"When," I said, still breathless. "When are you moving?"

"It won't happen for a few more months. So I've still got awhile. I need to save up as much money as I can. That's why I got the job bartending--it's not cheap to live in New York."

I thought about what to say next. Nothing came to mind.

"So that's my news," Maddy said. "Your turn. What did you want to tell me?"

"Nothing," I quickly said. "It was nothing. Just forget about it."

"You sure?"

"Yes," I said. "I'm positive."

# # #

Maddy's admission came at the start of dinner, before we'd even received our entrées, and I spent the rest of the meal feigning interest as she talked about her move. She spoke of her adventures in apartment hunting for a place in New York, and about the various neighborhoods and which ones she'd prefer to live in. She talked of the dilemma of whether she wanted to take her car with her or sell it. I tried to hold up my end of the conversation but I could barely concentrate.

137

When dinner ended, we bid each other farewell and I walked over to Westfield Mall. It was relatively late in the night, well past ten, and the only people in the mall were a few workers at assorted stores finishing their closing duties. I walked down the mall's main walkway and went straight to the arcade.

Ed had covered my shift and he'd already closed down the arcade for the night, so I unlocked the security gate and flipped the main power switch in the back of the arcade. Every machine powered on. I walked up and down the two main aisles, looking over the selection. Eventually, I came to a stop in front of an old standby: Pac Man.

I dropped a quarter into the slot and started playing. The familiar *wokka-wokka-wokka* noise sang from the speakers as I maneuvered Pac Man throughout the maze.

Such a simple game. Eat all of the dots before the ghosts eat you. If you accomplish that objective, you win. If you don't, you lose. Why, I wondered, couldn't life have such a simple, clearly-defined objective? I still felt shell-shocked from the news that Maddy would be moving. Both her and Willie, gone. I tried to look on the bright side of things, but there was no bright side.

For the first time in awhile, the thought of returning to college entered my mind. Maybe see if my coursework from Northwestern would transfer to a college somewhere in Indianapolis, and start taking classes again. As recently as a year ago, such a thought was unfathomable. Westfield Arcade was such a special place, and working here was just too much fun to consider simply throwing it all away to go back to college. But the magic of the arcade had started to wear off once the regulars began coming around less and less. And now both Willie and Maddy would soon to be gone from my life.

Still, college held little appeal. I'd chosen Accounting as a major all those years ago not because of some love of numbers, but because I couldn't think of what else I'd like to do. Balancing the books for Ed at the arcade was fine, but sitting in a cubicle and doing that for other businesses, day-in, day-out, was not for me. At least, I didn't think it was.

Before long, the rhythm of the game took over and my mind cleared. I escaped into the game, solely focused on it, the utter concentration that Pac Man required causing the outside world and all of its problems to momentarily disappear. Nothing else mattered as I remained by myself in the arcade and expertly maneuvered the game's joystick to direct Pac Man around the screen.

I played forever, in my own little world, before a voice behind me startled me back to reality.

"Hey."

My body involuntary jumped and I turned around. Ed stood behind me, leaning against the Gorf cabinet.

"What are you doing here?" I said, stepping away from Pac Man.

"Forgot my jacket earlier," he said, holding up the jacket in his hand.

"Was it a good night tonight?" I asked, though I was sure I already knew the answer.

"No," he said, shaking his head lightly. "No, it was not."

"Things will pick up," I said.

"Things will pick up," Ed repeated. "That's been the refrain around here for awhile now, hasn't it? But business hasn't picked up."

For the first time, I noticed just how worn-out Ed looked. There were deep bags under his eyes. His hair had thinned out and was no longer black speckled with gray; it was almost entirely gray. He even looked like he'd lost some weight.

"You all right?" I said.

He let out a long sigh.

"No, I'm not," he said. "I'm starting to lose my ass on this place. We're pulling in one hundred dollars in quarters a week--that's on a good week--and that just doesn't cut it. Not even close. The bills and lease payments keep coming and I'm not earning anything to pay them."

He slowly shook his head as he looked back out at the newer games towards the front of the arcade.

"The games," he said. "That's what the problem is. They've been shit lately."

He turned back towards me.

"Lemme ask you a question," he said. "What made Pac Man such a great game? Donkey Kong? Space Invaders? What was it about those games that made people stand at the cabinet for hours on end and pump quarter after quarter into them?"

"They were fun."

"It was more than that. They were *original*. That's what made them good. No game that was even remotely similar to any of those games had been released before they came along. And that just doesn't happen anymore. All of a sudden, it seems like there's no originality left.

"Just look at the games that have come out over the past few years," Ed continued, picking up steam, the tone of his voice increasing. "Super Pac-Man, Pac-Man Plus, Jr. Pac-Man, Lady Bug, Mouse Trap--all of them were identical to the original Pac-Man. After Donkey Kong, came Donkey Kong Jr., Donkey Kong 3, Mr. Do's Castle, Kangaroo. Donkey Kong clones, each and every one of them. Centipede spawned Millipede, Jackler, Caterpillar, countless other rip-offs."

"The arcade still has some good games," I said. "Out-Run's fun. Commando, too. Marble Madness isn't bad."

"Sure, those are good games," he said. "But games like that are few and far between. Everything else is just a

140

copy of a successful game with a few minor alterations. That's not gonna cut it. You have to have originality to survive. It's like any industry--the market has to evolve to maintain people's interest. You can't just keep releasing games that are basically identical to one another and expect people to spend money on them. I mean, you saw what happened to the home video game market."

A few years previously, around the middle of 1983, the home video game market—mostly comprised of consoles from Atari and Coleco that plugged directly into one's television and allowed users to play various games on cartridges that were compatible with those consoles—had flat-out imploded. The crash of the home video game market had been swift and sudden, and sales had simply disappeared. In 1983, the industry had 3.6 billion dollars in sales; two years later, in 1985, that number had dropped dramatically to $300 million; by 1986, that number would drop all the way to under $100 million. Atari and all of their closest competitors had gone bankrupt. Cartridges that had once sold for thirty dollars a piece were thrown in the clearance aisle and marked down to less than five dollars a game...and still didn't sell. It had been an astronomical drop that had all but decimated the home video game market. And the main culprit in the disappearance of the home video game market was the fact that the games released for those systems had gotten stale and unoriginal. People, quite simply, had gotten bored.

"My greatest fear," Ed said, "is that the exact same thing is going to happen to the arcade industry. And if it does, Westfield Arcade is done. Finished."

"All it takes is a few great games, and people will come back," I said. "It's just temporary."

"I'd like to think it's temporary," he said. "But I don't know if it is. I honestly don't."

141

"Things will pick up," I repeated again, as if by repeating this phrase, business would simply, magically return tomorrow.

"Things better pick up," Ed said. "And soon."

8. Golden Axe

For as long as I could remember, my grandpa's favorite day had been the opening day of the baseball season.

He viewed the day as nothing short of a national holiday. While he was raising me, he'd always let me take the day off from school, and we'd order pizza, grab a few sodas, and sit around the television to watch that afternoon's Cubs game on WGN. He'd talk endlessly of the promise the forthcoming year held for the Cubs, how all it'd take was one or two prospects to start playing up to their potential for the season to be a special one. It was always great fun, skipping out on school and spending the entire day with lounging around with my grandpa.

When I showed up to my grandpa's room for opening day a few weeks after my dinner with Maddy, I found him lying in his bed. The television was off, yet he still stared blankly into the darkened screen. His room was completely silent.

"Grandpa," I said.

He looked over at me for a second, then turned back towards the television.

"It's opening day," I said, sitting down in the recliner next to his bed. "Are you excited?"

"Opening day," he repeated. "When is opening day?"

"It's today."

He looked over at me.

"Do the Cubs play today?"

"Yes. In a few minutes."

"It's opening day," he announced. He smiled. It'd been awhile since I'd seen a true, genuine smile from him.

"Can I turn on your television?" I asked my grandpa. I knew better than to do anything to the television without asking his permission. A few weeks ago, I'd turned off his television when his therapist had come into the room to ask him a few questions, and he turned agitated and petulant until we turned the tv back on.

"Yes, yes," he said. "The Cubs. It's opening day."

I turned on his television and flipped the channel to WGN. The evening news was just ending. The broadcast cut away and a picture of Three Rivers Stadium in Pittsburgh appeared (the Cubs were opening the season with a road game). Harry Caray's familiar voice came through the television speakers, sounding half-drunk, welcoming fans to another exciting year of Cubs baseball.

"Do you think it will be a good year this year?" I asked my grandpa.

He didn't respond or acknowledge the question. He was entranced by the television. Harry Caray kicked it over to Steve Stone, who gave a brief overview of the main players for that year's team, as each player's picture flashed onscreen. Keith Moreland. Ryne Sandberg. Lee Smith. Rick Sutcliffe.

"Big Red!" my grandpa exclaimed upon seeing the picture, using his nickname for Rick Sutcliffe, the Cubs redheaded starting pitcher. "Show 'em the sinker, Big Red."

The brief pre-game show ended and Larry Bowa, the Cubs leadoff hitter, stepped to the plate.

"Play ball," my grandpa exclaimed. "My two favorite words!"

Here he was--the grandpa I remembered, the grandpa I grew up with. I hadn't seen my grandpa this enthusiastic or clear-headed in a long time. His condition had continued to worsen over the past few months, and he was constantly impatient, borderline senile at times. During other visits, he was confused and disoriented. But seeing his old self shine through on that day was a welcome change.

The game began and we watched. The first few innings passed by quickly with the Cubs leading 2-0.

"What do you think of the game so far?" I asked my grandpa during a commercial break between innings.

He didn't respond.

"Grandpa, what do you think of the game so far?" I asked.

"Good, good," he said.

"Big Red is having a good game," I said.

"Big Red will win the Cy Young!" my grandpa said.

We continued watching, with the Cubs extending their lead to 5-1. At one point, the announcers briefly talked about the Cubs upcoming homestand, and a picture of Wrigley Field flashed onscreen. My grandpa looked at it then turned towards me.

"Do you remember when we went to Chicago for opening day?" my grandpa asked.

I looked at him. I was shocked that he remembered. When I was in eighth grade, he'd surprised me with tickets to that year's opening day game. That morning, we'd driven up to Chicago and went to watch the game at Wrigley Field together. It had been a beautiful seventy-degree day and we'd gorged on ballpark food: hot dogs, peanuts, sodas. For the entire day, we were out in the bleachers, the sun beating down on us as we watched the game, while everyone else I knew was stuck in school. The day was still one of my fondest memories of spending time with him.

"I remember," I said.

"That was fun. We ate hot dogs."

"We did," I said.

"I want to go there again. I want to see Big Red pitch."

"Maybe next month," I said to my grandpa, knowing full well that his doctors would never allow such a visit.

We continued watching the game. A nurse showed up at one point to check-in on my grandpa.

"We're going to Chicago," he announced to her.

She looked at him and smiled.

"We're going to eat hot dogs."

The game finally ended and the Cubs won, which delighted my grandpa.

"This is the year," he said when it was over.

I was delighted, too, but not because of the game's outcome. It had been a good visit with him, one of the best I'd had in awhile. His lapses in memory had been minimal. There were no fluctuations in his mood.

But as great as it was to see his vibrant self return for a moment, I knew that he could be in a completely different mood when I showed up tomorrow. Every visit was a roll of the dice, a wild card. The difficult thing about the disease was that I never knew what to expect.

"I'll see you tomorrow, Grandpa," I said as I left.

# # #

I saw little of Maddy in the months that followed our night at Giovanni's. She'd started to bartend five nights a week to save up money for her move, leaving her no free time to drop by the arcade and watch MTV. I visited her at Sam Goody during my lunch breaks as often as I could—although it was great to sit around and talk about music with her when I visited, these interactions were usually brief and constantly interrupted by customers asking her questions. On a couple of nights, I'd stopped by the bar she worked at, but the place was usually so busy that she had barely any time to talk.

I was alone in the arcade one night when she showed up for the first time in weeks. Standing at the Out-Run cabinet, one hand holding the game's steering wheel and the other holding the gear shifter, I was driving the Ferrari down a desert highway when I heard her behind me.

"Don't crash," she said.

I immediately looked over and my car onscreen did just that: it crashed, flipping in the air a few times after colliding with another car.

Maddy stood behind the metal security gate, wearing a mid-length denim skirt that ended just above her knees and a black t-shirt that depicted the artist Prince on a motorcycle, a still from his Purple Rain album cover. Over the t-shirt, she wore her black leather jacket.

"How's it going?" I said, walking over and unlocking the security gate.

"Good," she said. She entered into the arcade and walked over to the television. As usual, the channel was switched to MTV, and the video for "Sara" by Starship was playing.

"Busy day today?" she asked, taking off her leather jacket and hanging it on the back of her chair.

"No," I simply said.

Business at the arcade still had not picked up. The games we'd received over the past few months had been neither memorable nor successful, and each had been sold back to a distributor at a significant loss shortly after receiving them. Making matters worse, a new home video game console had been released and it had, so far, proved to be a moderate success. The Nintendo Entertainment System, it was named. The home video game market, which a year earlier had looked to be completely dead after the bankruptcy of Atari, was showing signs of life once again, which further cut into the number of visitors to the arcade.

Maddy and I watched the video for "Sara," seated in front of the television. I looked at her out of the corner of my eye. The glow from the television reflected against her skin, and a small strand of hair hung over her forehead. Her lips moved ever so slightly with the lyrics to the song as she watched the video. *Sara, Sara, storms are brewing in your eyes.*

The song finally ended and MTV cut to a commercial break. Maddy looked over at me.

"So tomorrow's the big day," she said. "I'm leaving for New York."

"Really?"

"Yep. Last night was my final night at the bar, and today was my final day working at Sam Goody. There's no turning back now."

So it was official. From the moment that she dropped the bomb on me at Giovanni's on that night so many months ago, I knew this day would come. I'd held on to the distant hope that something would get in the way of her plans, that she'd change her mind. But I knew it was a long shot, and now, what little hope I had was gone.

"So, this is goodbye," I said. "This is really goodbye."

"Goodbye--that word sounds so final," Maddy said. "It's not goodbye. We'll still keep in touch."

We watched the commercial break for a brief moment. I barely registered any of it.

"So do you have any grand farewell speech for me?" she asked.

"Not really," I said.

"Well, you should. Something about how you're positive that I'll succeed, that you believe in me. Something about how, despite my fear that I'm going to fail miserably and get my ass handed to me by the city, I'm not making a mistake at all."

For a brief moment, I considered giving her the exact speech I'd planned to during our dinner at Giovanni's. I'd practiced the speech so much that I still remembered every word of it. But giving the speech now would be too little, too late--it would lead to an awkward goodbye and little more than that.

"I'll miss you," I said.

She waited for a moment.

"That's it?" she finally said.

"Yeah. That's it."

"Three words. Not much of a grand speech."

"It was concise. To the point. I really do mean it, too--I'll miss you a ton."

MTV returned from break, and the video for "Take my Breath Away" by Berlin started playing.

"Your turn," I said to Maddy. "Do you have a grand farewell speech to give?"

"I do."

"Lemme hear it."

She looked at me and paused for a moment. "Take my Breath Away" continued playing in the background.

"I'll never forget you," she began. "I'll never, ever forget you. I don't know what will happen in New York. I guess that's the exciting thing. Maybe I'll stay there forever. Maybe I'll crash and burn and move back home with my tail between my legs--my parents certainly think that's what will happen. But whatever happens, we will always stay in touch. You're too great to let go of."

I sat there, looking into her mesmerizing eyes, not sure of what to say in response.

"Wow," I finally said. "That was a million times better than my speech."

"It was more wordy, at least," she said.

"It was amazing."

"I'm glad you liked it," she said. Maddy turned back towards the television and we watched in silence for awhile. The video for "Take my Breath Away" came to an end but neither of us broke the silence by guessing what the next video would be. It ended up being "Love Walks In" by Van Halen, and we watched Sammy Hagar and the other band members dance around on stage for a moment.

Halfway through the song, I heard a soft whimper coming from Maddy's direction. I looked over and saw that she was lightly crying.

"What's wrong?" I said.

She sniffled her nose, then reached into the pocket of the leather jacket hanging on the back of her chair and pulled out a Kleenex. She dabbled at the corners of her eyes with the Kleenex.

She looked at me. Her eyes were bloodshot. She tried to smile through the tears.

"I'm scared," she said. She sniffled her nose again. "It sounds so stupid to say. I'm practically an adult. But I'm scared that I'm going to fail."

"You'll be great," I said. "I know it. You're the best."

"I just don't know what is going to happen," she said. "My future after today is one big question mark. And if this doesn't work out, the dream is over. It'll be time to find something else to strive for. And I have no idea what I'd shoot for if I didn't have acting. It's the only dream I have."

"You're going to be awesome," I said. "And in a few years, when you turn into this huge star, you're going to look back on this night and remember how scared you were and you're going to laugh. You're going to laugh that you ever doubted yourself."

Maddy smiled.

"Thanks," she said.

She wiped at her eyes with the Kleenex again.

"Can I get a hug?" she said.

I stood up and walked over to her. I looked into those eyes, still beautiful even if they were bloodshot and stained with dried tears. At the corner of her eyes were small lines, imperceptible from even a few feet away but just barely visible up close.

She extended her arms out to me and I wrapped my arms around her. I ran my hands over her back, felt the bony protrusion of her spine through her thin cotton shirt. Her body was warm, radiating heat.

We hugged for an extended moment before she pulled away. For what seemed like the longest time, we just stood there in the arcade, right in front of the television, only inches apart from one another. She looked at me with those mesmerizing eyes, and I held her gaze. Neither of us said anything.

She closed her eyes and leaned in towards me. Her lips found mine and we kissed. I tasted the sweet taste of her lipstick, could smell the faint scent of her perfume. My heartbeat rocked my whole frame, the moment more intense than any game of Robotron: 2084 or Pac Man ever could be.

I draped my arms around her once again and held her tight. I could feel her hands on my back, then she ran one hand through my hair. She snaked her tongue past my lips and our tongues intertwined.

It only got better after that.

# # #

We lay there on the ground, in Westfield Arcade. In the throes of passion, we had ended up in the rear of the arcade, back by Pac Man and the other relics. Coming from every direction were sound effects from the arcade games surrounding us—the wokka-wokka-wokka from Pac Man, the "Prepare to Qualify" synthesized voice from Pole

151

Position, the steady heartbeat-like sound effects from Space Invaders.

Both of us were still naked, and she was snuggled up against my body, my arm around her. A thin sheen of sweat separated and connected our bodies, and I ran my hand along the smooth skin of her back. I didn't want to think about the germs and parasites and God-only-knew what else that lived and festered in the carpet underneath our naked bodies.

We just lay there in silence, on our backs and staring at the ceiling, listening to the sound effects all around us. I looked at Maddy out of the corner of my eye. She was snuggled in close to my body and her eyes were closed.

"That was fun," I said, breaking the silence. Jesus. That was fun? We'd just had sex, not gone on a rollercoaster together.

Maddy pulled away from my body and turned her head up towards mine.

"That was fun?" she said, smiling. "Wow. That's the best you can come up with?"

"Sorry. That was amazing."

"That's better."

"That was incredible."

"I agree," she said.

"That was...what's a descriptive word that's stronger than 'incredible?'"

"Unbelievable?"

"Yes. That was unbelievable."

Maddy smiled and got up from the ground. She rounded up her clothes, which had been strewn all over the floor of the arcade.

"I should be going," she said. "It's late."

I gathered up my clothes and neither of us said anything as we got dressed. I continued trying to wrap my mind around what had just happened.

When we were both finally dressed, we silently walked over to the entrance of the arcade. I reached over and held her hand, and she looked over at me and smiled. We reached the entrance, and I unlocked the security gate and pushed it upwards. I still had some closing work to do, numbers to record, but it would have to wait until tomorrow. Work was the farthest thing from my mind at the moment.

I exited the arcade with Maddy and locked the gate behind me. We walked through the dead mall, through the food court with the chairs all resting legs up on the table. Neither of us said anything. We walked down the main walkway of Westfield Mall, closed and darkened storefronts on both sides of us. I felt like I needed to say something but I had no idea what to say.

We continued walking down the main walkway of the mall, eventually reaching the main entrance. There were only a few cars in the parking lot outside.

I looked at Maddy.

"So did you really mean what you said earlier, that we'll always stay in touch?" I said.

"Of course I did," she said. "But I think it's best if we just let this night remain as is. If we try to make it into some long-distance thing it's just going to complicate everything."

"I agree," I said, though I wasn't sure if I was being truthful or not. "Good luck in New York. I can't wait to hear all about it."

"I can't wait to tell you all about," she said. "I'll be sure to write."

We hugged each other for a final time, and I watched as she walked over to her car and got inside. She waved goodbye and I waved back. She started up her car and I watched as she drove across the parking lot and disappeared into the night.

\# \# \#

"I'm closing Westfield Arcade," Ed said to me. "My lease is up in three months and I decided not to renew."

Ed stood across the arcade's front counter from me and looked directly into my eyes as he spoke those fateful words. He spoke in a calm, steady voice, as if it were no big deal, as if permanently closing a place that I regarded as nothing less than magical was a routine task for him.

We'd already closed down the arcade for the night and were the only two people inside. Upon hearing his words, it felt like we were the only two people remaining on earth at that moment. I looked at him across the counter, the full weight of what he'd just said sinking in.

"You're closing the arcade?" I asked Ed, barely able to talk.

"Yes," Ed said. "I am."

It had been a rotten month up to that point. Maddy's absence had settled into my life like an incurable disease. She hadn't been around much in the months prior to her move, but there was always that chance that she'd show up out of the blue on any given night, that hope that she'd surprise me with a visit. With her halfway across the country, that hope was gone.

I thought about her a lot, and thought about our final night together even more. It had been the greatest, a truly special moment, and I wondered if she felt the same way about it. For that matter, I wondered if she thought about me at all. I hadn't heard from her at all since her move, and I was filled with questions. Did she miss me? Did she think about me as much as I thought about her? Had she already forgotten about her promise to stay in touch no matter what? I had no answers to any of these questions, and thinking about her constantly did little more than remind me on a daily basis that she was gone for good.

It had been a dreadful way to spend the month, and now, the rotten month had gotten worse.

"Why?" I asked Ed, choking out that lone word.

"Why? Do you really have to ask that question? I'm not making money anymore. That simple. I'm bleeding money to keep this place open. I'm sick of it. I'm sick of losing money."

"So this"—I motioned out to all of the games on the arcade floor—"this will all be gone?"

"Yeah. I wanted to give you a head's up to get a start on a search for a new job. Use me as a reference. I'm more than happy to--"

"This is a lot to take," I said. I felt like I was going to faint. Or cry. "This is such a shock."

"Why is it a shock? You're here more than I am. The arcade isn't what it used to be. Not even close. I told you a few months ago that things needed to change, business needed to pick up. Well, it hasn't. And this Nintendo system looks to be the real deal. It's starting to sell. Kids are staying home and playing that instead of coming here."

I tried to come up with a counter-argument but I couldn't think straight. I was shell-shocked, catatonic. Utterly blown away. I knew business was bad. I wasn't blind. But I couldn't wrap my mind around the fact that Westfield Arcade was going to simply disappear and be replaced by a Hallmark store or a Foot Locker. It just didn't seem right. The arcade was too magical, too amazing. And it was soon to be no more.

Ed talked with me for a little while longer. He gave me the name of a friend of his who managed an electronics store and said he was looking for a full-time employee. He told me there might even be an opening at the fertilizer sales company he worked at during the day and promised to check for me.

155

But I barely heard any of it. All I could think about were his fateful words. It was over. Westfield Arcade was done. It'd be closing in a matter of months.

# # #

The decision to purchase Westfield Arcade from Ed was the biggest decision I'd ever made in my life. It was also one of the easiest.

There wasn't a single eureka moment when everything clicked, no lightbulb that suddenly turned on over my head. The idea had first popped into my mind the night Ed told me he was closing the place. I'd spent the night alone in the arcade after he left, slowly pacing up and down the aisles of games, looking at the hulking cabinets on both sides of me. Every single game I walked past triggered some sort of memory from my endless nights at the arcade over the years since I'd started working here. The Dig Dug cabinet that Willie and I had played until five in the morning on the night the arcade had received the game. The Pac Man cabinet that I'd popped my arcade game cherry on so many years ago and continued to play endlessly in the years that followed. I passed the Space Invaders cabinet that Willie had set a high score on the very first time I met him, and I remembered the crowd that surrounded to watch the game and the excitement and anticipation on all of their faces.

I dropped a quarter into Black Tiger. Played it for half an hour, then moved on to Commando. The games normally provided an escape for me, but not on that night. There was too much falling apart in my life to simply escape it. It felt like everything was imploding.

I continued playing. Gauntlet. Then Paperboy. A few games of Donkey Kong Jr. At some point--I don't even remember what game I was playing--I made the decision that I wasn't going to let the arcade close. I was going to buy it from Ed. There was no second-guessing the decision. I didn't grab a sheet of paper and write out the pros and cons of buying the arcade. All I knew was that I couldn't let the place die. It was as simple as that. Outside of my grandpa, Westfield Arcade was all I had.

That next day, I talked with Ed in the arcade and told him about my decision. I laid out my plans in simple detail, and he responded to those plans with a single-word response:

"No," he said.

"What do you mean, no?" I said, surprised, a little angry.

"I mean, no, I won't sell the arcade to you."

"Why not?"

"Plenty of reasons." He was hunched over the front counter, looking at a magazine, and he didn't even look up from the magazine as he spoke.

"Give me one."

"Because I like you," Ed said. "I'm preventing you from making a mistake. Buying this place right now would be a terrible investment. That simple. I'd feel awful if I sold you everything and you lost your ass on this."

"That's my decision to make, not yours."

Ed finally looked up from his magazine.

"Even so, there's the financial situation," he said. "You need a lot more money than a rainy day fund to keep this place open. Running a business like this requires some serious money. And that money has a tendency to disappear pretty quickly."

I had money, I told Ed. Not a ton of it, but there'd been an insurance payment when my parents had died. An inheritance, too. It was enough to purchase the arcade games that Ed owned outright from him, cover the monthly payments to distributors for the games that had been bought on credit, and handle lease payments to the mall for awhile.

"I've got enough money to keep my head above water until business turns around," I said.

And it would turn around. There was no doubt in my mind that it would. I wanted to keep the arcade open because I loved the place, but I also because I believed in it. I believed so strongly in Westfield Arcade, and I knew it could be great again. I could see it so very clearly in my mind.

"The games are dropping in quality," Ed continued. "And they have been for awhile."

"This place is about more than the games for me. It's about the arcade itself. The hangout. The camaraderie. I can't let it disappear."

Ed looked at me. His steely, indifferent manner softened slightly.

"There's a lot of behind the scenes work that goes into owning a small business like this," he said.

"And I already do practically everything for you. Balancing the books. Dealing with distributors. Taking ads out in the newspaper. I can handle it, Ed. I won't be in over my head."

"It's still a risk, keeping this place open," Ed said.

"Maybe so. I don't care."

Ed looked out at the arcade. It was almost six o'clock but the place was completely dead, not a single customer in sight.

"You're absolutely sure you want to do this?" Ed said.

"Positive. This place is everything to me. It can't go away. I won't let it."

"Well, there's nothing else I can say other than, 'Good Luck,'" he said. "Unfortunately, I think you're going to need it."

9. After Burner

Hi Mike,

Should I begin this letter with 'Hi,' or would something like 'Dear' be more appropriate? 'Hi' isn't too informal, is it? Hopefully not. And if it is, tough luck. Deal with it. I'm beginning the letter with 'Hi' whether you like it or not.

Well, I do apologize for taking awhile to write you after my big move. But it's been a busy time! I have arrived in The Big Apple. New York City. I'm far away from home, and it feels far away from home.

But I love it here! I found a roommate, and we live in Brooklyn. She's a painter, and she's actually introduced me to some of her friends who are involved in the theatre scene. I joined a theatre group that a few of them are a part of, but that, unfortunately, is the only news I have to report on the acting front thus far. 'Sensible Alternatives,' the play that my friend from Indy was involved with, had funding fall through and has been put on the kibosh. Still, I'm hopeful that I'll find something to act in at some point.

There's a small Italian eatery a few blocks from me, and I was hired for a waitressing position a few weeks ago. It's SUCH a cute little restaurant. So far, I love it.

What else? Oh, the decision to bring my car with me was monumentally stupid. It took me an hour to find a parking spot for it when I arrived here. In my first week in NYC, I received two parking tickets. Needless to say, I've since sold the car.

Saving the best for last, I have a crazy story for you. I saw Emilio Estevez the other day! I was walking around applying for jobs, and all of a sudden I look to my left at a crosswalk and Emilio Estevez is standing right next to me. Definitely not something that happens in Indianapolis. Plus, I know Breakfast Club is one of your favorites, and I imagine you're just seething with jealousy now.

Hopefully, my next letter will be a bit more exciting.

Miss you,
Maddy

     I sat in Westfield Arcade and read Maddy's letter a second time, then a third time.

     Even as my own life became overwhelmed with eighteen-hour days preparing the arcade for its reopening, I still thought about Maddy every single day. Receiving her letter brought a smile to my face. Her personality, the personality that I loved so very much, shone through in her letter. And Emilio Estevez! Maddy, Willie, and I had all gone to see The Breakfast Club in the theater multiple times during its release, and now Maddy had randomly ran into the star of the movie on the street. I wanted her to be here, right beside me, to tell me the whole story.

     "What'cha reading?"

I looked up and saw Gonzo in his red Radio Shack vest, standing across from me at the front counter.

"Nothing," I said. I took the letter and put it in a drawer behind the front counter. We remained at the counter and watched MTV on the television across the room for awhile. The video for "Hysteria" by Def Leppard was on. It eventually came to an end, and a black-and-white image of a lone girl walking along a beach appeared onscreen. "Wind Beneath my Wings" by Bette Midler started playing through the television's speakers.

"Jesus, this song," Gonzo said. "I can't escape this song. I swear to God, I was listening to a classic rock station the other day, and they were playing this song."

"MTV plays it all the time, too," I said. "I've heard it so much I know all the lyrics by now."

"Can you sing it for me?"

"Not a chance."

He smiled and threw me a quarter for a Coke. I walked over to the soda machine and poured him a cup, then handed it to him. He took a sip from the straw as he looked out at the arcade floor.

"Still can't believe how different this place looks," Gonzo said.

After purchasing the arcade cabinets from Ed and extending the lease with the mall, I'd put Westfield Arcade through a transformation. Décor-wise, the place hadn't changed at all since it opened up in 1980, and it was in dire need of a makeover. The walls were trashed. The carpet was stained from hundreds of spilled soda cups and imitation butter from overturned popcorn buckets. In the locations where the most-popular games had once been, the carpet was threadbare and entirely worn away from the crowds of people that had stood on it over the years.

So I'd closed the arcade for a month and spent some time moving arcade cabinets around the arcade as I tore up and replaced the carpet. Another week was spent painting over the drab maroon walls with a lighter blue color. The arcade's dim, dark lighting was replaced with bright track lighting that hid nothing. I'd even ordered a brand-new television, replacing the wood-grain monstrosity from the early 80s with a state-of-the-art, 60-inch television with a slick metallic black finish, complete with a VHS player, then ordered two black leather lounge chairs and placed them in front of the television.

The aesthetic renovation to the arcade was only part of the work required. There were endless meetings to deal with--meetings with officers from the bank, meetings with officials from Westfield Mall, meetings with insurance agents. Paperwork, too--lease documents for the mall, insurance waivers, application forms.

It had been a madcap month full of eighteen-hour days spent preparing the arcade for its re-opening. I visited my grandpa over the noon hour every day and that was the only break I had from getting the arcade ready.

Gonzo's gaze drifted away from the arcade games and out towards the walkway in front of the arcade.

"Are you ever going to take that that 'Grand Re-Opening' banner down outside the arcade?" he asked. "That thing's been up for at least a month now. The grand re-opening has come and gone."

"But it gets peoples' attention. Hopefully, it interests them enough to check the place out, see what's changed."

"So you're just going to keep that up from now until forever? Fifty years from now, when people are showing up in flying cars like in The Jetsons, that Grand Re-opening banner will still be out there?"

"The moment someone comes into the arcade in a flying car, I'll take the banner down, how's that?"

"Works for me."

We continued watching MTV, and Gonzo looked out at the other people in the arcade. In total, there were two people in the arcade other than Gonzo and I, both posted up at the Cabal cabinet. Outside of those two, the arcade was empty.

"Dead night," Gonzo said.

"I'm aware," I said.

"Everyone must've missed the 'Grand Re-Opening' banner out front."

Gonzo chuckled, but I didn't feel like laughing. Grand Re-opening banner or no, the first month at the newly-reopened Westfield Arcade hadn't been very different from the final months of the previous Westfield Arcade. The visitors were sparse. The evenings were dead. The crowds were nonexistent.

I'd done everything in the first few weeks of the re-opening to generate hype and re-establish Westfield Arcade as *the* local hangout for teenagers and young adults. I'd taken out ads in the local newspaper every single day when the arcade was closed for renovation, counting down to the re-opening date. I'd posted flyers around the mall once it had re-opened. I'd even offered free plays on all games for the first hour of the day the arcade re-opened, and while that had drawn in a pretty significant crowd, that crowd hadn't stayed much longer than the hour of free gaming before leaving. Instead of a GRAND RE-OPENING, as the banner hung out front proclaimed, the months since the arcade had re-opened had been far from grand. The complete opposite of grand, to be honest.

"The arcade really does look good," Gonzo said, looking out at the new carpet, the freshly-painted walls, the gleaming television in the corner.

"Thanks," I said.

"Look at the bright side--if you lose your ass on the arcade, at least you could have a second career as an interior designer."

# # #

When my grandpa had first been admitted to the senior care center, one of the nurses had taken me aside to talk to me about Alzheimer's disease and give me a brief summary of what I could expect as the disease progressed. The most difficult thing about Alzheimer's, she told me, was that just when you accepted the effects of the disease and felt like you could handle it, the disease got worse.

She was right.

My grandpa's disease had started to progress at a noticeable rate. Before, flashes of the disease's progression would pop up every once in awhile during conversation. Now, the disease had taken over. Instead of flashes of the disease, there were only flashes of the person he'd been before it took hold. He was detached, constantly confused. Everything I said to him was always accompanied by a question in my head, a question of whether what I'd just said actually registered in his mind or if it was just a meaningless jumble of words.

Just as the nurse had said, his condition always seemed to worsen at the moment that I started to get accustomed to his current state. And the most difficult thing was that there was no miracle cure, no hope of him magically improving. His doctors and nurses were powerless to stop the progression of the disease.

"I want to watch the Cubs," he said one day I visited him. As usual, he lay in bed, propped up by a mountain of pillows behind his head. I sat in the recliner next to his bed and we watched a news broadcast on television.

"The Cubs aren't on, Grandpa," I said. "It's the off-season."

He watched the news for awhile in silence.

"The Cubs..." he said, offering no elaboration beyond that. This was something that had started to happen with more frequency also. He'd start a sentence and his words would trail off, leaving his thought unfinished.

We continued watching television. I looked over at my grandpa, lying in his bed, watching the television with distant, empty eyes behind his thick glasses. Flecks of gray stubble dotted his cheeks. Thick strands of uncombed silver hair hung over his deeply-lined forehead.

My grandpa yawned, and for a moment, I thought he was going to fall back asleep. It wasn't just his memory that had started to falter as the disease progressed. His energy had started to disappear, too. It seemed impossible for him to stay awake for two or three hours straight before drifting off to sleep.

"What are you having for dinner tonight?" I asked him.

"Dinner," he said. I couldn't tell if he'd said the word as a question ("Dinner?") or just a statement.

"Dinner," I said. "Do you know what you're having for dinner tonight?"

"Mashed potatoes," he said.

"That's your favorite, right?"

"Mashed potatoes," he repeated. "I like mashed potatoes but I don't like coleslaw."

"I don't like it either," I said.

On the television, the newscaster talked of a local zoning ordinance that was going to be put to a vote in a week.

"Remember when we went to opening day?" he asked me. "I let you skip school and we drove up to Chicago and went to the game."

"I do remember that," I said, surprised that he could recall the memory.

"You were supposed to be in school but I never told your teachers that I let you skip."

"That was a great time," I said.

166

We watched the television for a little while longer, and I eventually told my grandpa that I had to go.

"Where are you going?" he said.

"To work."

"Where do you work?"

"The video game arcade. Remember, Grandpa? I bought the video game arcade."

"What's that?"

"It's at the mall. People come and pay quarters to play video games."

"Are you home from college?"

"No, Grandpa. I work full-time now."

"How many hearts did you break this semester?"

"None, Grandpa."

He looked at me for a moment.

"Oh," he said.

I got up from my chair and walked over to him. I brushed a few strands of hair to the side of his forehead, then leaned down and gave him a kiss on his forehead.

"I'll see you tomorrow, Grandpa," I said before I left.

# # #

In the annals of pop culture, 1989 is one of those overlooked years, a year that isn't usually perceived as being as defining as the influential years in the mid-80s. Which is a shame, because, for pop culture, the final year of the 1980s was a year that was as groundbreaking as any other year of the era, a perfect end to an unforgettable decade.

In television, both Seinfeld and The Simpsons premiered in 1989, the latter proving to be nothing short of a nationwide sensation for its edgy humor and crude jokes. Saved by the Bell, the first non-cartoon Saturday morning tv show, premiered. The Cosby Show, Roseanne, and

Cheers were still going strong. Dynasty, Miami Vice, and Family Ties (three of the most defining shows of the entire decade) each ended their series within a two-week period in May.

In movie theaters, Batman blew everything away. The third Indiana Jones film was released. Lethal Weapon, Ghostbusters, and Back to the Future each had a sequel released. Iconic films that still hold up to this day came out every few weeks in theaters--Field of Dreams and Major League in April, When Harry Met Sally... in July, Uncle Buck in August, Look Who's Talking in October, Christmas Vacation in December.

But for me, 1989 had another distinction: 1989 was the year that the popularity of Nintendo positively exploded. The NES home console had been released a few years prior and had turned into a moderate success, more of a novelty than anything, an advanced system that a few fortunate kids owned. But in 1989, the machine turned into a sensation. Every kid had a Nintendo in his (or her) home. It didn't matter their age--college students, teenagers, even those in grade school. Spurred on by hits like Super Mario Bros. 3 and Legend of Zelda, the machine rose to levels of popularity that had never been seen before. The home video game market, which had all but disappeared in the mid-1980s, was back with a vengeance.

To compete with Nintendo, arcade games started getting more complex, gimmicky even. Arcade games began to become more about grabbing people's attention as they walked past and less about the sheer fun and challenge of the game itself. Driving games no longer had just a steering wheel--they now had a full cockpit that players sat in to mimic the effect of sitting down in a sportscar, complete with gear shifter, accelerator and brake pedals. Shooting games no longer consisted of a player piloting a ship on screen with a joystick. Now, they, too, had full cockpits for players to sit down in and first person views that made it seem as if you were flying them; many had seats that rumbled and moved along with the action onscreen. In the span of a few months, Sega released Laser Ghost, a shooting game with 3-light guns mounted to the cabinet that used angled glass to create a laser light on the screen; After Burner, which was a fighter jet game with a full fighter cockpit for a player to sit in that rumbled and shook based on the plane's movement in the game; and Hang-On, a motorcycle racing game that didn't have any traditional controls at all--instead, the game's "controller" was a life-size imitation motorbike mounted to the cabinet that the player sat in and leaned to the left or right to control the character onscreen.

And all of that was fun. It was different. But it also got away from the simple joy of playing a simple game with a joystick and a fire button and nothing more to rely on than your own instincts and reflexes. Throw in the fact that almost all new games were $.50 to play, and it became increasingly easier for me to see why people had shunned the arcade for the simplicity of the Nintendos connected to their home televisions. The games on Nintendo were nowhere near as elaborate as the newer arcade games, and the graphics on arcade games were light years more advanced than anything on Nintendo, but Nintendo games had a simple, easy-to-play-but-hard-to-master nature to them, the very characteristic that had made Pac Man, Donkey Kong, and countless other games from the golden age of arcade games so popular.

# # #

Mike,

How is 1990 treating you so far? It's going well for me. The 90s are here! Can you believe it?

169

Still no phone--and even if I had one, I couldn't afford the long distance calls. It is EXPENSIVE to live here. My waitressing job at the eatery covers rent and little more. And despite that, I love living here so dearly.

As for celebrity-spotting, I had two great ones this month. I saw...

The guy who plays Cameron in Ferris Bueller's Day Off walking in Central Park. Seriously, I saw him! I don't even know the name of that actor, but that doesn't matter. I saw one of the actors from my all-time favorite movie!

And...I waited on Dustin Hoffman! How cool, right? He's in town filming some movie, and he stopped by the eatery for lunch the other day. Even if he stiffed me on the tip, I can now tell people that I waited on Dustin Hoffman. I tried to wow him with my acting skills but there's no real dramatic way to deliver the line, "Here's your Caprese salad, sir."

On the acting front, I have some news. Nothing major, but any news is better than no news. I will be appearing in an off-Broadway production of a play named The Midnight Indiscretion. I play a nurse who helps deliver a baby in the middle of the play. I have a total of two lines. "Push! You can do this!" and "I've delivered hundreds of babies in my life, and this one here's the cutest I've ever seen." I've practiced saying both of those two lines roughly nine hundred million times.

I hope the arcade is doing well. If it isn't, I hope you're thinking about moving on and doing something else.

Miss you,
Maddy

\# \# \#

Maddy,

I have to apologize, first. Didn't realize that it has been over three months (!!!!) since I last wrote. So very sorry, but there is a reason I haven't written.

I've been busy. Really busy.

Everything, for me, is going wonderfully. After a rough start, business at Westfield Arcade has finally turned around. You should see it. Every night, it's just as packed as it used to be, back in the early 80s. I'm busy, but in a good way. It's nonstop, but I wouldn't want it any other way.

The arcade is just fantastic and doing gangbusters. The constant busy days remind me of why I kept the place open in the first place. It's---

    I stopped writing. I re-read everything I'd written. Seated at the counter, I looked out at the arcade floor. Friday night, 7 pm. Three people in the arcade. One teenager played Altered Beast as another looked over his shoulder with a bored expression on his face. A third teenager wandered around the arcade by himself--and had been wandering for awhile. He was either deciding which game he wanted to play or determining if there was anything of value in the arcade that he could steal.
    Truth was, the letter to Maddy was an absurd exaggeration. Doing gangbusters? Nothing could be further from the truth. The 80s had ended not with a bang but with a whimper for Westfield Arcade.

Of course, there were little teases from time to time, brief reminders of what the arcade once was, of what I hoped it could be again. A side-scroller game based on the Teenage Mutant Ninja Turtles line of toys had been released, and the game had been extremely popular for awhile. Four players could play the game at the same time, each one as a different character, and for weeks after the game's release, teenagers would show up and crowd around the cabinet every single night, mashing attack buttons with their index fingers and maneuvering their joysticks. A similar game based on The Simpsons television show was released a few months later, and it proved to be equally as popular. But the novelty of the games wore off quickly. The appeal in the games was no longer to get a high score; the appeal was in beating each stage of the game and ultimately defeating the game's final boss. Once that objective was achieved, there was little reason to continue playing the game.

A handful of moderately popular games with little replay value weren't going to save the arcade. I knew that. I'd tried other means of drawing people in. I'd attempted to host tournaments every Saturday, a different game every weekend. $5 entry fee, player with the overall high score takes all. I'd envisioned hundreds of players coming from all over the area, the best of the best, all descending on Westfield Arcade and pumping quarters into arcade cabinets for the entire day like old times. But the first weekend after I'd advertised a Space Invaders tournament in the local newspaper, a measly five people had showed up. The next weekend, not a single person showed up for a Donkey Kong tournament, and I abandoned the idea. Other promotions failed just as miserably.

And now, here it was, a new low: Lying to Maddy about how great the arcade was doing. Lying my ass off because I was too embarrassed to tell her the truth. We'd stayed in touch strictly by mail over the past year, and every few weeks, I'd receive a letter from her. I'd often read her letters four or five times upon their arrival, and I'd kept them all in a little drawer behind the front counter. When the day was especially slow, I sometimes spent an hour going back through her letters and reading them one by one. Some of the letters, I'd probably read close to one hundred times.

She'd reacted to my purchase of the arcade with excitement and encouragement at first. But as I continued complaining about the lack of business in each letter I wrote, she'd started to politely question whether keeping the arcade open was the right decision. Maybe I'd be happier, she told me, if I simply closed the place and found something else to do. As much as I wanted to have the arcade succeed and prove her wrong, it was getting more and more difficult to disagree with her point of view.

I took my letter to Maddy, wadded it up into a ball, and threw towards the garbage can. A hand reached over the counter and grabbed the wadded-up sheet of paper from mid-air as it soared towards the basket. I looked over and saw Gonzo's smiling face. He threw the wadded-up sheet of paper back at me.

Gonzo showed up around once every week, and he was the only one of the original crew who came in with any sort of regularity. Rufus, Bearclaw, all the other regulars-- none of them ever came to the arcade anymore. I knew Rufus had gone away to college, though I had no idea where. Gonzo had told me that Bearclaw followed his girlfriend to Cleveland when she'd gotten a job there, but I didn't know if that was the case or not. Willie had simply disappeared after he'd said his final goodbye--no-one had heard from him since he'd moved back to California. Other regulars from the arcade's early days had gone on to different things. Some lived in other cities. Some still lived in Indianapolis but were too focused on their careers to stop by the arcade.

"Anything exciting happen tonight?" Gonzo asked, looking out at the three other people in the arcade.

"What do you think?" I responded. It was all I needed to say.

"Up for kicking Shredder's ass in a game of Teenage Mutant Ninja Turtles?" he asked.

"Don't really feel like it," I said.

"Come on. I'll even let you be Donatello."

"No thanks. You're on your own tonight."

I watched as Gonzo walked across the arcade's floor and deposited fifty cents in the Teenage Mutant Ninja Turtles cabinet. I remained at the front counter, watching the entrance to the arcade, on the lookout for any customers. But there was no-one. The three people from earlier had left, leaving Gonzo and I as the only two people in the arcade.

With nothing to do, I walked over to the Teenage Mutant Ninja Turtles cabinet and watched Gonzo play for awhile. His turtle walked upright around a burning building, jumping around the screen and attacking hordes of foot soldiers. Gonzo was so zoned into the game that he didn't realize I was standing behind him.

I glanced over at the game next to Teenage Mutant Ninja Turtles. Final Fight, read the marquee. The demo screen was playing, and I watched as two computer-controlled characters progressed through the game. The characters took out a group of three enemies, who flickered then disappeared away. The game scrolled sideways. They took out three more enemies. The game continued scrolling sideways. Another wave of enemies. Then another. I blankly stared at the vast endlessness of the demo screen for a long time, transfixed by the sight for reasons I couldn't even explain.

I eventually tore my eyes away from the screen and looked out into the food court outside the arcade. I saw four teenagers sitting at a table, wearing stonewashed jeans and brightly-colored Pacific Coast Highway t-shirts. Each teenager had a small, rectangular gaming device named a Gameboy in their hand, holding the devices in close to their faces to make it easier to see the device's monochrome screen.

Not content with ruling the home video game market, Nintendo had recently released their portable Gameboy device. It was the first handheld gaming device with interchangeable cartridges, and it proved to be just as popular as their home video game console; it flew off the shelves. Everywhere you looked, kids and teenagers had their faces buried in front of Gameboys.

I silently watched the four teenagers in the food court for awhile as they each concentrated on the screens of their respective devices and mashed their thumbs down on the device's directional pad. They talked with one another as they played. One of the kids pumped his fist in celebration, then continued playing. After awhile, they each got up from the table and walked back towards the mall's main walkway. None of the teenagers so much as glanced in the direction of Westfield Arcade.

I turned back towards the arcade and looked around me. Gonzo and I were still the only two people in the arcade. Friday night, almost 8 pm. The arcade used to be a madhouse. Now, it was a ghost town. I silently stared out at the arcade for a very long time, at all of the games, each one running demo screens with computer-controlled characters attacking enemies and speeding around in cars and fighting aliens in an endless loop.

"I'm lost, Gonzo," I finally said. I ran my hand through my hair, closed my eyes, and let out a long, dejected sigh. "I am totally fucking lost."

"What's wrong?" he said. He looked away from his game and turned towards me. There was genuine concern in her eyes.

"What isn't wrong? Look around. It's Friday night and the arcade is dead. It's always dead. I'm losing my ass on this. The money is disappearing."

"Is it that bad?" he asked.

"Hell yes, it's that bad. It's not good when you have bill after bill to pay and no money coming in to pay those bills. It's not good at all."

My financial situation was, to put it mildly, turning into a mess. The money I'd inherited wasn't much, but it was something. I was still keeping my head above water. Barely. But month by month, as I continued to buy the latest games and continued to receive bills in the mail, that money was disappearing.

"You know how people say you can have whatever you want if you just work hard?" I said, frustrated. "Well, all I want is for Westfield Arcade to be as successful as it once was. That's all I want. And I'm out here working my ass off, every single day of every single week…and it's not helping out at all. I'm doing everything I can, and it's just not enough."

"I'm sorry, man," Gonzo said. "I really don't know what else to say."

I didn't either. There was really nothing else to say. I knew that I'd just sound like a bitter fool if I kept complaining. But I didn't care.

"What kills me is that I was so sure about this place," I continued. "Ed told me it was a bad idea to keep it open. But I was so sure of this place. I believed, man. I believed so strongly in this place. And the stupid thing is, I *still* believe in this place. For whatever reason, I still believe it can be great again. I'm sure of it."

I shook my head disgustedly.

"Maybe I'm just blind," I said. "Maybe I'm just a delusional idiot. I don't know. I'm…"

The word trailed off.

"I'm just lost," I continued. I could think of no better description to use. Lost. To be so sure that the arcade's fortunes would turn around, to have that undying belief that the place would return to glory, and then to be so astronomically wrong was a frustration unlike any I'd ever experienced.

Again, I sighed, ran my hand through my hair. I looked over at Gonzo and saw him staring back at me.

"I don't know much, but I know one thing: You're not lost, man," Gonzo said. "You're the farthest thing from being lost. You've got something you're passionate about, something you believe in. Some people spend their entire lives trying to find something that they believe so strongly in, and most people never even find anything at all. But you've found yours. So you're not lost. Not by a long shot."

I let his words soak in.

"Maybe not," I said. "But I still feel like it."

I looked back around at the deadened arcade. I shook my head disgustedly as I looked at the pitiful selection of newer games up front. A.B. Cop. Bonzana Brothers. Dragon Saber. Even the quality games like Final Fight and Smash TV had proved to be little more than novelties.

"You know what I need?" I finally said to Gonzo. "A single game. That's it. Just a single, awesome, amazing game that is unlike anything else that's ever been released before. Something revolutionary. Something innovative. I need a game like Pac Man. Space Invaders. Donkey Kong. I need something that's just head and shoulders above any game that's been released before, something that is just so far beyond anything that Nintendo has. This place can be great again. I know it. I just need one special game to bring the crowds back and show everyone how amazing of a place the arcade can be."

I looked back out at the dead arcade, at the rows of games with their demo screens running and their sound effects blaring from the speakers and not a single person around to play them.

"Just one game," I said to Gonzo. "A single revolutionary game. That's all I need for everything to change."

In March of 1991, that game arrived.

January 5, 1997

       As he sits in the deadened arcade, Mike Mayberry looks out at the floor of Westfield Arcade. The afternoon has brought a number of individuals showing up to pick up arcade cabinets they've purchased, and the arcade is starting to clear out. Half an hour ago, a collector of arcade games showed up and hauled away ten cabinets on a flatbed truck, and now, for the first time all day, the arcade truly looks like a business that is about to close. Empty spaces are everywhere. Like a toothless grin, open gaps where games once were litter the arcade floor.

       He looks at his watch. Just after five o'clock. This is it, he thinks to himself. This is really it. Westfield Arcade, his beloved home for almost two decades, the only job he's ever known, is only a few hours from being gone for good.

       He walks out from behind the front counter and paces up and down the main aisle, past the games that remain. He's nervous. It's still difficult for him to wrap his mind around the fact that Westfield Arcade will be gone forever. The moment that he closes the arcade for a final time--what will that be like? He knows there's no turning back now, but he still feels overwhelmed when he imagines just how emotional it will be when he turns the lights out at Westfield Arcade for the final time.

But he's even more nervous about what will happen in the hours after he closes the place. The thought of the flight tonight fills his stomach with butterflies. Not the flight itself, but more the thought of what will happen once the flight lands. It's a moment he's thought about a lot over the past few weeks; the decision weighed on him heavily. He's prepared for it, analyzed whether it's the right thing to do, taken every precaution. Finally, that moment is almost here. And thinking about it is turning him into a nervous wreck.

Mike walks to the back of the arcade and comes to a stop at the Missile Command cabinet. An escape--that's what he needs. As he has countless times in the past, he needs to start up a game and have the world around him simply disappear as he concentrates on playing.

He deposits a quarter into the Missile Command cabinet and the game begins. He starts working his hand over the game's trackball controller, moving the cursor around to defend the six cities at the bottom of the screen against the onslaught of enemy missiles raining down.

He makes it to the eleventh stage before losing his first city, a great beginning to the game. He goes apeshit on the trackball as the speed and frequency of enemy missiles increases. He starts to feel a dull pain in the palm of his hand.

"Excuse me, do you work here?"

Mike abandons his game of Missile Command and turns around. In front of him is a guy, mid-thirties, Mike guesses, with close-cropped black hair and a goatee. The goatee is flecked with gray and, instead of looking fashionable, it makes the guy look a few years older than he would without it.

"Yeah, I do. Mike."

Mike extends his hand and the guy shakes it.

"Dan Franklin," he says, shedding himself of the large Columbia winter coat he wears, revealing scrawny arms underneath a plain white t-shirt. "We talked about your Street Fighter 2 cabinet."

"Right, right," Mike says. He smiles. "So you're the lucky dog who's soon to be the proud owner of the most classic fighting game of all time."

"Yep. As long as the machine's in good condition, that is."

"The cabinet's pristine," Mike says. "Here, follow me."

They walk over to the cabinet in the middle of the arcade. Dan looks the game over, examining the finer details of the cabinet.

"Great condition," he says.

He inspects the painting on the side of the cabinet.

"<u>Great</u> condition. Is this the original paint job on the side?"

"Yep. Hasn't been refurbished."

"It isn't scuffed or marked at all."

"This game is my baby," Mike says. "I've kept good care of her."

"Everything's in working order? Quarter slot? Joysticks?"

"Yep. Everything's fine. The game plays even better than it looks. Real responsive controls."

Mike steps up to the cabinet and inserts two quarters, one for each of them, then motions for Dan to join him. They select their characters--Mike goes with Blanka, Dan with Ryu--and play a game against one another. It goes on for a few minutes, and finally ends when Blanka delivers a strong-punch, forward-kick, roundhouse-kick combo attack that knocks Ryu out for good.

Despite the loss, a smile crosses Dan's face.

"God, I forgot how fantastic this game is," he says. "I can't wait to get this set up."

"Congrats," Mike says, walking over to grab the metal dolly. "This game is one of the great ones. A true classic."

It is a cash transaction. Dan returns with two friends and they load the machine onto the dolly, then wheel it out of the arcade. Mike watches through the window as the Street Fighter 2 cabinet is wheeled across the food court.

After they have disappeared, he looks back at his watch. It is six o'clock on the dot. Only three more hours before Westfield Arcade is closed forever.

10. Street Fighter 2

I turned thirty.

Big, scary number, thirty is. Thirty is the big leagues. Shit gets real when you turn thirty. It's one of those birthdays that matter, a milestone birthday that ushers in a new era of one's life.

For me, thirty resonated far more than any birthday I'd experienced up to that point. And not in a good way. Instead of bidding adieu to the uncertainty and disorganization of my twenties, I felt even more uncertain and disorganized when I turned thirty. Nothing in my life was working out. I didn't even want to celebrate my birthday, largely because there was nothing to celebrate.

I visited my grandpa on my birthday and watched television with him, as we did almost every single day. Twice, I mentioned to him that it was my birthday. The first time, he blankly looked at me and said nothing. The second time, he didn't even acknowledge my comment and remained staring straight ahead at the television.

I spent the day working at Westfield Arcade, and stayed late after I closed down the arcade. I pumped quarter after quarter into various games, alone in the arcade. It had been another dead day at the arcade. I couldn't even remember the last time the arcade had had a good day.

# # #

I was emptying quarters from the various cabinets one night when the phone in the arcade rang. I set the bucket of quarters onto the ground and walked over to the phone behind the front counter.

"Westfield Arcade," I answered.

"Mike, this is--"

"Maddy!" I interrupted. "I can't believe it."

"Believe it. I finally have a phone!"

Instantly, a smile broke out on my face.

"It's so great to hear your voice," I said.

"You, too," she said. "I just got the phone, and I figured I'd call to wish you a happy belated birthday. So, happy belated birthday, Old Man!"

"Thanks."

"Thirty, huh? How's it feel?"

"I'm still standing."

"Did you receive a walker as a present?"

"That, and a pair of orthopedic shoes. I figure I'll move in with my grandpa at the retirement community next week."

She laughed.

"You're the very first person I called on the phone, you know," she said. "It was literally hooked up twenty minutes ago."

"Wow, I feel so special," I said. I said the phrase in a half-joking tone, but it really did feel nice to know that I was the very first person she'd called.

"Good day at the arcade?" she asked.

"Yeah, it was ok," I said, though the truth was that it had been yet another lackluster day.

"What's going on with you?" I said, changing the subject. "Between us, you're the one who leads the exciting life. Hobnobbing with celebrities out in New York, working at a fancy restaurant, acting in plays."

"Please," she said. "I only wish my life were that glamorous."

Both of us laughed into the phone. It was so great to talk with her.

"I do have some pretty good news, though," she said. "One of the waitresses who works nights at my restaurant quit the other day, and my manager is giving me all of her shifts. So I'll be working nights now, and that's where the real money is. I'll be making double, easily, of what I make working days. For a change, I'm going to be able to look at my bank account and not burst into tears."

"That's so great," I said.

We continued talking. She told me about some smaller parts in a few off-Broadway plays that she'd had over the past few months. She asked about my grandpa, and I talked with her for awhile about the progression of his Alzheimer's.

"I have to get going," she eventually said. "Long-distance calls are not cheap, and even with evening shifts at the restaurant, I've gotta save as much money as I can."

"I understand," I said. "It was so great talking with you."

"You, too," she said.

There was a brief moment of silence.

"I miss you," she finally said.

She ended every letter she wrote with the same "Miss you, Maddy" phrase, but hearing her speak the words was so much more impactful. The words resonated with me, and I found myself unable to talk for a moment.

"I miss you, too," I said.

"I really mean it," Maddy said. "I miss you a ton."

Neither of us said anything for a few moments, then we said our final goodbyes and I hung up the phone. I stood there behind the counter in the arcade, looking at the phone, the smile never once faltering on my face.

It was the first time I'd smiled in awhile. It felt great.

# # #

"Is that new game any good?" Gonzo asked me one night, looking at the cabinet I'd just moved to the front of the arcade earlier in the day. I still continued buying as many of the latest games as I could, hoping, praying, that I'd stumble upon a game that would explode in popularity and magically rescue the arcade. But I wasn't sure how long that could go on. My financial situation was getting worse and worse with each passing month.

"I haven't played it yet," I said to Gonzo. "But it's supposed to a good one."

"You say that about every game that arrives. Every time a new game arrives, you talk about it like it's going to be the greatest thing this arcade has ever seen. You said it about Spy Hunter 2. You said it about Captain Silver. Just once, I want to hear you say, 'Hey, we just got a new game in, and lemme tell you, it is the shittiest game I have ever played in my life.'"

"I'm being serious about this one," I said. "It really is supposed to be a good one. It's huge in Japan."

"Huge in Japan. I think every arcade game is huge in Japan."

I grabbed four quarters from the cash register, then stepped out from behind the counter.

"Let's give it a shot," I said.

Gonzo and I walked over to the cabinet. It was a Wednesday night, almost closing time, and two other people were in the arcade, in the back alternating turns on Galaxian.

When we reached the cabinet, I looked it over. Street Fighter 2, the marquee read, yellow letters over a gray background. We watched the demo screen for a brief

moment--a muscled character in a white karate outfit was
battling against a massive, facepainted sumo wrester--and
then deposited the four quarters into the coin slot. I hit the
two-player button.

A Choose Your Character screen appeared with
eight different characters to pick from. Gonzo and I each
moved our character selection window around the screen--
past Guile, Chun-Li, Zangief, others who would become
household names to every video game player on the planet
over the next year. Gonzo selected Ryu, a character with
long blonde hair who wore a red karate outfit. I selected
Dhalism, an Indian character with a shaved head.

The game began. Gonzo's character stood on the
far left side of the screen, mine on the far right side. There
were no spaceships, no cars, no jets or aliens. Just two
characters, pitted one-on-one against each other. The
object of Street Fighter 2 became clear very quickly: beat
the living shit out of your opponent before he beat the
living shit out of you.

Feverishly, Gonzo and I tapped the six attack
buttons on the control panel, delivering combinations of
kicks and punches. Our characters jumped around the
screen as we tried to time our attacks perfectly. I delivered
a four-punch combo, topping it off with an uppercut that
sent his character flying across the screen. Gonzo
countered with a series of sweeping leg kicks.

We went berserk on the attack buttons, relentlessly
tapping them. At one point, Gonzo's character yelled an
indiscernible word and actually threw a fireball across the
screen at my character.

"How the hell did you do that?!?" I yelled at him
over the game's sound effects as my character did a
spinning backflip to avoid his attack.

"I have no idea!" he said. He sounded like he was
short of breath.

The game was a best two out of three format, and when my character finally finished his off in the third fight with a roundhouse kick, both of us looked at each other. Gonzo's face was flushed red and his chest expanded and contracted with deep breaths. My own deep breathing racked my body.

A smile broke out on Gonzo's face. He reached into his pocket and pulled out a ten dollar bill.

"Quarters," he said, handing me the bill. "Go get them. A bunch of them."

I practically sprinted over to the change machine. I couldn't stop thinking about what I'd just experienced. The intensity of the game was absolutely incredible. The sound effects were amazing. The graphics, without question, were the best I'd seen. Everything about the game was so far beyond any game I'd ever played.

I added a ten-dollar bill of my own to Gonzo's, and walked back to him with twenty dollars worth of quarters weighing down my pockets. We each dropped four quarters down the slot and played another game, Gonzo as Guile, me as Zangief. When that frenzied game ended, we played another. And another. And we kept playing and playing and playing.

We stayed in the arcade into the late night, until almost two in the morning, and did nothing but pump quarter after quarter into the Street Fighter 2 cabinet and talk shit to one another as our characters fought onscreen. We played as every single character, observing the differences in their fighting styles. Eventually, we both determined who our favorites were--mine was Blanka, Gonzo's was E. Honda--and we fought each other in a series of matches with those characters.

When we finally decided to call it quits, I turned off the main power switch in the rear of the arcade and we exited the arcade. Both of my hands throbbed in pain--my left one from ramming the joystick in various directions, my right hand from relentlessly tapping the attack buttons. Gonzo and I had each dropped over thirty dollars worth of quarters into the game.

I pulled down the metal security gate and looked back in at the blank screen of the deadened Street Fighter 2 cabinet in the front of the arcade.

"This is it," I said to Gonzo. "This is the game that going to save the arcade."

# # #

I ran an ad featuring Street Fighter 2 in the local newspaper a few days later. The ad proclaimed that the new game was "unlike anything you've ever played," but that wasn't hyperbole--it was the honest-to-God truth. I'd continued playing the game with Gonzo late at night for the past few nights, and I'd fallen in love with the nonstop, unpredictable nature of the game even more. We'd even started to uncover button combinations to perform a few of the special moves that each character had.

The evening after the ad ran started out slowly, no different from every evening over the past few years. Around seven o'clock, two teenagers I'd never seen before entered the arcade. One wore a half-zip pullover Starter jacket with PACERS stitched on the front pouch and the NBA team's logo displayed on the back. The other had on a pair of oversized denim overalls with one strap left undone.

There was not a single other person in the arcade when they walked in. The two kids spotted the Street Fighter 2 cabinet at the front of the arcade and walked over to it. I sat behind the front counter and watched them. The one in the Starter jacket zipped open the front pouch and pulled four quarters from inside. He inserted the quarters into the coin slot.

189

I continued watching from the front counter as they selected their characters and started playing the game. They got into the game, mashing the various kick and punch buttons and maneuvering their character around the screen with the joystick. Wide smiles crossed both of their faces as they intently stared at the screen and fought each other onscreen. When their final round ended, the kid in the overalls gave a triumphant "Yes!" and pumped his fist. His friend in the Starter jacket pounded the cab in frustration with an open palm, then immediately walked over to the change machine and inserted a five-dollar bill.

For the entire rest of the evening, they fed quarter after quarter into the cabinet, each of them making two separate trips to the change machine to get change for five-dollar bills. They talked trash to one another and gloated after every victory. They debated which of the eight characters were their favorites. The unadulterated joy of playing beamed on both of their faces for the entire night, right up until I had to kick them out at closing time.

The next night, the same two teenagers showed up with two others with them. They went straight for the Street Fighter 2 cabinet and all crowded around. The two kids from the previous night played the first game, then two others played after them, then the winners of both matches played head-to-head. For the entire night, the group posted up at the Street Fighter 2 cabinet, sucking down Cokes and playing the game.

The weekend came, and an even bigger crowd, around ten people in total, showed up and played the game for the almost the entire day. At one point, one of the members disappeared out into the mall for a moment and returned with three large pizzas from the pizza shop in the food court. He placed the pizzas on a small table next to the Street Fighter 2 cabinet and the teens continued to play as they ate slices of pizza. A few members of the crowd wandered around the arcade and started playing other games as they waited their turn at Street Fighter 2.

From there, the game took off. There was nothing, absolutely nothing, that even came close to Street Fighter 2 on Nintendo. Every weekday at four o'clock, right after local schools had let out, group after group of teenagers would show up to play Street Fighter 2. I bought a second cabinet, then a third one, and from four o'clock to close during the week, there wasn't a moment that any of the Street Fighter 2 machines were open. On the weekends, there would be groups of people standing outside of Westfield Arcade before I even opened the arcade, anxious to be first in line to get their Street Fighter 2 addiction satisfied.

I kept waiting for the novelty of the game to wear off and it never did. Instead, the popularity grew and grew. Street Fighter 2 was the embodiment of competition in its most primal form: You versus your opponent in a battle to the death. One winner. One loser. In games of the past, achieving a high score or defeating groups of computer-controlled enemies was always the primary objective when playing, but with Street Fighter 2, there was no need to keep track of a high score, or even pay attention to the game's scoring system at all. Beating the snot out of your opponent and emerging victorious was the only thing that mattered, and the true beauty of Street Fighter 2 was how the head-to-head format of the game brought out the competitive nature of all who played--getting killed by a computer-controlled player or failing to get a high score in a game was certainly frustrating, but it was a completely different level of frustration to lose a head-to-head battle to a close friend standing next to you (a friend who, more often than not, was more than willing to gloat about his victory to your face).

The format of Street Fighter 2 lent itself perfectly to a tournament set-up, and I started putting together tournaments on the weekends. That first weekend, I'd set up a sixteen-player tournament and over forty people showed up to the arcade to participate in it. From there on out, I set up sixty-four person, single-elimination tournaments every single weekend, and as word got around, I still had to turn away people from participating.

The game absolutely raked in money, and since there were eight separate characters in the game to play, each of whom had different fighting styles and special moves to learn, the replay value of Street Fighter 2 was off the charts. Good players had a single character that they'd mastered and played game after game, but the true champs of the game were the ones who were adept at playing every character and had memorized every single special move for each one of those characters.

The crowds had once again returned and it was glorious to see. After being gone for the past few years, Westfield Arcade was finally back.

11. Mortal Kombat

Dear Mike,

So this is going to be a departure from my typical letter. Because, shock of all shocks, I actually have some good news to report. And not good news in the sense that I got another promotion at my job, or good news that I saw a celebrity. I'm talking about good news on the acting front.

Yes, my acting "career," the reason I moved to New York in the first place, finally had something good occur.

I met this director of a play. Real up and coming guy. He's been the assistant director for a number of plays in the past, and in a few months, he's going to begin casting for an off-Broadway play he wrote. And he told me he wants me to play the lead character. The lead!

Long story short, I could have big news in a few months. Right now, he's trying to secure funding for the play, and once he gets that, casting will begin. He tells me that I'm perfect for the part. I feel like I shouldn't even be talking about this, like I'm going to jinx myself if I actually dare to believe that something good might happen for me. Like I'm getting my hopes up only to have them crushed once again in a few months. But whatever. If it doesn't work out, it doesn't work out.

Sorry for not calling, but those long distance calls are expensive. Gotta save up as much money as I can.

Miss you,
Maddy

# # #

If Street Fighter 2 led the renaissance of the arcade, then Mortal Kombat was right behind it in line. It was a one-on-one fighting game just like Street Fighter 2, and Mortal Kombat had even more special moves and secret characters than Street Fighter 2. But what made Mortal Kombat stand out was the violence of the game. Every time you punched or kicked an opponent, streams of blood would shoot from their face and pool on the ground. That in itself was neat enough, but Mortal Kombat also had fatalities, special moves that could be performed on a defeated opponent to end a fight with an excessively gory final attack. Separating an opponent's head from their shoulders with a vicious uppercut, for instance, or ripping an opponent's heart from their chest and holding it in the air like trophy.

The fatalities were so overly violent that they stirred up controversy amongst various parenting groups and even led to Senate hearings on video game violence. But no-one in Westfield Arcade was appalled by the game's gore. We thought it was...
"Awesome!"

I stood behind the front counter of the arcade, watching the crowd of fifteen people at the Mortal Kombat cabinet go crazy with excitement after witnessing Sub-Zero perform his fatality onscreen, in which he uppercutted his opponent and, in a geyser of blood, ripped their head from the rest of their body, spinal cord still dangling from the neck.

"So bad ass!" I heard one observer yell.

The kid who had won the game wore a Pacers Starter jacket, and he turned to the crowd and accepted a few high fives. He was the same kid who'd come into the arcade with his friend and played Street Fighter 2 right after the arcade had received the game. Timmy was his name, and he was a freshman at one of the local high schools. He reminded me a little of Willie, brashly confident and always running his mouth. He'd become a mainstay at Westfield Arcade, and no-one could compete with him at Street Fighter 2 or Mortal Kombat. I'd even taken him on a few times and gotten my ass kicked.

"Winner stays, loser pays," Timmy said, turning back towards the game. The next challenger stepped up to the game and deposited fifty cents, and another game began.

It was a Saturday night, and the arcade was rocking. MTV's weekly Top 20 video countdown played on the television with "To Be With You" by Mr. Big currently showing. A group huddled around the television and watched the video. At the front of the arcade were the three Mortal Kombat and three Street Fighter 2 cabinets, and a mob of people stood around each one of the six cabinets. In the row directly behind the fighting games, there was a line five-deep to play Virtua Racing, the first racing game to offer truly realistic 3d polygon graphics as well as a choice of four different viewpoints players could choose from while racing. It was also the first game to cost a full dollar to play, but the game was so much better than any racing game that had been previously released that people were willing to pay a dollar to play it.

To the left of Virtua Racing was the X-Men cabinet, a game based on the popular comic book. X-men had two twenty-five inch monitors displayed side-by-side in the cabinet, making the cabinet twice as wide as most other games. The sheer size of the cabinet allowed a whopping six players to play at the same time, each as a different character from the comic book. At the moment, there was a crowd around the game. I walked over and watched the game for awhile--it was always a sight to behold when six top-notch players were playing the game at the same time and the game's screen was a chaotic scene of their characters attacking waves upon waves of enemies. Beside the X-Men cabinet was the Terminator 2 cabinet, with two plastic replica machine guns mounted to the control panel. As I watched the chaos playing out on the X-Men monitors, I saw a lone teenager walk up to the Terminator 2 cabinet, put four quarters into the quarter slot, then grab a hold of a machine gun in each hand and start blasting away at terminators onscreen.

All in all, at least eighty people were in the arcade, either playing games or waiting for their turn in line. The crowd was varied. Many were teenagers. Some were in college. But the mania of Street Fighter 2 and Mortal Kombat had infected much older folks as well, and there were a few people in their thirties and even forties in the crowd.

There was another commotion at one of the Mortal Kombat cabinets as another fatality was performed. I looked over and saw Timmy turn away from the cabinet and face the crowd, both arms extended in the air.

"This game is fucking up my childhood," he said, "and I love every second of it!"

The group around the cabinet started laughing, and Timmy turned towards the kid he'd just beat in the game.

"Go home and be a family man," he said, repeating a popular character's saying from Street Fighter 2. The phrase had become a tagline that many boastfully repeated after defeating an opponent in a fighting game.

The madcap day finally ended a few hours later and everyone left. I walked around the vacant arcade and emptied out each one of the cabinets. It had been a killer day. Virtua Racing, at a dollar a game, had brought in over one hundred dollars by itself. Each one of the Mortal Kombat and Street Fighter 2 cabinets had bested that figure handily. Even the X-Men game, with six people playing at the same time for a majority of the day, had approached one hundred dollars for the day.

I walked over to the front counter and logged the details of the revenue generated for the day, then noticed a stack of mail on the edge of the front counter. I'd been so busy during the day that I hadn't opened it when it arrived. I grabbed the stack of mail and thumbed through it. A couple of flyers from various distributors I worked with, advertising their deals on new games. A piece of junk mail from a Chinese restaurant a few blocks away, and another from a pizza place a few blocks away. The last letter in the stack was from Maddy.

I perked up when I saw the letter from Maddy. Despite the fact that she now had a phone, we'd strictly kept in touch my mail over the past few months. Even though most letters from her covered the same ground--an overview of whatever small acting part she'd recently been in, a recap of any celebrity sightings that had occurred since we last spoke, a general update on her waitressing job--it was always the highlight of my day whenever I received a letter from her.

I eagerly tore into her letter and started reading.

Mike,

Turns out that I didn't jinx myself after all--in a few weeks, on the 28th to be precise, I will be starring in a play named Rat Race. This is the play I told you about a few months ago, and I will be the lead in the play. It's official. The lead!

To say I'm excited is an understatement. In fact, I think it is humanly impossible to be as thrilled as I am right now.

I included the poster advertising the play. Under the list of cast and production crew, you might notice that the poster says 'Starring Maddy Fredrickson.' In case you forgot, that's me! My name!

I must go, but I hope the arcade is still doing wonderfully.

Wish me luck.

Miss you,
Maddy

Folded up with the letter was a small poster advertising the play. It was an all-black poster with light green writing and a caricature of a small rat on the left side. The name of the play--Rat Race--was scrawled across the top of the poster. Directly under that was a single line that said 'Written and Directed by Liam Worthington.' On the left side of poster was a CAST subheading, and Maddy's name was the first one listed.

I looked at Maddy's name for awhile, listed in front of all the other names. I set the poster down and read her letter again. Her enthusiasm jumped off the page. I thought about her, how excited she be, how she was surely walking around with her wonderful smile plastered on her face at all hours of the day. I wanted to see that smile. I wanted to hear her laugh. I simply wanted to be there for her, with her.

The arcade had been doing such great business that, for the first time in a long time, I actually had some extra money in my bank account. Without even contemplating the decision or giving myself the chance to second-guess it, I looked up the number to the Indianapolis Airport in the Yellow Pages and dialed it. After being transferred around a few times, I booked a flight leaving for New York City on the morning of the 28th, the day of her big play.

# # #

I still visited my grandpa every single day, and his room seemed to look more and more depressing every time I visited. The size of the place seemed to get just a fraction smaller, the lighting in the room just a little dimmer, the paint on the walls just a little more bland.

My grandpa's condition, too, continued to worsen with every visit. The differences in the room's dimensions and lighting was in my head, I knew, but no matter how hard I wanted to believe, the progression of his disease wasn't a figment of my imagination. The deterioration of his mental state was real and serious and on full display every time I visited.

"Grandpa?" I said on the morning after I'd booked my trip to New York, standing in the doorway of his room. He sat in his recliner in the middle of his sparse room, a couple feet away from the television, staring directly into it. A morning news broadcast was playing, the anchor delivering a story about the Mall of America, a shopping mall scheduled to open next month in Minnesota. The mall, according to the news broadcaster, was set to be the largest shopping mall in the world.

Upon hearing my voice, my grandpa slowly rotated his head towards me.

"Come in," he said.

He turned back towards the television and continued watching it. I walked into his room and sat down on the side of his bed.

"What are you watching?" I asked him. I asked him this exact question upon my arrival every single day, and this simple question was usually a good indicator of how our forthcoming interaction would progress. Often times, he'd be able to answer the question correctly, maybe even hold a brief discussion about whatever show he was watching. Other days, he looked at me as if he didn't understand the question. Still other days, he didn't even acknowledge the question and remained staring blankly ahead at his television.

On this, day, he didn't look away from the television.

"Grandpa, what are you watching?" I repeated, my voice a little louder.

He turned his head and looked at me, no expression whatsoever displayed on his face. After looking at me for a second, he returned his attention to the television.

"The Cubs," he said.

"You're watching the Cubs?"

"Yes."

"It doesn't look like the Cubs."

"I want to watch them."

"They're not on in the mornings."

"When are they on?"

"Later," I said. "This afternoon."

"They're in last place."

I watched the television with him for awhile. The story about the Mall of America ended, and the news anchor gave away to her male co-anchor for a story about Home Alone 2, an upcoming sequel to the popular movie from a few years ago.

"I'm going to be going on a trip soon," I said to him.

No response from my grandpa.

"I'm going to be going on a trip soon," I repeated.

"Where?" he asked, not looking up from the television.

"New York City," I said.

"Where's that?"

"It's a big city. Out east."

"Are you taking IndyGo?" IndyGo was Indianapolis's public transport service.

"No. IndyGo doesn't go to New York."

"Are you driving there?"

"No. I'm flying there."

He didn't say anything or register any sort of response. He simply focused on the news broadcast, which had now cut away to a commercial break.

"When I'm gone, I won't be able to come visit you," I said. "Is that ok?"

He turned his head towards me.

"Where are you going?"

"I'm going to visit a friend in New York."

"Why?"

"I'm visiting a friend," I repeated. My grandpa simply looked at me for a few moments and then turned back towards the television.

"Okay," he said. I wasn't even sure what this statement was in response to.

We continued watching television and I asked my grandpa a few questions as we watched, but he didn't respond to any of those questions. Lately, carrying on a conversation with my grandpa that lasted for longer than ten seconds was next to impossible. As difficult as it was to deal with the progression of his disease, the most difficult part was that I knew that it would only get worse.

Two weeks later. 7 pm. I walked up a set of cement stairs and reached the entrance to the theatre. All around me were the sounds of the city--drivers honking their horns impatiently, assorted chatter from pedestrians, random sounds that seemed to come from nowhere and everywhere all at once. Taped to the entrance door at the top of the stairs were posters for three separate plays showing at the theatre. One of the posters was the exact same poster that Maddy had sent to me. Rat Race, read the title at the top. I checked the cast list again, spotting Maddy's name instantly.

I opened the door and walked through the entrance, relishing the quiet and solitude of the theatre after a madcap day in New York. My flight had arrived at noon, and since Maddy had no idea I was visiting, I had the entire afternoon to myself. I'd spent it wandering around the city, getting lost every few minutes. I'd almost been run over by at least five separate taxi cabs. I'd been approached by roughly one thousand panhandlers on the street asking for money.

But I'd survived. And now, here I was. Maddy's big premiere. All day long, as I ambled around the city, my heart had raced in anticipation of seeing her for the first time since our final night together in the arcade. I'd bought a cute small bouquet of flowers--carnations, daisies and a few other flowers, neatly arranged in a small vase--and I held the vase in my hand, ready to present it to her after the show.

The entrance hall of the theatre was a small room. A row of five oak-colored ticket windows aligned the far eastern wall. Only one of the windows had someone behind it; the rest were shuttered. I walked over to a line in front of the one open window. As the line slowly moved forward, I thought about Maddy. My body practically vibrated from excitement. I wondered how she'd changed.

She sounded the same in her letters, but would she still be the same person I remembered?

My turn in line came and I walked over to the window and bought a ticket. After paying for it, I walked over to a bank of payphones in the corner of the entrance hall. I inserted eight quarters and dialed 1-800-COLLECT. After answering a few questions, I gave the operator the number to Westfield Arcade. The phone rang four times, then was picked up.

"Westfield Arcade," the voice on the other end of the line said.

"Gonzo," I said. "It's me."

"What's up, man?" Gonzo said.

Gonzo had the day off from Radio Shack, and I'd thrown him some money to work at the arcade for me. My return flight was leaving early tomorrow morning, and I'd be back in time to open the place by noon.

"How's everything going?" I asked him.

"Busy night," he said. "Timmy's cleaning up at Street Fighter 2. As usual. NBA Jam's been busy all night. Oh, and the screen for the Virtua Racing cabinet went blank and smoke started billowing up from the rear. Is it bad when that happens?"

"What?"

He laughed into the receiver.

"I'm just fucking with you, dude. Everything's fine."

Gonzo asked a few questions about what to do upon closing the arcade, then we said our goodbyes.

"And good luck with Maddy," he said at the end. "I can't wait to hear how she's doing."

I hung up the phone and walked through the door underneath a THEATRE ENTRANCE sign. It was fifteen minutes before the show was scheduled to begin, and the theatre was relatively packed. There were approximately twenty rows of padded seats in the theatre, and the first five rows were entirely full, with each subsequent row getting less and less crowded. I grabbed a seat in the third row from the back and set the bouquet of flowers in my lap.

At the front of the theatre was an elevated stage. Two large red curtains were drawn, and the stage was hidden behind the curtains. Sitting by myself, I watched those curtains, waiting for them to open. Random conversations took place all around me, but all I could think about was finally seeing Maddy again.

The theatre continued to get more packed as show time approached, to the point where there were only a few scattered seats open. And then, all of a sudden, the lights dimmed and the general conversation around me faded to silence. There was a brief pause, and the curtains opened up to reveal a domestic kitchen setting. A refrigerator and countertop were on the left side of the stage, and a dishwasher was on the right. A dinner table with four chairs around it was in the middle of the stage. Sitting alone at that table was Maddy.

She looked different but I recognized her instantly. Her hair was the first thing I noticed. It'd always been short and jet black, but now it was a little longer, not quite shoulder-length, and colored lighter to a brunette shade.

My heart skipped a beat in my chest upon seeing her. She gathered some dishes from the table then walked over to the sink and deposited the dirty dishes into it. She remained at the sink as she started scrubbing away at a plate. A child ran onstage.

"Mommy," he said, walking over to Maddy and tugging at the hem of her dress. "Lizzie stole my race-car toy. I want it back. I want it back, Mommy."

As the young child complained to Maddy, another child, a girl this time, appeared on stage holding a plastic race car in her hand. She waved it in front of the young boy, who started chasing her around the kitchen. Maddy followed them both, trying to round them up. As she did so, an older man walked into the kitchen, looked in the refrigerator, and started complaining to Maddy that there was no milk. Maddy tried to talk with him while simultaneously calming down the two children. It was a chaotic scene, full of yelling and screaming and the two children chasing each other around the kitchen. Finally, everyone left the stage except for Maddy. She looked out towards the audience with a worn-out, utterly exhausted expression on her face.

"My life hasn't always been this glamorous," she said, straight-faced. The crowd immediately laughed at the statement. A few people clapped. She waited for the laughter to die down before continuing.

"No," she said, "this is far more than I could have ever hoped for. As a young girl growing up in the mountains of West Virginia, I dreamed about this type of life."

The play lasted for ninety minutes. It was a mediocre play that would have most likely put me to sleep had Maddy not been in it. There were other characters, other actors, but my eyes never wavered from watching Maddy the entire night. She elegantly commanded the stage and was head and shoulders better than the other actors. Her natural charisma shone through, and she had a certain gracefulness to her that none of the other actors possessed. Every time she addressed the crowd and smiled, it felt like she was smiling right at me, though I knew that it was far too dark for her to be able to make out anyone's face in the crowd.

When the play finally ended, the curtains were pulled and the crowd started clapping. They continued to clap, as the curtains reopened and the entire cast and crew lined up side by side and took a bow.

After that, the curtains closed for a final time. Everyone in the crowd stood from their seats. Some lingered around and formed into huddled packs towards the front of the theatre, but most made their way to the exits. I remained sitting in my seat. Around ten minutes after the play ended, the cast appeared from the back and started making their way around the small crowds of people that remained.

I spotted Maddy instantly. She appeared and immediately walked over to a group of five people who looked to be around her age. She exchanged hugs with a few of them, briefly chatted to the group for awhile, a smile on her face the entire time. A guy who looked to be a few years older than Maddy walked over to the group and stood at her side. His hair was slick backed and he wore a black suit without a tie.

He said something to Maddy, she smiled, then she leaned over and they kissed on the lips. When the kiss ended, the guy reached behind his back and produced a bouquet of flowers. He gave them to Maddy, causing her smile to widen. The bouquet, I noticed, was full of red roses, at least a dozen of them. The extravagant arrangement dwarfed the feeble assortment of flowers in my vase.

A boyfriend. Of course. Why wouldn't she have a boyfriend? She was beautiful, she was charming, she was starring in a play, for God's sake. I watched as she hugged this man again, careful not to upset the vase of flowers. I looked at the pathetic flower arrangement in my hands. For the first time all day, I started to think that this trip might have been a mistake.

I got out of my seat, grabbing my bouquet of flowers, and started walking towards the stage. Maddy was now holding hands with the man she'd kissed, and they talked to the same small group of people around them. As I walked towards her--only about fifteen feet away from her now--she glanced away from her conversation and looked directly at me. She stared for a few seconds. Initially, I thought she didn't recognize me.

And then her eyes widened and her face broke out into a huge grin. She excused herself from the conversation and walked over to me. She didn't scream out loud or throw her hands in the air or cause a scene in any way. She simply walked over and stood a few feet in front of me.

"You're here," she said.

"I am."

She set the bouquet of roses on the ground and stepped over and gave me a big hug. Over her shoulder, I noticed her boyfriend eyeing us over.

"I can't believe you're here," she said once the hug had ended. "I mean, I really can't believe it. It's so great seeing you."

"You, too," I said. I meant it. The letters I received from her were great, but being in her presence, seeing her smile up close, was something I couldn't get from a piece of paper.

"So when did you get in?" she asked.

"This morning."

"What'd you do all day?"

"Mostly just walked around."

"And you survived NYC?"

"So far, I have. Almost got hit by about five different cabs, but I survived."

She smiled again, continuing to look at me.

"So what'd you think of the play?" she asked.

"In my expert opinion, you were incredible."

"Thanks."

"Seriously, of the all the people on stage, you were the best. Easily."

I looked down and realized that I was still holding the flower bouquet.

"These are for you," I said, handing them to her. "Obviously."

"Thank you."

"They're not red roses. So I'm sorry about that."

"Stop it. They're beautiful."

"I think there are some carnations in there. Maybe some daffodils. A couple of other flowers, too. I can't really remember all of the kinds that the florist mentioned."

"Well, they're lovely. Thank you so much."

Behind Maddy, I noticed her boyfriend continuing to eye us over. When I handed the flowers to Maddy, he started walking towards us.

"Looks like you're a popular girl tonight, Maddy," he said when he arrived, looking at me, then at the flower bouquet, then back at me. His voice had a certain smugness to it, an arrogant tone that I instantly disliked.

"This is Mike," Maddy said. "A friend from back home in Indy."

He extended his hand.

"Liam. I'm Maddy's boyfriend."

Boyfriend. Though I'd suspected as much, that single, vile word—boyfriend—was like a punch to my gut.

"Mike," I said, shaking his hand. He held eye contact with me as we shook hands.

"Liam is the director of the play," Maddy said.

"I thought it was great," I said, even though my actual opinion of the play, outside of Maddy's performance, was quite different.

Liam gave a halfhearted nod, as if he was used to--almost sick of--people heaping praise upon his play.

"I wrote the play, too," he said, offering no gratitude for the compliment I'd just given him.

"We have some catching up to do," Maddy said to me.

"I know," I said. "As long as you have time."

"If I have time? Please! Of course I have time."

She turned towards Liam.

"Drinks at Mahoneys?"

"Of course, babe," Liam said. Babe. There are some guys who can get away with calling a girl 'babe,' some guys who say that word and it just flows effortlessly off their tongue. The word sounds natural coming from those guys. Liam was one of those guys. I disliked him even more.

"Let's see if anyone else is up for it," she said, then turned towards me. "Be right back."

I watched as Maddy and Liam reached the group of people they were talking with earlier and said something to them. One of them made a comment that made Maddy laugh. That wonderful laugh.

Maddy and Liam finished talking with the group and returned to me.

"Looks like it's just us three," she said.

We exited the theater and Maddy hailed a cab from curbside like a true pro. The three of us got in the back of the cab with Maddy in the middle and took it a few blocks to a bar with a sign that said Mahoney's over the entrance.

The bar was a run-down, hole in the wall with a homey feel to it. I loved it the moment we walked in. There was a wood-grain bar that dominated the right side of the place, with a series of booths on the left side that extended to the back of the bar. Up front, near the entrance, was a corner with a dartboard and foosball table set up. Various framed pictures and movie posters hung from the walls.

There were only around twenty people inside, grouped in booths and sitting on barstools at the bar. Behind the bar was an older man with silver hair and tortoise shell glasses.

"Hey, Johnny," Maddy said to the bartender as we walked past the bar towards the rear of the place.

"Maddy, how'd it go tonight?" he asked.

She gave him a thumbs up sign.

"Thatta girl," he said.

We found an empty booth in back and sat down in it, Maddy and Liam on one side, me on the other. Liam put his arm around Maddy as he sat down in the booth. A waitress appeared and we ordered drinks.

"So are you two old theatre buddies from back home or something?" Liam asked.

"No, Mike worked at a video game arcade that I used to spend a lot of time at," Maddy said.

"A video game arcade, huh?" Liam said, a grin widening on his face. "Babe, I didn't know you used to be an arcade game pro. What's your high score in Pac Man?"

He laughed at his own joke. Even his laugh sounded condescending.

"I don't have a high score," Maddy said. "I can count on one hand the number of times I played an arcade game. We just hung out. Talked. Watched a ton of MTV. God, that's all we did."

The waitress appeared and set our drinks on the table. Liam picked up his beer and took a long swig from the bottle.

"I used to spend a lot of time in video game arcades," he said. "Of course, I was thirteen at the time."

"So have you seen Jurassic Park yet?" Maddy asked me instantly, not giving me the opportunity to respond to Liam's remark.

"Yeah," I said. "Loved it."

"So cool, right? I loved that scene when the T-Rex is chasing the car through the wilderness."

"My favorite part was when Newman from Seinfeld was in the car and he looked over and saw the dinosaur right next to him. And then the thing's neck expanded and went all crazy before it attacked him."

"That part gave me nightmares," Maddy said. "Such a great movie."

"The movie was just ok, guys," Liam said. "The characters were pretty transparent, to be honest."

Maddy asked me about a few other major releases that had come out over the past year. Mrs. Doubtfire, Sleepless in Seattle, Groundhog Day. When the conversation finally ended, Liam turned towards Maddy.

"So I'm thinking of rewriting the third act of Rat Race," Liam said, announcing this information to her as if it would cause the Earth to stop spinning on its axis.

"Why?" Maddy said.

"It can be improved."

"I think it's fine," Maddy said.

"I'm not shooting for fine, babe," Liam said. "I'm shooting for groundbreaking. I'm shooting for revolutionary."

Liam went on to give a ten-minute long explanation of his plans to make the third act of the play "sizzle" more than it did in its current form by giving it more of an edgy tone and reworking the dialogue. The waitress appeared as he finished his critique, and Maddy and I ordered another drink.

"Nothing for me," Liam said, standing up from the table. "I have to get going."

He pulled out his wallet and threw a twenty dollar bill on the table.

"Drinks are on me."

He turned towards Maddy and kissed her, telling her that he'd see her at rehearsal tomorrow. He vowed to have the rewrites completed by then. Before leaving, he turned towards me.

"Good luck with your little video game arcade," he said as he got up and made his way towards the exit, leaving Maddy and I at the table.

"He doesn't seem like your type," I said after he'd left.

"I didn't realize I had a type."

"I just envisioned you being with who's not…" I searched for the proper way of saying it. "…as much of an assface."

Maddy laughed.

"He's not always the most sociable guy, I agree." She shrugged. "He's an artist--all artists have a bit of an abrasive personality. Plus, he's been under a ton of stress lately, with the play debuting and all."

She took a drink of beer and then looked across the table at me.

"Anyway, let's talk about something else," Maddy said. "Movies, music, MTV—all the stuff we used to talk about."

For the next two hours, we did just that, talking back and forth nonstop as only two friends who hadn't seen each other in awhile can do. We talked about Nirvana and debated whether "Smells Like Teen Spirit" or "Lithium" had a better music video, then talked about a couple of other current favorite videos. We both loved watching "Wayne's World" skits on Saturday Night Live and we talked about the movie that had recently been released.

We ran the pop culture gamut from the past few years and crammed as much as we could into our discussion. Eventually, the topic shifted to Westfield Arcade, and I told Maddy all about the arcade's renaissance. We started reminiscing about the endless nights we'd spent at the arcade before she'd moved away.

"So do you still talk with anyone else from those days?" she asked me.

"Those days? You make it sound like it was forever ago."

"Only feels like it, I guess."

"To answer your question, no, not really. Gonzo stops in every week or so. He's watching the place for me today while I'm out here, actually. But everyone else has moved on."

212

She took a drink from her beer.

"Do you ever think about doing just that? Moving on?"

"Not really."

I paused, and a silence overtook the table.

"Why would I move on?" I said. "The place is doing great."

"I'm just wondering," she said. "Wondering if you've decided to try some other type of career out for awhile. I think you'd be surprised at how much you'd enjoy a real job."

"I own a small business--a small business I love. Why would I give that up to try something else out?"

"You're right. Forget about it." She grabbed her bottle of beer and shook it. "It's the alcohol talking."

I looked across the table at her, a little hurt and confused by her words.

"What do you even mean by that? A 'real' job?"

She sighed.

"What I mean is, is this really it for you? Is this all you want? Mike Mayberry, the guy who owns a video game arcade."

"You make it sound so unappealing."

"Am I supposed to make it sound appealing?"

A few seconds ago, I'd felt mild irritation. That feeling was quickly giving way to a slow-boil anger.

"I'm sorry, but it's the truth," she continued. "I think you're capable of so much more than working at the video game arcade for the rest of your life, even if you do own the place. When you kept writing me about how terrible the arcade was doing, I was just waiting for you to close the place and move on with your life. Go back to school. Finish your degree. Get out there and try something different. And now, I'm a little disappointed that things at the arcade have turned around, to be honest. I wanted the arcade to fail, so you'd have to do something else for a change."

"I love the arcade," I said, raising my voice. "It's the best, my most favorite place in the world. The memories I have from that place are endless."

"You're holding on to the past."

"No, I'm not holding on to the past," I said, starting to get pissed off. "Seeing the arcade thrive again, that's all I want. Westfield Arcade is my dream, just like acting for a living is your dream. Only difference is that I'm actually having luck, while you're barely scraping by and acting in some awful play that no-one will ever see."

The expression on her face crumpled and she recoiled from the words, like they'd come out of my mouth and actually slapped her in the face.

"I'm sorry," I said. I motioned to my beer bottle. "It's the alcohol talking."

The line sounded much more believable when she'd said it earlier.

"I'm serious--I'm really sorry," I said. "I didn't mean that."

But it was already out there. There was no taking the words back. The damage had been done.

"Just forget about it," she said. "I need to get home anyway. It's late."

She grabbed her purse and got up from the booth, leaving a nearly-full beer bottle on the table.

"Can I walk you home?" I said.

"I'm taking a cab," she immediately responded.

"Can I split it with you? I need to get one to my hotel, anyway."

She looked at me for a second.

"Please, Maddy."

"Sure."

Maddy said goodbye to the bartender and we exited out of the bar. She hailed us a cab and it pulled to the curb

214

right in front of the bar. She gave the cabbie her address and he started driving.

"I'm sorry if I hurt your feelings," I said. "I really didn't mean it."

"Don't worry about it. Seriously. I'm fine."

But she didn't seem fine, and the mood in the cab was somber as we rode in complete silence back to her apartment. When we finally arrived, she handed me a five-dollar bill for her half of the cab and got out of the cab. Before shutting the door, she bent down and looked in at me in the backseat.

"I didn't mean to be rude back there," she said. "But I meant what I said. I really do think you're capable of so much more. But if you're happy, I guess that's all that matters."

She smiled at me one final time, but the smile had nowhere near the exuberance of the smile I knew, the smile I loved.

"Have a safe flight back," she said to me, then closed the door and left.

12. Mortal Kombat 2

I quickly pushed the visit to New York to the back of my mind. At least, I tried to. It had not gone as planned, not at all, and I still felt terrible for insulting Maddy's acting career. The trip had ended on a sour note, and I simply wanted to forget about it.

I concentrated on running the arcade. The arcade industry was undergoing a revolution that rivaled the golden age in the early 1980s in terms of popularity. Just as Pac Man, Donkey Kong, and the other groundbreaking games from the golden age in the early 80s had countless clones and imitators, so too did the success of Street Fighter 2 and Mortal Kombat spawn a number of clones. Every manufacturer in the industry started releasing versions of one-on-one fighting games. But what made the imitators of Street Fighter 2 and Mortal Kombat different from those had copied Pac Man and Donkey Kong was that many of the Street Fighter 2 and Mortal Kombat imitators were exceptional games that were phenomenally successful in their own right.

Virtua Fighter was the first fighting game to feature full 3D graphics and it quickly turned into a sensation; many gamers preferred the methodical, hand-to-hand fighting elements of the game to the superhuman special moves and fireballs of Street Fighter 2. Tekken soon followed, taking the 3d graphics and gameplay of Virtua Fighter and improving upon them in every way.

Killer Instinct was released, a fighting game that focused on stringing together combination attacks against your opponent by hitting specific button combinations-- experienced players could sometimes pull off combo attacks of twenty or thirty straight moves, truly a sight to behold. Primal Rage was a fighting game with dinosaurs as the characters instead of humans, and it, too, gained a devoted following, as did King of Fighters and Samurai Warrior.

Mortal Kombat 2 had been released as a follow-up to Mortal Kombat. The ads promised more characters, more blood, more fatalities, and the actual game lived up to all three of those. It was incredible. The graphics had been improved tremendously, too. I ordered three Mortal Kombat 2 cabinets, set them in the front of the arcade, and stacked the money to the ceiling as it poured in.

But throughout all of the popular clones, nothing was able to top the popularity of the granddaddy of them all, Street Fighter 2. The game was considered the benchmark by which all gamers were judged--if you were good at Street Fighter 2, you belonged. The game still drew crowds, and was so popular that Capcom released multiple updated versions of the game every few months. Street Fighter 2: Champion Edition came out a few months after the original, which was followed by Street Fighter 2: Hyper Fighting, then Super Street Fighter 2, and eventually Super Street Fighter 2 Turbo. The games were updates more than they were sequels--a few tweaks, a few different characters, a slight improvement in gameplay. Even if the updates were essentially the same game as the original, the anticipation surrounding the arrival of a new version of Street Fighter 2 was an event rivaled by nothing else at Westfield Arcade.

Good games weren't strictly limited to the fighting game genre, either. The racing genre--first popularized by Pole Position, then Out-Run, then revitalized with Virtua

Racing--had its finest game released: Daytona USA. It took the 3D polygon graphics technology of Virtua Racing and improved upon it with realism unlike anything we'd ever seen. I bought a beautiful quad-cab unit with four sit-down cockpits next to one another for four players to race against each other at the same time. A few months later, Ridge Racer came out and, to everyone's surprise, had graphics even more realistic than Daytona USA. Then Cruis'n USA came along--while not as realistic as other current releases, the game put a wacky spin on the racing genre, with a variety of extremely different vehicles to race with (an ATV, a police car, and a school bus among them).

# # #

The mob arrived at four o'clock, as it always did. Teenagers in high school and junior high, their school day having just ended, showed up for their daily visit to the arcade. Most had on tartan flannel shirts with worn jeans, adopting the grunge look that had been popularized by Soundgarden and Pearl Jam and countless other alternative rock bands. Others wore bright colored t-shirts left over from the early 90s. Some wore Air Jordan hi-tops; others trudged around in Dr. Marten boots.

Upon arrival, many went straight for the cabinets at the front of the arcade. Cruis'n USA drew a large crowd--the sight of a souped-up school bus racing down a country road next to a Ferrari was impossible to simply walk by without stopping to watch for a few moments. There was a cluster of Mortal Kombat 2 cabinets in the corner, and many walked straight to those upon entering the arcade. Some went to play, others went to simply watch in the hopes that they'd see a fatality performed. A large group had already formed at the Tekken cabinet, watching as two teenagers expertly battled each other, the crowd around the cabinet yelling out with every piledriver and roundhouse kick and going even crazier when the final attack that had ended the match was replayed on the game's screen in slow motion. Still other teenagers ignored the arcade games and went straight for the television upon entering the arcade. Beavis and Butthead, a show that had recently exploded in popularity, was on.

A jam-packed Westfield Arcade was a daily occurrence, but seeing the crowds, the camaraderie, never got old for me. It served as a daily reminder of why I loved the place. I stood behind the front counter, soaking in the sight.

The after-work crowd arrived and the place got even more packed, the lines at the popular games lengthening. The day turned into the night, and quarter after quarter continued to be pumped into the various cabinets on the arcade floor.

The night passed quickly and I kicked everyone out once closing time arrived. I walked around the deadened arcade, emptying out the cabinets, then walked back up to the front of the arcade. I noticed a stack of mail resting on the front counter.

Even as the arcade's popularity soared out of this world, the arrival of the mail was always the part of the day that I looked forward to the most. I'd sent Maddy off a letter a short while after returning from New York, asking her how everything was going and apologizing once again for the acrimonious end to my visit. I'd yet to hear back from her. Despite her silence, I still thought about her all of the time. And as the early afternoon arrival time of the mail approached each day, I continued to hope that day would be the day I finally heard back from her.

I looked at the three letters in my hand. A letter from a phone provider. A letter from a cable company. And a flyer for a Chinese place that had recently opened up a few blocks away.

Nothing from Maddy.

I wadded the three pieces of mail into a single crumpled ball and threw it in the trash. I told myself that tomorrow would be the day I finally heard from her. Or maybe the day after. Definitely by the end of the week. But I wasn't sure if I truly believed this or not.

# # #

In April, I showed up to watch the Cubs opening day game with grandpa, continuing our tradition from long ago. It ended up being the final opening day game we ever watched together.

He sat in his recliner, staring at the television. The television wasn't even on; he simply stared into the black screen with a deadened, zombified look on his face.

The progression of Alzheimer's had been rapid in the past year. Carrying on a conversation with him was impossible. He rarely even talked any more, like he'd simply forgotten how to speak a language. On the rare occasions that he did talk, it was usually no more than a single word or monosyllabic utterance. At times, it seemed as if he didn't even know who I was when I showed up. But I continued to visit every single day, in the hopes that, in some distant portion of his mind, my visits still meant something to him.

"Grandpa," I said, sitting down on the edge of his bed.

I reached over and grabbed his hand.

"Grandpa, how are you?"

He slowly turned his head towards me. No smile. Then turned his head back towards the television.

"Are you ready to watch the Cubs?" I said, speaking loudly. I had no idea if the tone of my voice had any effect on his ability to process the words, but I figured it couldn't hurt.

My grandpa remained staring straight ahead.

"It's opening day," I said.

The television remote was on his bedside table, and I reached over and grabbed it. I turned on the television and flipped to WGN. The familiar faces of Harry Caray and Steve Stone came onto the screen. I looked at my grandpa. There was no sign that the sight of the two Cubs broadcasters registered with him.

The broadcast cut away from the announcers to a shot of Ryne Sandberg.

"The Cubs," he said. He didn't smile or show any emotion, but just those words were enough.

"The Cubs, right," I said, encouraged. "Did you know it's opening day?"

He didn't respond to my question.

We watched the game together and I continued talking with my grandpa as it progressed, trying to get some sort of reaction out of him. Almost every question I asked him was met with stony silence. A few times, he simply mumbled "The Cubs" in response to a question, regardless of whether the question had anything to do with the game.

His eyes never once wandered from the television screen as we watched. At one point, a thin strand of drool ran down his chin and onto his shirt. I grabbed a tissue and wiped it up for him.

In the seventh inning, his nurse walked into his room and greeted us.

"It's bedtime, John," she said to my grandpa.

"Can you let him stay awake to the end of the game?" I asked. "It's opening day. He likes it."

"Sure," she said, then smiled. "Just don't tattle on me."

She left the room and we watched the game to the end. My grandpa stayed awake for the entire game, which was pretty significant in itself.

221

"Did you have fun watching the game?" I asked him when it had finished.

He turned towards me, and a faint smile slowly crept across his lips. It faded as quickly as it appeared, and he remained looking at me.

"Opening day," he said, his voice weary.

I smiled at him. Those two simple words let me know that he wasn't entirely gone just yet. His condition was getting worse and worse, but, somewhere inside of that mind of his, there was still a little of the grandpa I knew and loved.

"Grandpa, I don't know if you can even understand me," I said. "But I just want to thank you. I want to thank you for everything you've done for me."

My grandpa remained staring at me, a dazed look still on his face.

"I've thanked you about a million times before, but one more can't hurt. So thank you. Thank you for raising me, for uprooting your life to be there for me when Mom and Dad passed away. I don't know what would have happened had you not been there for me. Being raised by you was the best. I owe you everything."

No emotion registered on my grandpa's face. But I didn't need to see any sort of reaction. I knew that somehow, some way, my words got through to him.

# # #

"Got a weird story for you," Gonzo said one late night at the arcade a few months later.

"How weird is the story?" I asked.

"Pretty damn weird."

"Weirder than the music video for that Jamiroquai song 'Virtual Insanity?'"

"Weirder."

"Weirder than the video for Marilyn Manson's 'Sweet Dreams?'"

"Not that weird."

"Weirder than—"

"Just lemme tell the story," Gonzo said, interrupting me. "So we just started carrying these new computers at Radio Shack. Quad-speed CD-Rom drive. 24-GB hard drive, Windows 95 pre-installed. 28.8 kbps modem."

"You're speaking in a foreign language, man. None of that means anything to me."

"They're state-of-the-art, that's what I'm saying. The big push now is demonstrating the advantages of the Internet for customers. So we've got this demo unit set up in the store. Have you used the internet yet?"

"No. I've heard about it."

"It's pretty amazing. You can get news right away from news website--like, if the President gave a speech, I could go on the internet right when it ended and read about what he said, instead of waiting for the newspaper tomorrow morning. And most companies have websites where you can learn about their new products. You can spend a lot of time on there."

"Great sales pitch, but I'm not buying a computer from you," I said. "I've got better things to spend two-grand on."

Gonzo laughed.

"No sales pitch. But one cool part about the Internet is search engines. You type whatever topic you're interested in, and these search engines search every single website on the entire Internet for any pages that mention that person or subject. You can search for anything. Anyone. So today I went to one of the search engines named Lycos and started searching for random topics to see what came up. And then, just for the hell of it, I typed in Willie Cardinal into the search engine."

I looked at Gonzo.

223

"And?"

"And this was one of the results," Gonzo said. He slid a folded-up piece of paper across the counter to me. I grabbed it and unfolded it. It was a news article he'd printed out. 'Revolution Studios Aiming for the Sky' was the title of the piece.

I read the first few paragraphs of the printout and saw that it was a profile of a video game development studio. Before I got any further in the article, I caught sight of the picture that accompanied it. It was printed in a grainy, uneven black and white tone, but I could still make out the smiling faces of eight Revolution Studios employees looking into the camera. Most wore shorts with flip flop sandals. A few had on flannel shirt and jeans. A guy in the back wore a vintage Pac Man t-shirt that depicted a cartoon version of the little yellow sphere chasing a few ghosts.

It was a wild picture. One guy, smiling at the camera, wore a large striped top hat, like the Cat in the Hat wore in Dr. Suess's book. Another had extended his arm behind a fellow developer's back and gave him bunny ears for the picture. A guy in the rear of the photo had jumped onto the back of the person in front of him and rode him piggyback.

In the middle of this rambunctious crew was a guy with a nonchalant, barely imperceptible smile. He wore a Nirvana t-shirt that depicted the naked baby swimming album cover for Nevermind, and had light, curly hair. He was in a wheelchair.

It was Willie. I knew it was him before I even looked at the box underneath the photograph that identified those in the picture. I hadn't seen him in such a long time—hadn't even thought him much, either, at least not lately—but I recognized him instantly. He'd aged slightly—his face was a little fuller, his hairline had receded a bit—but it was him.

I quickly skimmed over the rest of the article printout. Willie, as it turned out, was one of the three founding members of Revolution Studios, as well as being the lead designer for each one of the four games they'd released thus far.

"I'll be damned," I said once I'd finally finished the article.

"Pretty crazy, huh?" Gonzo said.

"Shocking."

"I'm really not that surprised," Gonzo said. "I always thought Willie could achieve big things if he put his mind to it. Put the devotion and drive that he played arcade games with into something else, something worthwhile."

I looked back down at the article. In a sidebar was a list of the games that Revolution Studios had released thus far. Each was an arcade game. Decimation. Moon Battle. Warriors United. Spectrum.

"I remember that Warriors United game," I said. "We had that in the arcade for awhile."

"Yeah, I played it a few times."

"It did pretty good business. Then Mortal Kombat 2 came out and people lost interest so I sold it. Had I known Willie created it, I would've held onto it."

I looked back down at the sheet of paper, at the picture of Willie with his co-workers. They all looked like they were having the time of their life. The picture reminded me of the photograph that Maddy had given me on New Year's Eve so many years ago, the framed photo of the Westfield Arcade regulars after our Ms. Pac Man tournament.

Seeing the photograph of Willie put Gonzo and I in a nostalgic mood, and we reminisced for awhile about those glory years in the early 1980s. We talked about the regulars from back then. We talked about the games, how archaic and simple they were compared to the 3-d graphics and detailed animations of the current games. We walked to the back and played against each other in a few of our favorites from the golden age era: Missile Command, Centipede, Asteroids.

It was almost one in the morning when we decided to call it a night. Before we went our separate ways, I stopped him in the mall's parking lot.

"Could you do a favor for me?" I asked him.

"Depends."

"Could you type Maddy's name out and search the internet for her? I want to see if there's anything on her."

I still hadn't heard from her. I'd sent off a few more letters, only to hear nothing in response. She had simply disappeared from my life, and while plenty of other friends and acquaintances from my past had simply moved on and departed, Maddy's absence resonated far more than anyone else's. I missed her. Dearly. I wanted an update on her life. I wanted to see how she was doing.

In the dim lighting of the mall's parking lot, Gonzo smiled back at me.

"Sure, I'll do a search for Maddy tomorrow when I'm working," he said. "I'll let you know what I find."

\# \# \#

He found plenty.

Gonzo walked into the arcade late that next night, after I'd closed down the place. He had a small stack of about ten sheets of papers under one arm.

"What'd you find?" I immediately asked.

"Lots," he said, holding up the stack of papers. "But first, what is it worth to you?"

"A couple games of Tekken on the house?"

"Done."

I set a small tower of quarters on the counter, and Gonzo scooped them up. He handed over the stack of papers.

"I found a bunch of reviews of plays that she's been in," he said. "A lot of publications have archives on the internet that you can search through. A few of the reviews are from the New York Post's website, but most are from random theatre publications I've never heard of."

I looked down at the stack of paper and anxiously started thumbing through them. I quickly noticed that Maddy's name was listed in the cast of every write-up, and that Liam's name was listed as writer/director for every play. I also noticed that each play had been performed at the same theatre as Rat Race, the play I'd attended. Two of the printed-out sheets were, in fact, archived reviews of Rat Race from separate publications.

"I'll be over here if you need me," Gonzo said, walking towards the Tekken cabinet, leaving me alone at the front counter.

I started reading through each review. There were a total of three plays that Maddy had been in since Rat Race, and the reviews of the plays were either lukewarm or outright negative. Despite the less-than-stellar reviews, almost every single article singled out Maddy as the standout performer. One review said she had "genuine talent," despite the play's "disorganized structure and non-existent second act." Another review was from two months ago, for a play named Devious Circumstances, and it identified Maddy as "One to watch."

The last review I read was one from a publication named NY Stagehand. The review lauded Maddy's performance, writing that her "effervescent person shone through in an otherwise mundane production." Accompanying the review was a black and white photograph of Maddy onstage, looking into the camera. Like the grainy photograph of Willie, the photograph of Maddy had been printed from a low-quality monochrome printer, but I could still make out her smiling face. She'd grown her hair, I noticed, almost to shoulder-length.

I looked over at Gonzo, mesmerized by his Tekken game, staring straight ahead at the cabinet and mashing the various attack buttons.

Suddenly, I knew that I had to talk with Maddy. Reading the reviews had reminded me just how great of an actress she was, but seeing her picture brought back a whole slew of other memories.

I had to talk with her. It was that simple. It had been far too long since we'd talked.

I immediately picked up the phone and dialed 1-800-COLLECT. After I answered a few questions from an operator, the connection switched over to a dead silence. It only lasted for a few moments, and was replaced by the ringing of a phone. It rang one, twice. A third time. I turned away from the arcade and looked out the window at the deadened food court.

Finally, the phone rang a fourth time and an answering machine picked up.

"Hi, this is Maddy and Liam," Maddy's voice said through the answering machine. I immediately froze. "If you have good news, leave a message and we'll call you back. If you have bad news, don't bother."

There was a brief pause, then a loud beeping noise.

I stood in the arcade like a statue--not moving, not even breathing. The phone receiver felt heavy in my hand. My mouth felt dry as a desert. For the briefest moment, I thought I might be sick.

Maddy and Liam, the message had said. The phrase kept repeating in my head. Maddy and Liam. Such a vile, sinister pairing of words. I knew I should just hang up and slam the phone into the receiver, but I couldn't bring myself to do it.

"Maddy, hey," I said into the receiver. I had no idea what to say next. In fact, I couldn't even remember why I'd called in the first place.

"It's Mike," I continued. "How are you?"

For a few moments, I waited for her to answer the question, then remembered that I was talking to a recording.

"Got a weird story for you," I said, only to realize that the story wasn't really weird at all. "Gonzo found all these articles on the internet about the plays you've been in. Reviews and stuff. And the reviews for your performances were so good. So I wanted to congratulate you. And I wanted to say hi. So…hi.

"And Willie! I almost forgot. Gonzo found a picture of Willie, too. He's a game developer, believe it or not. He makes the games that we have in the arcade.

"Anyway, call me," I continued. "Please do. It's been way too long since we talked."

I quickly hung up the phone. Gonzo had left the Tekken cabinet during my phone call, and was now standing right up by the front counter.

"Who were you talking to?" he asked.

"Maddy" I said. "Well, not her. Her answering machine."

"How'd it go?"

"Terrible," I said, grabbing a box of Mike N Ike candies from the glass display case, hoping the sugar rush might improve my spirits. "Maddy has this jackass boyfriend. I met him when I went to visit her, and this guy is just a complete tool."

I opened the box of Mike and Ike and poured a few out on my hand. I shoved them into my mouth.

"Apparently, Maddy now lives with this boyfriend of hers," I continued. "I wanted to call and congratulate her, chat for a bit. But hearing his name on the answering machine just threw me off. I sounded like a rambling fool on the message."

Maddy and Liam--the phrase from the answering machine kept repeating in my head. It was starting to make sense why she hadn't reached out since I'd visited. It wasn't because her overwhelming schedule left her no free time to call or write. It was beginning to look like Maddy, like so many others, had simply moved on.

"I'm sorry, man," Gonzo said.

Not as sorry as I was.

13. Time Crisis

"You seen this shit yet?" Gonzo said to me. It was a late night at Westfield Arcade, after I'd closed the place, and we were the only two people in the arcade. Gonzo was looking at a video game magazine, and he showed me an article.

"'Is Playstation the future of video gaming?'" I read from the article's headline. I looked up at Gonzo. "What the hell's Playstation?"

"A new home video game console. From Sony."

I looked back down and skimmed over the article. The answer to the question posed in the headline, at least according to the article, was a resounding 'Yes.' The article talked glowingly of the Playstation's ability to produce cd-quality sound and graphics that were far beyond anything that any previous home console had been able to produce. Towards the bottom of the article was a row of full-color screenshots from various games that were scheduled to be released for the system.

"I have to admit, the games do look good," I said. "When's this thing come out, anyway?"

"Not for a few more months. I had a conference call with corporate the other day, and they're expecting our initial shipment to sell out entirely. They have high expectations."

I flipped the page. On the magazine's next page was a giant sidebar that listed every game scheduled to come out for Playstation in the year after its release.

"Good list of games, too," I said. "Tekken, Air Combat, Ridge Racer."

"According to that article, the Playstation version of Ridge Racer is going to be identical to the arcade version. Exact same graphics, sound effects, gameplay. Everything."

"The arcade game just came out a few months ago," I said. "It's probably the most-advanced game we have in Westfield Arcade right now. No way a home video game console could do graphics like that."

"I'm just quoting the article."

"I'll believe it when I see it," I said.

Just then the phone rang. I glanced at the clock above the counter. It was almost eleven o'clock at night.

I reached over and picked up the phone.

"Westfield Arcade," I answered.

"Is Mike Mayberry there?" the voice asked.

"Speaking."

"Mike, this is Linda from Cedar Grove Retirement Comm--"

"Is everything all right?" I instantly asked before she could finish. I knew she wasn't calling at eleven o'clock at night to say hi or discuss a bill that needed to be paid.

"Your grandfather has suffered a stroke, Mike. It wasn't fatal, but it was very serious. I'm so sorry to be the bearer of bad news."

I had a million questions I wanted to ask but I remained silent for a moment. I'd prepared myself for this moment for awhile now. One of his doctors had, in fact, took me aside a few weeks ago and mentioned my grandpa's increased chances of suffering a stroke as his Alzheimer's continued to progress. But no matter how much I'd prepared myself for this news, actually hearing the news still send shockwaves throughout my body.

"I'll be right over," I finally said.

"No, your grandpa isn't here. He's at Lakeview Community Hospital. He was rushed to the emergency room."

I thanked her and hung up the phone.

"Everything ok?" Gonzo asked.

"No, it's not," I said.

"Your grandpa?"

"Yeah," I said. "I have to get going."

I hurried to the back of the arcade and flipped the main power switch. Gonzo and I exited the arcade and I locked the security gate in place.

"I hope everything is ok," Gonzo said.

"Thanks."

I ran down the mall's main corridor and out to my car in the parking lot. Lakeview Community Hospitals was five miles away from the mall, and I drove over as fast as I could. This late at night, there was no traffic at all on the interstate.

I followed the signs to the Emergency Care Unit and parked my car in a space by the entrance. I exited the car and hurried over to the entrance. I entered into the lobby, a smaller room with a single check-in desk right inside the entrance and a long hallway to the left that led down to a corridor with doors on both sides. On the right half of the lobby was a waiting area with cushioned seats and a table overflowing with magazines. No-one was in the waiting area at the moment.

I walked up to the front desk and introduced myself to the nurse sitting behind it. She looked at a packet of paper and read my grandpa's name from one of the sheets. She got up from her chair and told me to grab a seat in the waiting area.

She walked away from the lobby, disappearing down the hallway and entering one of the doors on the right. I walked over to the waiting area, but didn't sit down or grab a magazine to flip through.

Five minutes later, the nurse returned with an older man wearing hospital scrubs. The nurse walked back behind the front counter and the older man in the scrubs walked over to me.

"Mr. Mayberry?" he said.

"Yes."

"I'm Dr. Langdon, one of the doctors here. Could you come with me for a second?"

I followed him down the hallway and we walked into an empty room. It was a sparsely furnished room with a patient bed pushed up against the wall and a small desk in the corner. There was a chair in the middle of the room and Dr. Langdon motioned for me to sit in it.

"How is he?" I asked.

He looked me directly in the eye and his expression did not change in the slightest.

"I'm sorry," he said. "Your grandfather was rushed here after suffering his stroke. Unfortunately, it was a very serious stroke. He had already passed away when he arrived here. There was nothing we could do. I'm so sorry for your loss."

# # #

His death was easier to take than I thought it would be. I was busy in the days after it happened, which helped. Planning both the funeral and the visitation took up the bulk of my time. There were hundreds of little details to attend to and decisions to make for each service. I had to determine where the funeral was going to take place, when it was going to take place, and help plan out every aspect of the service. I had to reserve a cemetery plot, then shop for a headstone for his grave and write an inscription. I'd closed down the arcade for a few days and I was constantly on the go, finalizing every last detail for the service.

I knew that my grandpa was in a better place now, and this thought also helped me to deal with his absence. Towards the end, the disease had reached such an advanced stage that I couldn't imagine my grandpa enjoying any aspect of his life. His ability to communicate had entirely departed him, and even simple motor skills like operating the television's remote control and walking more than a few steps became impossible for him to perform without assistance. His death was sad, no doubt, but his life during the final stages of his Alzheimer's was no way to live a life.

The grandpa I knew and loved had passed on long ago, and the fact that his suffering was over was a relief. But I still missed him dearly.

# # #

The visitation for my grandpa took place three days after he passed away, the night before the funeral. It was held in a small side-room at the funeral home that was referred to as a gathering room. My grandpa's open casket was displayed towards the rear of the room, right next to a small table with a few of his treasured possessions. His baseball that he loved concocting stories about was placed in the middle of the table. A few of his favorite Cubs sweaters were laid out, as well as a Cubs pennant. Framed black and white photographs of him in his younger years hung from the walls. To the left of the table were ten bouquets of flowers that had been sent by various people, mostly acquaintances in Oregon who were unable to attend the funeral.

The visitation itself lasted for three hours and was sparsely attended. My grandpa had few friends in Indianapolis. He'd spent most of his free time raising me, and had little time for anything else. Plus, he was nearly seventy years old when he moved here, not exactly an age that is conducive to an active social life.

Of those who showed up, the attendees were mostly members of the local church we were members of. The senior care center loaded up a few residents and brought them to the visitation in a van. Each one of his nurses and doctors showed up throughout the course of the evening. A few of my friends dropped by--Gonzo included, despite the fact that he'd never even met my grandpa.

As the evening winded down and the visitation was ten minutes from ending, Maddy showed up.

The room was nearly empty, with only the funeral director and I in the room. The funeral director was a short pudgy man in his fifties, and he stood across the room from me, over by the collection of flower bouquets. I stood near the entrance to the gathering room, wearing the only suit I owned, up by a small table with an open visitation book for guests to sign as they arrived.

I locked eyes with Maddy the moment she walked through the door. Her face was a little puffier than I remembered and her hair was longer, almost to shoulder-length--just like it had looked in the black and white photo that Gonzo had found on the Internet. She wore a black dress that extended past her knees, with a black cardigan sweater over the dress. The sweater was unbuttoned, revealing Maddy's pregnant, swollen belly that strained against the midsection of her dress.

She walked over and stood in front of me for a moment. I was speechless. I couldn't believe she was standing directly in front of me. I couldn't believe that she was pregnant. I couldn't believe that this all wasn't just a big dream.

"Wow," I said. "You're here."

"I'm here."

"I didn't expect to see you," I said.

"I wish it were under better circumstances," she said. "I'm sorry to hear about your grandpa."

I nodded in response to the statement.

"How are you holding up?"

"I'm fine," I said. "I really am."

We looked at each other for a moment.

"I like your hair," I said. "I believe that's what they call The Rachel."

"For the record, I cut my hair like this before 'Friends' debuted."

"So Jennifer Aniston copied you?"

"She did. I'm still trying to figure out a way I can sue for royalties."

I smiled at her, then looked at the clock on the wall and saw that it was nine o'clock.

"Do you have anywhere you have to be? I'll be done here soon. Maybe we could talk for awhile."

"Of course," she said. "I'd like that."

Maddy exited back out into the hallway. I walked over to the funeral director and spoke with him for a few minutes, mostly about the funeral tomorrow morning. He wished me a good night, and I left the gathering room. I found Maddy sitting on a chair in the hallway, right outside the door.

"Wanna walk around the neighborhood for awhile?"

"Sure," she said.

We exited out of the funeral home and into the night. The funeral home was located in the downtown district of a quiet neighborhood on the outskirts of Indianapolis. Various shops and restaurants surrounded the funeral home, most of which were closed for the night. It was a brisk Fall evening--not quite winter-jacket weather, but close. A light breeze blew through the air. Above us, thousands of stars glimmered in the night sky.

We started walking down the sidewalk, past businesses with their lights off and front windows darkened.

"How's the arcade doing?" Maddy asked.

"Just great," I said. "As busy as ever."

"Good to hear," she said.

"And you? The acting? Are you lining your mantel place with all of the awards that critics are handing you?"

"Hardly," she said, giving a slight chuckle.

"I read about a few of your plays on the internet. Gonzo has this computer at Radio Shack that he looks stuff up on for me."

"Right, I got your phone message. Sorry I didn't respond."

We continued walking on the sidewalk, past a shoe store and a Mexican restaurant that had both closed for the night. A few cars slowly drove by us on the street.

"The internet," Maddy said. "It's amazing what's out there. That's how I found out about your grandpa. I still check the Indy Star website every day that I'm able to. I saw his name in the obituaries and I knew that I had to come back."

"Well, thanks," I said. "I appreciate it. I really do."

We continued walking in silence for awhile.

"So," I said. "You're sort of pregnant, I noticed."

"Yes, I am. Well, not sort of. I am. Pregnant."

"Congratulations."

"Thank you."

More silence between us as we kept walking. In the distance, a car honked its horn.

"Liam," Maddy eventually said. "The guy you met when you visited. The director of that play I was in. He's the father."

I'd already made that assumption, though I still felt a twinge of disappointment upon hearing Maddy confirm it.

"He wasn't able to make it out with you?" I said. "Working on his latest masterpiece, I assume. Or has he moved on to Hollywood now? Replacing Spielberg for the next Jurassic Park, maybe?"

She was silent. Her expression didn't change at all in response to my good-natured joke.

238

"I'm kidding around," I said. "Just teasing. I didn't mean to sound—"

"We're not together anymore," she said. "Liam and I. We don't talk anymore."

Now it was my turn to be silent. I had no idea what to say.

"Maddy, I'm sorry."

"Don't be. Nothing for you to be sorry about."

Maddy came to an abrupt stop, then walked over to a park bench a few feet away. She slumped down in it. I walked over and sat down next to her. Across the street was a small park, skeletal trees and dark shadows dimly lit by a few streetlights. She silently looked out at the park with a saddened, defeated expression on her face.

"It's over, Mike," she said quietly. "Everything is over. My relationship with Liam. My acting dream. Just, my life. That's what's over. My life."

For a moment, I thought she was going to start crying, but she paused and the moment passed.

"Everything will be fine," I said, mostly because I could think of nothing else to say.

"No," she said. "It won't. I haven't acted in months--there isn't exactly a ton of demand for a pregnant stage actress--and I don't know when I'll be able to go back. What happens when I have the baby? Take her--or him, I still don't know if it will be a boy or girl--to daycare while I work during the day, hire a nanny to work every night I have rehearsals? Basically have a bunch of other people raise my kid? I can't even afford that, let alone do I even have any desire to do that. And I don't know what I'd do without acting. I honestly don't."

She sighed.

"Liam," Maddy said. "Such a fucking asshole."

I didn't say anything.

"We didn't plan for this to happen, and when I told him that I was pregnant, he said he had too many irons in the fire to worry about a child. He actually used that expression. Irons in the fire. I walked out on him when he said that. I've talked with him once since then, and his stance hasn't changed. He's gone."

"I'm so sorry."

"Don't be. Forget him."

She looked at her pregnant belly and ran her hand over the top of it. She leaned to the side and rested her head on my shoulder. We both stared out into the shadowy, deadened park across the street.

"Feels like old times," Maddy said. "Us sitting around and talking late at night."

"All we need is a television showing MTV," I said.

She lightly laughed at my comment.

"I miss those days," she said.

"Me, too," I said.

We remained sitting on the park bench for awhile, Maddy resting her head on my shoulder the entire time. Neither of us spoke. The night was so quiet and serene that I almost nodded off to sleep at one point.

"I have to get going," Maddy eventually said, standing up from the park bench. "I'm staying with my aunt and she's probably wondering where I am. Plus, I have an early flight tomorrow."

We walked back to the funeral home. Tree branches and leaves rustled in the distance. Her hand brushed up against mine as our arms swung as our sides. I eventually grabbed it, and we held hands as we walked down the sidewalk.

Her car was the only one left in the diagonal parking spots that bordered the street in front of the funeral home. It was a white 4-door Chevy Lumina, and when we arrived at it, I noticed an Avis Car Rental sticker in the corner of the windshield.

Maddy turned towards me before entering the car.

"It was great seeing you again," she said.

"You, too. Keep me posted on the little one."

"You'll be the first to know," she said. "Well, not the first. I'll probably call my parents before you. And some family members. Maybe a few other friends. But I'll get around to telling you eventually."

She smiled at me and I smiled back at her. She unlocked the car and sat down in the front seat, but before closing the door she looked up at me.

"I'm sorry for not responding to your letters," she said. "And your answering machine messages."

"No problem. You were busy."

"That's no excuse. I feel terrible. I always meant to call. I really did. Then, things got hectic, and the pregnancy happened. Everything started going downhill, and I didn't want to call you up and spend the entire call complaining about my life falling apart."

"I'm just glad you came tonight," I said.

"Me too," she said.

She closed the door and started up her car. She looked out the windshield at me and waved. I waved back, then watched her car as it traveled down the street and disappeared into the night.

# # #

A month later, I talked with her again. It was another busy evening at the arcade, and I stood amongst the crowd gathered around the Time Crisis cabinet, the latest and greatest game the arcade had in stock. Across the arcade, the phone behind the front counter rang. I hurried over and answered it.

"Westfield Arcade," I said.

"Josephine Kay Fredrickson," was the very first thing I heard.

"Great name," I said. "When did you give birth?"

"Yesterday," Maddy said. "I'm at my apartment now. My parents are here. My mother's already driving me up the wall. But I'm home safe. And the little one is doing great. Question: Do you like Josie or Jo as a nickname for Josephine?"

"Jo," I said. "Definitely. It's brief. To the point."

"That's seven total votes for Jo, five votes for Josie. It's a close one."

Maddy and I had kept in touch since my grandpa's visitation. Every week or so, she'd send off a letter containing general updates on her pregnancy and recaps of visits to the doctor. She eagerly talked of the emotions she felt, and her anticipation skyrocketed as the weeks ticked away and the big day approached. I loved reading her weekly updates and tried to provide as much support as I could. Even though I was seven hundred miles away, I felt like I was, in a small way, experiencing it with her.

"How are you feeling?" I asked.

"I've been better. I don't think I've slept in over twenty-four hours. But I survived."

"And the little girl?"

"She's doing great. Everyone says that she looks like me, that she has my eyes. Thank God. If she had Liam's eyes, I'd make her wear sunglasses for the rest of her life."

She laughed into the phone.

"I adore her so much. She's a cutie. Pudgy little face. Always smiling. She even has a few strands of dark hair on her head."

"That's great," I said. "Congratulations."

"Thanks," Maddy said.

On her end of the phone, I heard someone yell Maddy's name in the background.

"Hold on for a second," Maddy said to me.

Her end of the line went silent, and she returned a few moments later.

"I have to get going now," she said. "The little stinker needs a diaper change, and I'm just the one to give it to her."

"Sounds fun," I said.

"You know, I'd love for you to visit and meet her sometime."

"You just want a babysitter so you can go out on the town, right?"

"But of course."

We both laughed, and then said our goodbyes.

I hung the phone up and a smile crept over my face. I'd been anxiously awaiting that very phone call. Maddy's due date had been two days ago, and when it had come and gone, I'd spent the last forty-eight hours wondering when she'd call with some sort of update. I'd even phoned her twice yesterday and left messages both times, seeing if she had any news.

Well, she had news, all right. She was now a mother of a baby girl. Her very own child to love and comfort, to be there for, to raise into a woman. Playtime was over for Maddy. Everything had changed for her.

And now, it was official--she'd taken that final step into adulthood.

14. Maximum Force

The Sony Playstation home console was released later in the year, and it was a blockbuster from the moment it came out. It sold-out nationwide on its release date, with many people waiting in line for hours outside of stores to get their hands on the system. The Internet had just started to truly go mainstream, and AOL chat rooms and message boards were filled with people enthusiastically discussing and praising the machine. An enormous marketing campaign ensured that commercials for Playstation ran constantly. Billboards and magazine advertisements for the system were everywhere. And in the months after its launch, the system continued to fly off the shelves, becoming the fastest-selling console in the history of video gaming.

"Playstation," I told Gonzo one Friday night, looking out at the practically empty arcade floor, "is absolutely kicking Westfield Arcade's ass."

"I bought one myself the other night," he said. "Saved fifty bucks with the Radio Shack employee discount."

"How do you like it?" I asked him.

"It's pretty damn amazing," he said. "It really is."

I remained looking out at the practically empty arcade floor. The effect of Playstation on the arcade had been as sudden and deadly as a snakebite. The crowds had simply disappeared. The rush of teenagers arriving at the arcade upon the school day ending, the groups of people spending entire weekend days at the arcade, had all but vanished. Everyone had started to stay home and play their Playstations to get their video game fix.

"Dead night," Gonzo said, noticing me looking out at the arcade floor.

"Thanks for pointing that out, Captain Obvious."

"You'll be fine," he said. "This isn't the first dead stretch the arcade has gone through. You survived Nintendo. You survived Genesis. You'll survive this."

"I don't know," I said. "This feels different."

"How so?"

"In the past, there was always a clear distinction between arcade video games and home video games," I said. "Arcade games were simply more advanced. The Nintendo and Super Nintendo and Genesis all had plenty of good, fun games, but those consoles didn't have the hardware to produce the advanced graphics and sound effects of arcade games. In the past, you look at an arcade game and a video game for a home console side-by-side, there was always a huge difference. The arcade games were always more advanced and realistic. By a wide margin.

"But these Playstation games are just as advanced as anything we have in the arcade. More advanced, in some cases. That's never happened before, where a home video game console has more advanced games than the arcade does."

Also, I told Gonzo, I'd read that the cd's that Playstation games were stored on could be mass-produced for less than a dollar per cd, whereas it required hundreds of dollars to assemble an arcade game, not to mention the man hours needed to build the cabinet and hook up the complex wiring inside. Consequently, game manufacturers had started to flock to Playstation to produce games for it.

I'd always believed that the camaraderie and social aspect of Westfield Arcade would enable the arcade to succeed no matter what obstacles I encountered. But that confidence was starting to waver.

# # #

I started up the vacuum cleaner, the device's motor humming to life, and began vacuuming the carpet of the arcade, starting by the newer games up by the entrance. I excused myself as I vacuumed around two kids standing at the Mortal Kombat 3 cabinet, then made my way towards the vintage games in the back of the arcade, the vacuum sucking up bits of popcorn and particles of dirt along the way. I carried a spray bottle of Resolve carpet cleaner and a worn rag in my hand, and sprayed and scrubbed away at any stains on the carpet that I encountered.

When finished, I unplugged the vacuum from the wall and gathered up the power cord, setting the vacuum in the back closet. I walked up to the front counter and ran a damp cloth over the glass of the countertop, polishing the surface. I felt like a bachelor getting his apartment in perfect shape to make a good impression on a big date. The analogy wasn't entirely inaccurate.

There were only a few people in the arcade—the two kids at the Mortal Kombat 3 cabinet continued to play, there were another two teenagers at the Virtua Fighter 2 cabinet, there was a lone older guy in the back plugging quarters into the Galaga cabinet—but the place looked great.

It was a day I'd been looking forward to for awhile. Maddy had sent me a letter a few weeks ago, saying that she was briefly visiting Indianapolis for a family reunion.

We'd made plans for her to visit the arcade today at 4:30 in the afternoon. 4:30 was five minutes away.

I took a final walk-through, making sure I hadn't missed a stain anywhere, then returned to the front and looked out the arcade's entrance. I saw a girl walking towards the arcade, pushing a stroller past the tables of the food court.

Maddy spotted me in the arcade and waved, keeping one hand on the stroller. I smiled and waved back. I was anxious, nervous, excited. Maddy finally arrived at Westfield Arcae and I walked over and hugged her.

"Maddy," I said.

"Good to see you," she said.

I knelt down to look at her little girl in the stroller. She was asleep, with her eyes closed and mouth hanging open, her head lifelessly tilted to the side. Her face was so pudgy and cute. There was a pink bow in her short, stringy hair. She wore a green onesie with a cartoon alligator on the front.

"Cute outfit," I said.

"Oh God, don't get me started on that thing," Maddy said. "My aunt bought her that exact outfit and sent it to me, and all she's talked about for the past month was how much she can't wait to see little Jo wearing her alligator outfit. Thing is, I forgot to pack it. I stopped by four different stores before I came here until I found an identical one at a Babies-R-Us."

Maddy looked around at the arcade.

"This place looks different," she said. "When did you remodel?"

"Years ago, when I re-opened the place," I said. It suddenly struck me that this was the first time Maddy had been in the arcade since she moved to New York. "It's not normally this clean, though. I did some vacuuming and cleaning for you."

"I'm impressed."

I walked over to the front counter and grabbed a wrapped present that I'd set behind it earlier.

"This is for you," I said, returning to Maddy and handing her the present. "Well, not for you. It's for Jo."

"Well, thank you. On behalf of Jo."

Maddy examined the exterior of the present, then tore into the wrapping paper. She pulled the present out and looked it in her hands. It was a small t-shirt with a picture of a blocky enemy from Space Invaders screen-printed on it. Underneath the picture was an inscription: Future Video Game Champ.

Maddy looked at the tag attached to the shirt, then looked back at the front of the shirt.

"Future video game champ," she read. "I think it's safe to say that little Jo will never, ever wear this for as long as she lives."

I laughed.

"Oh, come on. What's wrong with it?"

"For starters, she's a girl. She's not a future video game champ. She's a future princess, or a future ballerina. And second, it's a size Newborn. She's already outgrown all of her Newborn clothes. It's too small."

"I had to guess on what size she wore," I said.

"Well, you guessed wrong. A for effort, though."

"I bought it at that baby store on the other side of the mall, if you want to return it. I won't be offended."

"I'll hold onto it. I'll find some use for it."

I looked back down at her little girl, asleep in the stroller, mouth hanging open, her miniature little body expanding and contracting with her breathing patterns every few seconds.

"She's so cute," I said.

"Thanks."

"She really does look like you."

Maddy smiled.

"I think so, too."

Jo's eyes suddenly jumped to life and she woke up. She blinked a few times and opened her mouth and yawned. Her wide eyes looked at me, then around the arcade, her head on a swivel. Maddy knelt down beside me and made a funny face at Jo, and the baby's face lit up with a smile. She reached out towards Maddy, flailing her tiny hands and kicking her feet.

"No way, sweetie," Maddy said. "You're staying in the stroller."

I walked around the arcade with Maddy and Jo, giving them a small tour. As we walked, Maddy told me about her ex, Liam. After his latest play had been a disappointment, he'd been unable to find work. Broke and penniless, he'd been evicted from his apartment and had to move to Vermont to live with his parents. Currently, he was working as a barista at a coffee house. According to a theatre friend of hers, he burned a few bridges when he left and would most likely never get another job in the New York City theatre scene.

She told the story with a sly, pleased smile on her face, clearly delighting in the karma that had come his way.

"Speaking of the theatre, have you started looking for work?" I said.

"Not yet," she said. "I don't know if I'm going to go back or not."

"Why?"

She paused, looked out at the food court then back at me.

"I just don't have the time to start acting again," she said. "Not now. I've got a job lined up at an insurance agency that I start in a couple weeks--a real job, with benefits and a steady paycheck and everything. I won't have any time left for acting. There are only so many hours in the day."

"You could move back here," I said.

"I thought about that," Maddy said. "But this isn't home. Not any more. My parents live in Florida now. Practically everyone I know is gone from here. New York is my home. I couldn't leave it."

Maddy sighed.

"It's tough," she said. "Everything was going so well. I was starting to network and meet some really good contacts. I really, honestly had a shot at a few supporting roles in Broadway plays. After that, who knows what would have happened?

"Acting was my dream. Still is. Dreams die hard. But sometimes you have to sacrifice something you love for something you love even more."

She looked down at her baby.

"We'll figure something out, won't we, Jo?" she said, reaching down and pinching the baby's small foot with her thumb and index fingers, giving it a little shake. "Just you and me, taking on the world."

# # #

I'd always loved the movie Back to the Future 2, one of the few movie sequels I deemed worthy of the original, and my favorite scene took place towards the middle of the movie. Marty McFly has been transported to the future, an advanced world full of flying cars and shoes that tie themselves, and there's a scene where he walks into a diner named The 80s Diner, a restaurant full of artifacts and memorabilia from the long ago decade of the 1980s. There's a Rubix Cube, a video featuring Max Headroom, Michael Jackson music playing from the speakers. One of the artifacts from the 1980s is an arcade game named Wild Gunman.

McFly walks over to the game and starts playing as two young kids look on. Both of the children are perplexed by the hulking arcade cabinet--"My dad told me about these," one says. They regard it as something from the stone ages, a long-forgotten relic from another era. They quickly lose interest in the arcade cabinet and walk off.

When I saw the movie in the theater, I'd found it to be a funny scene, purely because it was so far-fetched. The notion that arcade games would simply disappear and children in the future would have no idea what they even were was ludicrous. But as the weeks at Westfield Arcade continued to pass, I started to wonder whether or not the movie might just be spot-on with that particular prediction of the future.

Business at the arcade had gone from bad to worse since the introduction of Playstation. Many game developers had started exclusively producing games for Playstation, and fewer and fewer arcade games were being created. There were still a few quality arcade games released throughout the year--Street Fighter Alpha, Dead or Alive, Tekken 2--but each of those games had an arcade-perfect version released for Playstation shortly after being released in arcades. It simply didn't make sense for people to drive halfway across town and pay .50 per game when they had an identical version of the game at their own homes, available to play on their Playstation whenever they wanted to.

Good games were the lifeblood of the arcade. As much as I loved the camaraderie and the sense of belonging that the arcade fostered, the games were what drew people in. With few good games, the arcade was rendered all but irrelevant in the eyes of teenagers. The problem, I knew, wasn't exclusive to just Westfield Arcade--the arcade's closest competitor, an arcade a few miles away that opened up during the fighting game boom of the early 90s, closed its doors due to lack of business.

And yet, as the arcade industry crumbled before my very eyes and the business I loved started to falter, I found myself thinking, more and more, not about the arcade and what I'd do to combat Playstation, but of Maddy.

We'd both gotten email addresses, and we constantly communicated back and forth. Maddy had started her new job at the insurance agency and kept me abreast of the daily going-ons in her office. She still adored her little girl, and sent constant updates on Jo and how she was doing. Maddy sent a hurried, flushed email when Jo had taken her first step--she was so excited that the email was borderline incoherent. She'd excitedly told me about a tooth that had started to form in the back of Jo's mouth.

Maddy talked about acting, too. She missed it greatly. She still kept in touch with her theatre buddies and reported their achievements to me via email. Her friend Sally had starred in an off-Broadway production named "Midnight Oil." Her friend Michael had finished writing his first play. Jess had secured a supporting role in a Broadway production that had been nominated for a Tony Award. The names of her friends meant nothing to me--I'd never met any of them--but the fact that many of their careers had started to take off made Maddy proud of them. And a little jealous.

Acting was something that had always been a part of her life, Maddy told me in an email, and not being involved with the theatre scene left her with an emptiness. As much as she loved Jo, not even her little girl could fill that void.

# # #

The letter from Maddy arrived in the mail a short while later, during another slow afternoon at Westfield Arcade. The day's mail consisted of a flyer from Sears (their latest specials on Playstation games were featured prominently), a piece of junk mail from an electric company, and a single white envelope with Maddy's name and address in the upper left-hand corner. I grabbed the envelope with Maddy's name on it and discarded the other two pieces of mail. I looked over the outside of the envelope, intrigued. We'd been communicating entirely by email for months--it had been ages since she'd sent me anything in the mail.

I tore into the envelope and pulled out the contents: a Polaroid photograph and a small piece of paper. I looked at the photograph first. It was a glossy Polaroid that showed Maddy smiling into the camera while she held Jo up, both hands wrapped around the baby's belly. Jo looked into the camera, her mouth open in a wide smile, wearing a small pink t-shirt and a cloth diaper. I could make out the words Future Video Game Champion on the cloth diaper, although the last half of each word was folded back along the side of the diaper.

I set the photograph on the front countertop and picked up the note that had been included with the photograph. Found a good use for your shirt, it read in Maddy's familiar handwriting.

I smiled. I looked at the photograph again. It was such a cute photograph. Maddy, smiling an exuberant smile and holding Jo up right next to her. And little Jo! She'd grown up so much since Maddy had brought her into the arcade during her last visit. Her hair was longer and even darker than it'd been then.

I recalled the day that Maddy and Jo had visited the arcade. It had been so great seeing Maddy, meeting Jo--it had, in fact, been one of the few memorable days at Westfield Arcade over the past six months. I recalled something that Maddy had said on that day, a line that had stuck with me ever since. Sometimes, Maddy had said when talking about sacrificing her theatre dreams for the sake of raising her little girl, you have to give up something you love for something you love even more.

The words had resonated with me. I'd done the exact same thing so many years ago, when I'd dropped out of college to be there for my grandpa. I was only a year away from graduating and had already put countless hours into obtaining my degree. At the time, I'd enjoyed college, was looking forward to graduation. But I knew that I had to be there for my grandpa. The decision had been easy. Sacrificing for him had been a no-brainer.

I looked out at the arcade floor, lit up like a carnival with the glow from nearly one hundred arcade monitors. Westfield Arcade. The place I loved. The only job I'd ever known, my home for my entire adult life. It was so full of magic, so full of memories--not just for me, but for thousands upon thousands of others who'd spent time here over the years. So many people had spent countless hours at Westfield Arcade as they grew up, hanging with their friends, screwing around, having fun.

There was, I knew, still a chance that the arcade could return to prominence once again. Playstation was kicking ass, but there was always that possibility that the arcade could get a revolutionary game that could single-handedly save the industry and bring the crowds back. It had happened before. It could happen again.

But I also wasn't sure if I cared as much as I used to.

I looked back down at the picture of Maddy and her little girl, just stared at Maddy's smiling face and Jo's expression. The ability to email back and forth and be in near-constant communication was great. But I still missed her. Instead of strengthening our relationship, hearing from her constantly through email made me miss her even more.

I thought, once again, about what she'd said: Sometime you have to give up something you love for something you love even more. I looked back out at the floor of Westfield Arcade, every game powered on with no-

254

one around to play them. I stared out at my beloved arcade for a long time.

And right then, right there, I knew that it was time.

As I stood alone in the arcade, I decided to close Westfield Arcade forever.

January 6, 1997

  It's been a busy few months for Mike Mayberry since he made the decision to close Westfield Arcade for good. There have been meetings with officials from the mall and infinite amounts of paperwork to fill out. He's had to contact all of the various distributors and vendors he works with and settle up any outstanding balances. And selling off the stock of arcade games has been a pain in the ass—fielding countless calls from interested parties with questions regarding the arcade cabinets, coordinating times for them to examine the games, negotiating with those who wanted to haggle over price.

  Closing a small business, he's found, requires almost as much work as opening one.

  But now here he is. Westfield Arcade's final day of business. The clock strikes seven, marking only two remaining hours until the arcade is closed for good.

  Standing behind the front counter, he looks out at the arcade floor. The arcade has practically been gutted. Over three-fourths of the arcade's stock is gone. Only around twenty games remain, and those few games are intermittently scattered throughout the arcade floor, surrounded by open, empty gaps where their counterparts once stood. A few of the games are in the back section of the arcade. A few are in the front up by the entrance.

  "I heard this place was closing."

  Mike looks up and sees Gonzo, standing right inside the entrance to Westfield Arcade. Two other people are at

Gonzo's side. The guy on his left is a diminutive guy with thick glasses and short hair. His shoulders are slightly slouched forward as he stands there looking at Mike with a sheepish smile on his face. The guy on Gonzo's right has light-colored, curly hair. His skin has a deep tan to it. He's in a wheelchair.

Mike recognizes them both instantly, and he stands there and looks at the two of them. They're not quite middle-aged but certainly not the teenagers they were the last time they set foot in Westfield Arcade so many years ago.

"You gotta be kidding me," Mike says, walking over to them. He reaches the guy in the wheelchair first, and shakes his hand.

"Good seeing you, buddy," Willie Cardinal says.

"You too." Mike turns towards the other guy-- Rufus. He can tell it's him even though he hasn't seen him in over a decade.

"Rufus," he says.

"Hey."

Mike looks at both of them, in disbelief that they're here.

"This numbnuts tracked me down on the internet," Willie says, pointing to Gonzo.

"We've been exchanging emails back and forth, and I let him know that Westfield Arcade was closing," Gonzo says.

"When he told me that, I just knew that I had to come back," Willie says.

"I wasn't going to miss it, either," Rufus says.

Willie looks out at the depleted, practically empty arcade floor.

"If that isn't one of the saddest sights I've ever seen," Willie says. "This place is a graveyard."

"People have been picking up games all day," Mike says.

"Graveyard or not, there's still a few good games left," says Rufus. "You guys can stand here with your thumbs up your asses if you want, but I'm getting a few games in."

"Mortal Kombat 3," Gonzo says. "You're on."

They both walk over to the MK3 cabinet, leaving Willie and Mike by themselves at the front of the arcade.

"This is certainly a surprise," Mike says. Willie smiles back up at him, that ear-to-ear grin that Mike remembers from so long ago.

"We've got some catching up to do, that's for sure," Willie says.

"Gonzo showed me the article from the internet," Mike says. "You're designing video games now?"

"I was. Not anymore. Sold the company to a larger development studio a few years ago."

"How the hell did you even get started in that?"

"When I moved away from here after the crash, I started working as a video game tester--when a company finishes a game, they have a bunch of kids play the game for hours on end, looking for bugs in the game, giving feedback on what they like and don't like about the game, that sort of thing."

"Sounds like a dream job."

"It was…for awhile. Got old pretty quick."

"Playing video games all day and getting paid for it got old? Shit, you have changed."

Willie laughs.

"See, the thing about that job was that I had no say in what game I played. I had to play both the good games and the bad ones. Spending four straight hours playing 'Altered Beast' or 'Commando' and getting paid for it was great. But spending four straight hours playing a piece of shit like 'Araknoid: Revenge of Doh' or 'Missing in Action'? Not cool, man. Not at all."

"Point taken," Mike says.

258

"But I made a few contacts on the job and started spending nights at a few game developers' offices, learning the programs they use. That's all I did, every single night, and I got it down cold before long. Long story short, I started designing games, a few friends left to start up their own development house, and I joined them. We were doing pretty well for awhile."

"We had a copy of Warriors United in here for awhile, actually."

"That was my favorite game we did," Willie says. "After we had a few hits, we sold our company to a larger studio. I tried staying on, but couldn't handle being constantly told what to do."

"Why am I not surprised?"

Willie smiles.

"So I quit. I made enough from the sale of our company to take it easy for awhile. The wife got a job in Philadelphia, so we moved there and haven't left since."

"The wife," Mike says. "So you're married?"

"Yep. I don't know how she puts up with me. Her, or our two little ones."

Mike looks over at Gonzo and Rufus, both hunched over the Mortal Kombat 3 cabinet and playing the game with feverish intensity.

"And Rufus?" Mike says. "What's he up to?"

"He lives in Philly, too. Randomly ran into him at the airport a few years back, and we've stayed in touch. When I told him about Westfield Arcade closing, he insisted that he join me for a final visit."

Willie starts wheeling out towards the arcade floor and Mike follows him. They pass by Gonzo and Rufus at the Mortal Kombat 3 cabinet, both of them focused on the game, in their own little world.

"So this is it?" Willie says. "Westfield Arcade. It's gone."

"It's gone, all right."

They pass the Time Crisis cabinet, and Willie stops for a moment and looks at it before continuing on.

"We had us some Wild West times here back in the day, didn't we?"

"Sure did."

They pass a few more games and a few empty spaces where games once were before coming to a stop in front of the Time Pilot cabinet.

"Time Pilot," Willie says. "Man, I forgot all about this game."

"It's underrated. One of the good ones."

Willie wheels past the Time Pilot cabinet and continues on past a few more open spaces.

"Burgertime," Willie says, reading the marquee off the next game he comes to. "An arcade game about a chef making a fucking hamburger. Can you believe how insanely stupid that sounds?"

"That didn't stop us from playing it back in the day."

"Damn right," Willie says. "Still pisses me off that the guy has an H on his hat. Peter Pepper is the name of the chef. Burgertime is the name of the game. So why not a P or a B on his hat? Why an H?"

"One of life's great mysteries," Mike says.

"All these years later, and it still bugs me."

He wheels past Burgertime and a few other games and reaches the Pac Man cabinet towards the rear of the arcade.

"There she is," Willie says. "My baby. This game is a national treasure."

Willie watches the demo screen for awhile.

"How many hours of our lives did we spend playing this game when it first came out?"

"Oh God, I have no idea," Mike says. "At least twenty hours a week. A part-time job, really."

"I don't regret a second of it. Those were some great times."

Towards the front of the arcade, Mike hears Gonzo and Rufus at the Mortal Kombat 3 cabinet, grunting and swearing as they battle each other.

"We're not about to let them have all the fun, are we?" Willie asks

"Let's play."

So they play. Pac Man is up first. They alternate games at the cabinet, chatting with each other as they play, reminiscing about the countless nights they spent in Westfield Arcade, catching up. Gonzo and Rufus finish at the Mortal Kombat 3 cabinet and move towards the back of the arcade, back where the classics are. Donkey Kong and Space Invaders are both gone, but Frogger remains, and Rufus and Gonzo start alternating games at the Frogger cabinet.

When their games of Pac Man conclude, Mike moves to the Centipede cabinet and starts up a game alone. Willie wheels over to the Robotron: 2084 cabinet, his old nemesis.

"Wouldn't this be a fitting end?" he says to Mike. "On the arcade's final day of business, I set a high score in the one game I never could back in the day."

"No chance," Mike says. "The game hasn't gotten any easier over the years."

Willie laughs.

"You think I can finally beat Mikey's high score, Rufus?"

"Sure," comes Rufus's response, though he has no idea what he's agreeing to. He is deep into the game of Frogger. The world around him has disappeared.

Willie doesn't even come close to breaking 100,000 points in Robotron: 2084, let alone challenging Mike's 1.2 million high score. He plays with neither the concentration or vigor that he once played with. Instead of kicking the

261

machine in frustration or yelling obscenities, Willie simply wheels away from the cabinet when his game ends, a smile on his face.

The four middle-aged men continue to play, just like old times. The television has already been sold, so they can't blast MTV from its speakers. Even if the tv was still in the arcade, Mike doubts that MTV would even be showing music videos.

Eventually, the four of them leave the back of the arcade and move towards the front to play a few of the newer games. First up is the Teenage Mutant Ninja Turtles arcade game. The four of them start playing at the same time, crammed in next to one another at the cabinet, plugging quarters into the slot every time they die. They beat the game in under half an hour.

From there, they wander around the arcade and play whatever they feel like. Rufus grabs a plastic gun from the Time Crisis cabinet and starts blasting away at enemies onscreen. Gonzo sits down at the Ridge Racer cabinet and starts piloting the car onscreen with the steering wheel mounted to the control panel.

Mike and Willie head over to the Tekken 2 cabinet and play a few games against one another.

"Fun game," Willie says as they move away from the cabinet after their final game, "but they don't make 'em like they used to."

"Jesus, you sound old," Mike says, and Willie laughs at the comment.

Before long, the four men find themselves at the front of the arcade, up by the entrance.

"Damn, my hands are ruined," Willie says, stretching out his left hand as if squeezing an invisible stress ball. "Been way too long since I've played an arcade game before today."

"My forearms are killing me," Rufus says.

They stand around for a short while, looking out at the arcade. Then it becomes time to say their goodbyes. Willie and Rufus both leave their email addresses and phone numbers, telling Mike to stay in touch. Mike has already exchanged contact info with Gonzo a few days ago.

"Hold on for a second," Mike says before they leave.

He walks over to the front counter and opens up a cabinet. He pulls out a medium-sized chalkboard: the high-score chalkboard from so long ago. He took it down after he bought the arcade and performed the renovation, and never bothered hanging it back up. But he couldn't bring himself to throw it away, so all these years, it's been stored behind the front counter.

Mike carries the high score chalkboard over to the three men. The writing has faded and smudged over the years, but the WLC's that cover the chalkboard are still faintly visible.

"I want you to have this," Mike says to Willie. It seems like a fitting end to the visit: the man who once ruled the arcade being bestowed with a commemorative keepsake to forever remind of the era when he was king of Westfield Arcade. Mike expects Willie to accept the high score chalkboard with heartfelt gratitude.

"I don't want that piece of shit," Willie says instead, and starts laughing. "What the hell am I going to do with a four foot by four foot chalkboard? My wife would kill me if I showed up back to our place with that thing."

And Mike can't help but laugh. Good old Willie. Leave it to him to take a sentimental moment and turn it on its head.

Gonzo, Rufus, and Willie leave the arcade, and Mike watches them walk through the nearly-deserted food court. Willie gestures his hands around as he animatedly tells a story, and both Gonzo and Rufus laugh at him.

When they're out of sight, Mike walks over to the front counter and sits back down in the chair behind it. Once again, he is alone in the arcade. And, perhaps, he thinks, this is how it should be. This is how Westfield Arcade was meant to come to an end. Not with a group of friends standing around and playing games against one another, not with a rush of customers storming the arcade with quarters jingling in their pockets for one final time, but with the man who's stuck it out over all of those years, alone with the arcade that he has devoted his life to for that entire time.

He looks around the arcade, the roughly twenty games that remain casting illuminated glows from their monitors. By this time tomorrow, the movers will have arrived and packed up the remaining games and taken them to a storage shed across town, and the arcade will be completely empty.

Mike grabs the manila folder off of the counter. Opens it up, just to verify that everything is still inside. It is. A plane ticket. United Airlines. Leaving tonight. Destination: New York City. And a single piece of paper with an address in Brooklyn written on it.

Mike looks back at the clock. 8:58. This is it, he thinks. In the months since he made the decision to close Westfield Arcade, he's thought a lot about this one moment, the moment when he closes the arcade for good. He's wondered what it would feel like, and he's envisioned a tearful goodbye, a heart-wrenching scene during which his emotions get the best of him and he's so distraught that he can barely function.

Instead, he feels few emotions. He feels nostalgic, sure. That's the predominant emotion he feels. It is impossible to spend such a long time working at a place and not feel nostalgic when it finally comes to an end. Closing the arcade will mean closing a connection to his past, closing a connection to the greatest years of his life--

it's only natural to feel nostalgic when something like that comes to an end.

But the nostalgia he feels isn't a sad nostalgia. And the fact that he doesn't feel sad at all during his final moments in Westfield Arcade only confirms that closing the place really is the right thing to do.

He takes a look out into the food court and sees that it is almost empty. A janitor has started sweeping the floor, putting the chairs legs-up on the tables as he sweeps. The repetitive, pre-recorded music that plays throughout the mall during the day has been turned off. The neon signs above a few businesses in the food court are dark, the workers scurrying around behind the counters and performing closing duties.

Mike turns away from the food court and starts walking to the back of the arcade. One final trip down memory lane, though the sparsely-furnished interior barely resembles the place he's worked at for the past seventeen years.

Each game he passes, every single one of them, brings back memories from the period of time when they were released. He passes the Mortal Kombat 2 cabinet, standing all alone next to gaping holes where the Street Fighter 2 and Tekken cabinets were before they were picked up earlier today. Fall of 1994, that was, when Mortal Kombat 2 came out. The fighting game craze was in full effect, and booming business had finally returned to Westfield Arcade.

He passes by a few more open gaps and comes to the cabinet for Altered Beast--Winter of 1988. That bleak period when there was a dearth of quality games and Maddy had already moved and the arcade was leaching money from his bank account. Tough times, those had been, but through it all, he believed in Westfield Arcade. He continues walking, past a few open gaps and reaches Millipede--the summer of 1983, when he'd stay late in the arcade with Willie and Maddy almost every night and didn't have a care in the world. The best time of his life, that glorious summer of 1983 was.

His trip from the front of the arcade to the back is like seeing the evolution of arcade games in reverse. The digitized voices and crystal clear sound effects of the modern games in front meld into a warbled collection of simplistic blips and bleeps as he reaches the rear. The images onscreen go from 3-D graphics so advanced they look hardly different from a movie to screens that depict little more than a few rudimentary shapes and lines.

When he reaches the rear of the arcade he walks over to the lone door in the back. The Space Invaders and Asteroids cabinets that were sandwiched around it at the start of the day are both gone. He turns the knob and pushes the door open a crack. He snakes his hand inside and finds the main power switch right on the wall.

He flips the switch and just like that, every single game shuts off instantly. The arcade goes completely silent as every sound effect cuts out abruptly. The glow from the monitors of the few games remaining in Westfield Arcade go black, and the arcade is shrouded it darkness.

Mike walks back towards the front of the arcade, past the few games that remain, their monitors empty and silent. Mike reaches the arcade's entrance and steps outside. He pulls down the metal security gate and locks it into place with his key.

Without looking back, he walks away from Westfield Arcade, through the empty food court, and out of Westfield Mall forever.

# # #

Mike's plane touches down at LaGuardia Airport at one in the morning. Unable to sleep on the plane, he takes a cab straight to his hotel and is out cold the moment he lays down in his room.

He awakes early the next morning, eats breakfast alone in the lobby, and takes a cab out to Brooklyn just after ten. New York City may have changed in the years since he last visited, or the city may not have changed at all. He doesn't know. He can barely remember what the city looked like during that last visit.

The cabbie arrives at the address Mike gave him. Mike pays him and gets out of the cab. It's a nice, quaint neighborhood, far removed from the hustle and bustle of Manhattan. Three-flat brownstones and brick walk-ups are packed tightly next to one another. Cars are parallel parked on the left-hand side of the street. In the distance, he hears a train rumbling along the tracks.

He finds the piece of paper in the pocket of his parka and looks at the address printed on it.

Maddy Fredrickson
140 W. Durant #5
Brooklyn, NY 11245

He looks at the three brass numbers above the entrance to the walkup directly in front of him: 140. This is the place.

It's a Saturday, and he's pretty sure that she's home. He knows that she spends most Saturdays holed up in her apartment with Jo--in multiple emails, she's sarcastically referred to her "exciting" Saturdays spent playing and watching cartoons with Jo. He hasn't told Maddy about his visit today, nor has he told her of any details of the plan he's been working on for the past few months. He wants to tell her in-person and discuss it face-to-face--it's far too important of a decision to discuss over the phone or in a few hastily-written emails.

The apartment building is set back from the sidewalk, with a cobblestone path that cuts through a small yard in front. He walks up the path to the entrance. There is an intercom system to the left of the building's front door. Eight buttons, one for each apartment in the complex. Maddy's name is written next to the fourth button from the bottom.

Mike presses the button and he waits. Nothing happens for what seems like at least a minute. At the moment he reaches out to hit the button again, a voice speaks from the intercom.

"Hello?" It's a tinny, hollow voice, but he can tell that it's Maddy.

He leans in close to the intercom.

"Maddy?" he says.

"Yes. Who is this?"

"It's Mike."

There is a moment of silence, dead air over the intercom.

"Mike?" she eventually says.

"Yeah."

"What are you doing here?"

He does not answer immediately. What the hell is he doing here, anyway? It's too complicated to explain over the intercom.

"I wanted to talk," he says, keeping it simple.

"I'll buzz you up," Maddy's voice says through the intercom, apparently satisfied with his answer. "Third floor, door on your left."

There is a loud buzzing sound and Mike hears a mechanical click from the door as it unlocks. He opens the door and walks into an entryway. The entryway looks ancient, but it's not run-down or dilapidated. Just old. Beige vinyl wallpaper with a baroque pattern adorns the walls. A bank of mailboxes line one side of the entryway, apartment numbers written on the front of each one. An old ornate staircase in the corner winds up to the floors above.

Mike walks over to the staircase and ascends the stairs up to the third floor, the wooden steps creaking underneath him. There are two doors on the third floor that look identical to one another, except for the fact that one has a brass 5 displayed above the knocker and one has a 6. He walks over to the door with the 5 and knocks.

She answers the door instantly. Maddy wears a pair of oversize gray sweatpants and a plain red pocket t-shirt. She has no makeup on, but the natural glow of her skin still looks vibrant. She wears a pair of black-rimmed glasses that Mike has never seen her wear before. Her eyes look at him from behind those glasses, wide and disbelieving.

"It's really you," she says.

She takes a step out into the hallway and hugs him. He hugs her back.

"I was halfway worried that I just let a mass murderer into the building," Maddy says once the hug ends.

"Nope. Just me."

"Come in," Maddy says.

She leads him into a living room that is located just inside the doorway. The living room has plain, off-white carpeting that is worn in a few places. A television rests on a stand at the front of the room. It's a smaller tv, no bigger than 30 inches. Two mismatched couches--one blue with white vertical lines running lengthways, the other a solid black--face towards the television from opposite sides of the room. In the corner is a desk with a large desktop computer sitting on it. Various papers and folders are strewn about on top of the desk.

Next to the desk is a makeshift play area with all sorts of toys covering the ground. There are various Barbies and some clothes for the Barbies. Square building blocks litter the floor, and a few have been unevenly stacked on top of one another to form some sort of triangular structure that looks as if it could fall over at any moment. A crumpled pink blanket rests beneath a stuffed teddy bear.

Maddy takes Mike's coat and hangs it in a closet. They both sit down in the living room, on opposite couches. She looks over at Mike, just stares at him for a moment.

"So how have you been?" she finally asks. "What are you doing here? Is everything ok? I have about a million different questions."

"First question first. I'm good. You?"

"Good. Busy. With the little rascal, mostly. I apologize if I'm boring you to death with all of the email updates I send off."

"Not at all," Mike says. "I love hearing about her."

As if on queue, a little girl, knee-high, comes bounding out of an adjacent room on her two feet. She wears a small pink t-shirt with a rainbow on the front and a pair of denim overalls. Her legs move too quickly for the rest of her body and she stumbles to the ground, but she gets back up immediately and trudges over to Maddy.

"Up-py!" she pleads, extending her arms upward. "Up-py!"

Maddy reaches down and picks up her little girl.

"Do you remember Mike?" Maddy asks Jo, turning the child to face him.

Jo looks at Mike, then back at her mother.

"Binky!" she says.

Maddy smiles, then her eyes start scanning the living room.

"Binky!" Jo says again, louder this time.

"Mommy's looking," Maddy says. She turns towards Mike: "Do you see a blanket anywhere? Pink with lacy stuff around the edges."

"Underneath the teddy bear over there," Mike says.

Maddy spots it and walks over, setting Jo down in the pay area. The little girl picks up the blanket in one hand and the teddy bear in the other. Maddy walks back over to the couch and sits down.

"So you're here because you want to talk?" she asks.

"Yeah."

"And this conversation couldn't have taken place over email? Or the phone?"

"I suppose it could have," Mike says. "But I'd rather do it in person."

He looks at her. He doesn't feel nervous or uneasy, which surprises him. Instead, he feels calm, in control.

"I closed Westfield Arcade," Mike says. "Yesterday was the final day of business."

Surprise registers on her face.

"What happened?" she asks.

"Business dried up. People stopped coming in."

"Wow," Maddy says. "I'm sorry."

"Don't be. It was my decision. I could've kept it open if I wanted to, found a way to scrape by. But it was time."

Mike pauses for a moment.

"But I didn't come here to tell you about the closing of the arcade," he says. "I came to talk about something else.

Again, Mike pauses. He looks at little Jo in the corner of the room. She has set her teddy bear and blanket to the side, and has started to stack a few of her blocks on top of one another.

He looks back at Maddy, sitting across the room from him.

"Do you remember that night we went to that Italian restaurant?" he asks. "The night you told me you were moving to New York?"

"Sure," she says. "Giovanni's, right?"

"Yeah."

"What about it?"

He pauses.

"So that night, I wanted to tell you something. But I didn't get a chance to."

"I remember," she says. "We had that rock paper scissors contest to see who got to go first."

"Right," he says. "You won. You told me you were moving to New York. And I just froze up. I was so shocked I could barely talk. But I never did tell you what I wanted to say. So I came here to tell you."

He still has the speech memorized. All these years later, he remembers the speech that he wanted to give to her that night, the speech he'd spent countless hours crafting and fine-tuning. At their dinner on that night, he'd been so nervous, so terrified of delivering it. But he feels none of that now.

He clears this throat and starts speaking.

"I think you're amazing," Mike says. "You're the greatest person I know. The absolute best. By far. No-one else even comes close."

He looks at her. She stares back. A slight smile creeps over Mike's face.

"I'm in love with you," he continues. "In fact, that seems like an understatement. Love isn't a strong enough word. I'm in awe of you. I'm in awe of everything about you. Your smile, your personality. Everything."

Maddy's mouth is slightly open. In the corner, Jo knocks her stack of blocks to the ground. She picks one up in her small hand and throws it a few feet.

"I think I'm going to move here," Mike continues. "To New York. I found an apartment on the internet, on a realtor's website. I have to head over and sign the paperwork later today."

Maddy continues to wordlessly stare at him.

"I just want to be around you," Mike says. "I miss you."

Maddy stands up and walks over to him, and Mike gets up from his couch. They stand a few feet from each other for a moment, face to face, and then Maddy reaches over and hugs him. He hugs her back.

"I've been waiting for you," she says, her voice as low as a whisper.

They continue to hug for a moment. The moment is a special one, but it passes quickly. Maddy lets go of him and smiles before walking back over to her couch.

"What are you going to do when you're here?" she asks.

"College," Mike says. "That's the plan, at least. I've talked to a few places, and most of my coursework from Northwestern will transfer. A couple places even mentioned scholarship packages. I'm not even sure what I'm going to study, but I've got a few things in mind. Running a small business for the last decade has shown me what I like. And what I don't."

"When?" Maddy asks. "When are you going to move?"

"A couple weeks from now. I still have to move my stuff out of my apartment in Indianapolis, throw away what I don't want, move what I do want."

"This is incredible," Maddy says.

They continue to talk. Maddy asks him about the apartment he found online, and he describes a few details to her. With a laugh, she tells him that his monthly rent is two-hundred dollars too much. He hasn't signed any paperwork yet, and Maddy vows to help him find a different place. In the corner, Jo begins squealing for "Up-py!" and Maddy walks over and picks her up. She walks over to the couch and sits back down, Jo on her lap.

"Also, I think you should start acting again," Mike says. "I can watch Jo. I'm not saying I'd be good at it, but

I can learn. I want to help you. You're too good to simply stop acting. I've lived my dream for the past seventeen years--I loved going to work every single day. Now I want to see you live your dream."

Maddy looks at him.

"That would be…incredible," she says.

Jo starts kicking her feet, and Maddy sets her back on the ground. The little girl stumbles over to the toys in the corner and picks up her Binky.

Mike and Maddy continue to talk, both of their enthusiasm growing as the time passes. Maddy talks of a few acting friends she plans on contacting regarding getting a part in an upcoming play. She speaks with a feverish enthusiasm. Mike talks about a few colleges he's reached out to.

They continue to talk into the early afternoon. There is no passionate reunion filled with savage lovemaking or snuggling naked in the bed. Just two friends, who may in fact be more than that, talking about the wonderfully uncertain future that lies ahead.

Neither of them is quite sure what to expect.

But it is beginning.

Made in the USA
Lexington, KY
16 October 2013